Jacques

Tanya Ravenswater was born in County Down, Northern Ireland in 1962. After working as a nurse and a bereavement counsellor, she started writing fiction and poetry for both adults and children. She has published a collection of short stories for women, and has also been short-listed and published in the Cheshire Prize anthologies. Her children's poem, 'Badger', was the winner of the 2014–15 Cheshire Prize for Literature.

Tanya Ravenswater

Jacques

twenty7

First published in Great Britain in 2015

This paperback edition publlished in 2016 by

Twenty7 Books
80–81 Wimpole St, London W1G 9RE
www.twenty7books.com

Copyright © Tanya Ravenswater 2015

A CIP catalogue record for this book is available from the British Library.

Paperback ISBN: 978-1-78577-010-4
Ebook ISBN: 978-1-78577-011-1

1 3 5 7 9 10 8 6 4 2

Printed and bound by Clays Ltd, St Ives Plc

Twenty7 Books is an imprint of Bonnier Zaffre,
a Bonnier Publishing company
www.bonnierzaffre.co.uk
www.bonnierpublishing.com

For my inspiring parents, Margaret and Jack.
And for Fergus, always remembered, with love.

Prologue

There are few people to whom we really matter. To most people, our lives are like facts: noted, skimmed over, quickly forgotten. They might feel some sense of responsibility if we collapsed on the street, or if we asked them directly for help. Otherwise, to the majority of those we come across, the quality and details of our lives are largely irrelevant.

Such observation need not result in loss of faith in humanity. To live, holding all other worlds of feeling and thought in mind, is clearly impossible. We must choose the few to whom we give our time and love.

It is possible, of course, to survive without mattering to another person. But it is only when we matter, when we are seen and truly loved, that we know what it means to fully live. When we can find our home and accept the thought of our death. When we can be at ease and let the ambient music carry us on.

Uncle Oliver, as I once called him, used to tell me that it was wrong for a person to hold onto the past. 'The world needs us

all to be facing the front. Never taking our eyes off the ball.'
A good man should refuse to retrace his steps. Retrospection,
Uncle Oliver said, was a form of 'avoidable death'. In spite of
his advice, I had to decide from the age of eleven, that I had no
other choice. I could only live by 'dying', could only carry on
by deliberately trying to remember those priceless moments of
childhood that stitched me into the heart of life with threads of
love, the unforgettable love of my own Papa and Maman.

Now, more than twenty years on, I am glad that as a boy
I was able to trust and follow my heart. I carried my memories
forward as talismans. The feeling that, from birth, I had been
appreciated for who I was allowed me to hope that in the future
I might be valued in such a way again. To this day, through all
the challenges and losses I have had to bear, the love that gave
me life stays with me.

PART 1

1

Uncle Oliver wasn't my real uncle. He was the legal guardian chosen by Papa to look after me, in what Papa had described as the 'unlikely event' of his own untimely death. I had to accept that so-called 'unlikely events' were destined to be among the likely facts of my life. In 1984, Maman died from a sudden brain haemorrhage. When I had gone with Papa to see her laid out in her nightdress at the hospital, at first I was momentarily relieved. The doctors were wrong, I thought. She was very pale, but my mother had always been pale, especially if she was asleep or too cold. It was a long time before I would listen to Papa telling me that she was dead, that her heart and breathing had stopped, that there had been no mistake. I had nightmares for months afterwards. Images of Maman, calling for me from her coffin, entangled with imaginings of scenes from a story a boy had once told me at school, about a man burying a hibernating tortoise in a box, by accident, and only realising what he had done weeks later, when it was too late.

While highly imaginative and mentally agile in conversation, physically Papa was much less robust. As a child he had been very ill with rheumatic fever, which had affected his heart. I noticed that he would become quickly breathless. He tired much more quickly than Maman when we were playing. It was nothing for me to worry about, they had both kept reassuring me. Papa just needed to rest a little more and make sure that he always looked after his health. Every morning, with breakfast, he would faithfully take the pills that he joked would one day help him win an Olympic Gold for France.

Still, following Maman's death, Papa became anxious to ensure that sound legal arrangements were in place for me to be cared for, should anything happen to him. His options were extremely limited. Apart from a few acquaintances that he and Maman saw very little of, my parents had tended to spend their spare time simply in each other's and my company. Like me, Maman and Papa were both only children. They had become parents in later life. Three of my grandparents had died before I was born. My maternal English grandmother, who had been placed in a nursing home in Paris since the onset of a debilitating type of presenile dementia, wasn't competent to look after herself, let alone anyone else. I think Papa wanted to feel certain, for his own sake as well as mine, that, whatever happened, my future would be secure. Naively, I reassured him that there was no need for him to worry. I was sure that Madame Dupont would be happy to carry on looking after me as usual. She was a kind, interesting person who knew what I needed and where everything was in our apartment. She enjoyed talking and listening to my stories and understood exactly what I liked to eat and drink. There would be no need for her to actually adopt me. There was a girl at school who had been adopted and who had had to change her name. I didn't want that to happen to me. I would never have any other parents apart from Papa and Maman, whether they were alive or not, I said. I would always be called Jacques Lafitte.

Papa had employed Madame Dupont to supervise me after school. She would also stay with me sometimes when Papa had to travel abroad on business. She was a solidly built, plain-speaking woman, probably in her late fifties, with whom I had come to feel at ease. Occasionally Madame and I would take the metro to the 17th arrondissement to visit her hapless husband in their tiny apartment smelling of dog food and cigarettes. He would be sitting in front of the television, smoking, unshaven, always wearing the same kind of grimy sleeveless cotton vest. Their own family had all left home, Madame explained, wistfully. God had decided that her life's purpose would be to carry on caring for children. Monsieur Dupont, on the other hand, she confided, had turned to gambling.

Madame Dupont was undoubtedly a kind person who was very fond of me, Papa acknowledged. However, it wouldn't be possible for her to take full responsibility for me, should the unthinkable happen. I wouldn't have to be adopted, but I would need someone to make important decisions and arrangements for me until I was old enough to make them for myself. Papa's work colleague, Oliver Clark, had officially agreed to be my guardian. They had both worked for many years for the same international electronics company. Papa was based near our home in Neuilly-sur-Seine – a *commune*, or what the English usually refer to as a suburb, of Paris. While he travelled frequently to the company's headquarters in France, Oliver Clark was based and lived in Cheshire. Their relationship had always been more of a professional rather than a personal one, but Papa had regarded him as a knowledgeable and dependable colleague. He also had two children of his own and a wife who was a surgeon. If the worst happened, she would automatically become my joint guardian and I would at least be brought up in a family home. It was almost impossible for Papa to think about it, he told me, but he had to.

The conversations that Oliver Clark had with Papa always seemed to revolve around a constant exchange of numbers and were full of technical terms that I didn't understand. I don't think Maman did either. She would try to engage him, in English, on the subject of his family life instead. He would smile politely, baring tobacco-stained teeth edged with gold, and briefly mention how his children were excelling at school. His wife Anna seemed to manage 'perfectly well' without him, he said. I was puzzled then by the way he said it, as if it was a joke and at the same time not. I couldn't imagine Papa talking to someone in the same way about Maman. Oliver Clark would thank me reliably each time I offered him pistachios or another piece of ham to eat with his aperitif. Otherwise, it seemed to me that he was only vaguely aware of my existence. He certainly didn't strike me as the sort of person who would be at all interested in looking after a child. However, while at times I wanted to question Papa's decision, I told myself that we would always be together and would have no need to rely on anyone else but each other.

As time told, Papa's awareness of his own mortality and planning for my future in the event of his absence proved to be tragically prescient. In June 1985, just a year after Maman's death and days after my eleventh birthday, Papa was killed in a head-on collision on the Boulevard Périphérique, one of the busiest roads in Europe.

I wasn't allowed to see him after the accident due to the severity of his injuries. It was best that I remembered him, I was told, the way that he had been that morning when he had left me at my school gates.

As Papa had planned, Madame Dupont came to stay in our apartment until Oliver Clark arrived. I didn't need to return to school for the moment, she said. We could read together, take nice picnics outside, or do anything else I wanted, she offered gently. She understood that I would be very upset, but she also was sure that my parents would want me to do my best to carry on living and enjoying myself. While I knew that she was right, I didn't want to do anything, or go anywhere. Although being in the apartment without them made me feel constantly on the edge of crying, I also felt a comfort in that sadness, which held me as close then as it was possible for me to be to Maman and Papa. However kind and familiar Madame Dupont was, I just wanted it to be the three of us again, having breakfast, sharing detailed stories of our days over dinner, kissing each other every morning and night. My whole world had been built on what I trusted would be the unshakeable ground of their presence, my daily life framed by proof of how much I was cherished.

Those early days after Papa's death are blurred together in my memory. I seemed to spend most of the time, alone, by choice, between constantly playing scales on Maman's piano until I was exhausted and then curled up tightly on my bed, hoping to escape into sleep and turn back time.

I do remember clearly how I would repeatedly close my eyes, trying to fix a permanent image of Papa's face in my mind. His kind brown eyes. The broad, open expanse of his furrowed forehead. The craggy line of his nose. His overlapping front teeth. His short, wiry beard, black hairs curled with white. The image kept slipping from my grasp. I had seen that face so many times, moving, changing. Each feature had had its own limitless repertoire.

From the day that he came to Neuilly to take me back to live with him in England, the same day that he suggested that I call him Uncle Oliver, my guardian seemed intent on convincing me that I couldn't remember much about my previous life. 'You can't possibly remember those details! Someone else must have told you about that!' he said, when I tried to recount some episode. While, in due course, I would discover that when it came to other people's feelings Oliver lacked imagination and empathy, at the time I couldn't understand his remark. He gave me absolutely no encouragement to reminisce. Discussion and storytelling had been central to my life with Maman and Papa.

In many ways, they had treated me as an equal in conversation. They had never made me feel less important because I was a child. They encouraged me to talk about everything, from myself and my feelings to questions of art, literature, philosophy and science.

I would soon observe that Uncle Oliver behaved similarly with his own children as he did with me. Whether his approach derived from the style of his upbringing, I still don't really know. He was the kind of adult who genuinely didn't believe that a child was capable of real thought. He also seemed to find conversations about most things, apart from his work and his personal experiences and opinions, uninteresting and inconvenient distractions.

Uncle Oliver saw no reason to keep much from our Neuilly apartment. He brought me two compact suitcases for my clothes and other essential belongings. Some of our furniture and paintings were very valuable, he told me. Maman's piano, her beautiful grand Bechstein, would fetch a good price. He would arrange to return again to Paris as soon as he had taken me to Chester. He would complete funerary and all other arrangements for Papa himself. There would be no need for me to return. He would also sell as much as he could and add the proceeds to the rest of my parents' estate, for my future maintenance. Everything else would be cleared and the property put up for sale as quickly as possible.

I ran in different directions through the apartment. First to Maman's piano, my fingers flitting, light with panic across the keys. Then to the kitchen. Scanning the shelves, our coffee bowls, our eggcups, sprouted cress drying on blotting paper on the windowsill. Bewildered, nauseous, crying. Words ricocheting in my head. I didn't know where to go next, what to take. I lifted Mous, my old bear, from my bedroom and held him tightly against my chest.

There were so many important things. Things that had made me feel important. The riches and treasures of our own kind of palace. Papa's and Maman's books! Too many for the corner of a suitcase. I searched frantically, my fingers racing across their spines, unable to find the ones we had always looked at together. Maman's *Comical Nursery Rhymes*, which she had been given by her mother, with its fine black-and-white engravings of characters such as 'Quarrelsome Kate' and 'Jeremy Nobbler the Cobbler'. Her *Stories for Children*, full of carefully groomed, contented boys and girls flying kites, feeding doves, playing with mermaids. Papa's gilt-edged Hans Christian Andersen, the *World Atlas*, which his father had given him as a birthday present. Books that my parents had always said would be mine, to pass on to my children.

Maman's precious ornaments! The two translucent china birds on the mantelpiece that had been a wedding present. The stooped Chinese fisherman with the kind face and trailing beard. The Dutch clogs tied together at the backs of the heels with ridged red ribbon. The carved goats from Switzerland. The embroidered house in a frame that Maman had made when she was only seven. Full of mistakes and probably worth nothing to anyone but our family, she would always say.

Since Maman's death, Papa had continued to keep most of her things in their bedroom. Her smell was held captured in the collection of perfume bottles on the dressing table. Strands of her dark brown hair still wove through the bristles of her brush. Maman and Papa – roses and lilies, cigar smoke and hair cream, on the clothes, in the wardrobes, the drawers. Thoughts and images multiplying in every room, gathering in layers, around everything.

'You don't have to take anything at all, of course, if you don't want to,' Uncle Oliver stated. I could tell he was irritated by the way I was dashing about. I had tucked Mous under my arm with my box of watercolours and paper block. In one hand I was gripping the wooden handle of Maman's brush, in the other I had Papa's striped black-and-white silk tie.

'Why don't you take this little cigar box of photographs? Bring the things you're carrying as well. We can probably squeeze them in with your shoes and clothes. Whatever you decide, make it quick. We need to go. We can't miss the flight.'

I couldn't think what else to choose.

It was too onerous a decision for a child. The entire contents of the apartment were steeped in the history of my childhood. I didn't have the experience to know what would most matter in the long run. It was all so important.

2

On our flight to England, Uncle Oliver spoke cheerfully of Cheshire and of how optimistic he was that I would settle in quickly. His wife, Anna, and his children, Matthew and Rebecca, would be delighted with me, of course. Rebecca was twelve and Matthew fifteen. In spite of our age differences, we were bound to have things in common. They were both at private schools with good reputations. A place had been arranged for me at Matthew's school. There was no reason why we shouldn't all grow up and be successful together, Uncle Oliver suggested.

Whereas previously he had spoken to me in French, Uncle Oliver announced that from then on we would be speaking entirely in English. It was only fair to everyone. For someone of my age, he said, I had a remarkable command of the language. Although Maman had lived most of her life in France, her mother was from England and she had been born there herself. She had done an excellent job of teaching me, Uncle Oliver pointed out. I owed it to her to become completely fluent, as quickly as possible.

Whatever Uncle Oliver assumed and expected of me, however much I had become accustomed to speaking English frequently with Maman, I suddenly felt overwhelmed by the situation in which I found myself. I could hardly speak, overpowered by fatigue and a reality foreign in almost every respect. I had been feeling vaguely unwell since Papa's accident. The closest to it that I had experienced before was carsickness. It seemed as if I had entered an unreal nightmare, which could only end if my parents were to return. It was impossible to escape. I had moved from one world to another. The door between had become part of a wall. Memories were my only keys.

Even if I was too young then to articulate what I felt I needed to, I still suspected that in order to preserve something of my own identity in my new life with Uncle Oliver, I would have to divide myself between an inner sanctuary of private feeling and a steady outward show of interaction.

Anna, Matthew and Rebecca Clark met us outside Manchester airport. In contrast to Maman, who was soft like a brioche, Anna Clark was tall and as thin as a stem. Her hair was blonde, short and sharp. She wore a sweeping beige raincoat with an upturned collar and an olive-green silk scarf. 'Hello, Oliver.' I was surprised by the coolness of Anna's tone. It wasn't how I expected a wife to welcome a husband. There was no kiss, no embrace. Without removing her tight black leather driving gloves, she shook my hand briefly, greeted me formally. 'Pleased to meet you, Jacques,' she said brusquely. 'Welcome to England! Say hello, please, Rebecca and Matthew! He won't bite!'

Matthew was as tall as his mother, and had her colouring and long bones. He hung back, acknowledged me with a slight nod, but kept his head down otherwise. Rebecca, on the other hand, sprang forward. 'Bonjour, Jacques! *Je suis très heureuse de faire ...*'

Her voice was lively and genuinely welcoming. I thought at once that she was very pretty. Her hair was a much darker blonde than her mother's, an exuberant head of swarming, tangled curls. She had even darker eyebrows and lashes, and piercing blue eyes. She was obviously interested in me and her warmth made me feel more at ease. Until Uncle Oliver intervened.

'Rebecca! In English, please. Jacques needs to speak in English more than you need to speak in French. There's plenty of time for that at school.'

'Sorry, Dad. Hi, Jacques. I'm Rebecca. We are very sorry about your parents.'

'Rebecca! Enough said. Jacques has had a long journey. I'm sure he won't want to talk much now,' Uncle Oliver corrected again, more impatiently.

In spite of what Uncle Oliver said, I desperately wanted to reach out to Rebecca. I trusted that she would want to listen and understand. I wanted to confide in her, in French, about how isolated and fearful I felt; to go through every detail of what had happened since Papa had gone.

'I am very happy to meet you as well,' I said. 'Thank you for letting me come to your home.'

'Excellent, excellent,' Uncle Oliver acknowledged, automatically. 'Now, where did you park the car, Anna? Matthew, take one of Jacques' cases, will you? I need to get home as soon as possible. All this has set me back. A lot. I hardly have any time before I have to fly back again. I'm going to have to work all night to get on top of things.'

'The old, old story?' Anna commented. Even I could feel the bitterness. The green of her irises seemed to intensify with the rise of her emotion.

'You know how it is,' Uncle Oliver shrugged, apparently impervious.

'Well I think that's fairly obvious. Which is why I told you … Oh, never mind!' she finished, closing her eyes and waving her hand dismissively in the air. 'This way to the car, please, Jacques!' she snapped. She grabbed my hand and turned abruptly, walking stiffly ahead of the others, across the road, towards the car park. 'Short drive and we'll be home. Have a good journey, did you? Straight to bed after supper when we get there. You must be too tired for anything else!'

'Yes,' I replied, guessing that it wouldn't be in my interests to disagree.

At the age of eleven, even in a foreign country, I could see that I was no longer as welcome as I had been at home. My parents would have eagerly invited me to stay up and talk with them after dinner for as long as I could. I hadn't even arrived at the Clarks' house yet and it seemed that already, in Anna's mind, she wanted me in bed, asleep, as soon as possible. Within such a short time, it felt as if the foundations of my life, which I had expected would always be solidly the same, were being dismantled, whether I agreed to it or not.

When you think about it, it can be difficult to pinpoint exactly what makes places, which appear superficially to share many similar details, feel, in experience, significantly different. Subtle distinctions and particular arrangements of elements give an environment its own character and atmosphere, that can make its inhabitants feel more or less at home. The same applies to people. While as humans we have certain features in common, our personal histories, the places we come from and our physical chemistry make us specifically who we are. Papa once told me that he thought people were like grapes, coming from their own ground, their *terroir*. The soil and climate of one region, however close to another, would give its fruits their particular qualities and subtle variations in flavour. Although when transformed into wine, the grape would travel elsewhere in the world, it would continue to speak, in its own language, of the *terroir* that created it.

The Clarks lived in Chester, close to the River Dee. A European city, with both modern and historic buildings. Schools, churches and libraries. Tourist attractions, parks, museums, restaurants, cafes, moneyed leafy suburbs, poorer and much less elegant areas. On paper, in many ways like Paris. I felt, however, as soon as we arrived, that it was really quite different.

Like all those living in their place of origin, I had become accustomed to my surroundings, to the point of taking them for granted. I was used to the street-facing apartments and shop fronts, buildings in warm cream-grey stone, the familiar architecture, old and modern, of Neuilly and the centre of Paris. Tree-lined broad boulevards. The background hum of city traffic, the babble of voices, French voices, everywhere. Buzzing street cafes, often with red awnings, open from early until late into the night. Aromas of strong coffee and cigarettes. Smells of cooking herbs, breads and patisserie. All the small details in the way things looked, sounded and were made and done, the characteristics of my own *terroir*.

As we drove into Chester, there was no doubt it had its own charm, but mostly then I felt its foreignness. It seemed much smaller and quieter than what I'd been used to. Many of the individual houses on the outskirts, which had their own gardens, drives and gates at the front, were built in red brick. Towards the centre, there were strange old buildings painted white with black woodwork. There was traffic and people on the streets, but nothing like the roar and commotion of Paris. There were trees, but different ones, and nowhere did I see a line of plane trees.

The Clarks lived in what I could tell was a richer area of the city, with big detached houses, set back from the street, in their own large gardens. We arrived at their home at around seven that Sunday evening. It was still light, not the vibrant, intense light of Neuilly, but an English summer evening and warm nevertheless.

My immediate impression was that the towering, formidable building was, in many ways, like Anna Clark herself. It was surrounded by high fences, cropped, rolled lawns and lean, shadowy weeping willows. There were apple, pear and cherry trees and clipped shrubs, but few flowers or decorative features. The lines of the concrete steps and paths were straight, uncompromising, free from lichen or moss. The front drive and forecourt were thickly gravelled with grey chippings.

Inside, the house had four storeys and a steep, carpeted central staircase with white, thickly glossed banisters. The rooms were high-ceilinged, papered mainly in deep reds and browns, furnished with heavy, hard-wearing fabrics, dark teak and mahogany. The floors were mostly bare, polished wooden boards with functional rugs and mats.

Matthew was instructed to take my cases up to my bedroom and to come down straightaway to join the rest of us in the kitchen. There were a few things that needed to be said before I went to bed, Anna explained.

The kitchen, its windows overshadowed by the weeping willows outside, was chilled and dim. It was stone-flagged, with grey and white marble work surfaces, two deep ceramic sinks and an extended wooden table with solid bench seats.

'Please sit down, Jacques,' Anna Clark told me curtly, pointing to the table. 'Will you have a glass of milk or a cup of tea?'

I hated tea. My mother had occasionally made Lipton tea for Papa's English guests, but they usually had fresh coffee while I drank hot chocolate.

'Milk, please … Aunt Anna?' I just managed to say, nervously, swallowing uncomfortably.

'You can have some bread and butter with it if you'd like. And there's no need to call me Aunt, Jacques. Anna is perfectly adequate. We don't have to pretend,' Anna added matter-of-factly. She poured my milk and set the small glass precisely on a coaster in front of me. 'Where are they? Oliver? Matthew?'

Rebecca had followed us into the kitchen and slid down onto the bench opposite me.

'I'll have the same as Jacques, please,' she said. There was a roll of white kitchen paper in front of her on the table and she started to play a game, peeking at me from alternate sides of it.

'Don't be silly, please, Rebecca,' Anna said bluntly. 'You'll have to have tea with the rest of us. There isn't any extra milk.'

'So, what's it like in Neuilly, Jacques? Is it a lot different from here? I'd love to visit one day,' Rebecca persisted, pronouncing Neuilly slowly and deliberately.

'Give Jacques some peace, please, Rebecca.'

Anna clicked off the kettle before it had time to boil properly, filled a practical but ugly aluminium teapot and banged it down on the table beside a half-filled jug of milk. She was still wearing her coat and gloves.

'Oliver? Now, please! The tea's ready.'

Uncle Oliver and Matthew appeared together at the door.

'About time!' Anna commented, resentfully. 'Matthew, bring the mugs from the cupboard, please.'

'Could I have my tea in my room, Mum?' Matthew asked, nervously. 'I'm revising for maths.' He blushed as soon as he began to speak, rubbed his hand vigorously against his face, as if trying to smooth the pocked surface of his acned cheek.

'Yes. Make sure the cup comes back to the kitchen, will you? If you wait, your father will be pouring the tea in a minute.'

'I was just checking my mail,' Uncle Oliver offered, by way of explaining his delay. 'There's something else I'll have to see to this evening.'

'Don't you think I've got things to see to as well? Oh, and by the way, a girl called Amanda called from work for you. Unbearably bubbly little thing. Sounded like she couldn't wait to talk to you. Asked if you could call her back whenever you had the chance. No other message. One of your new little teasmaid people, is she?'

I couldn't have imagined Maman speaking to Papa in the cold tone Anna Clark used with Uncle Oliver.

'One of our new secretaries,' Uncle Oliver replied, nodding, making his way to the table without looking at Anna. He sat down beside Rebecca, his back turned to his wife. 'Amanda's a good girl. Very polite, eager to please. Not a quality you get in everyone nowadays.'

'I suppose it's easier when you're an airhead,' Anna stung back. She strode over to the sink and stared out of the window. 'With not much of a thought in your pretty little brain – apart from making yourself indispensable to the boss?'

I was struggling to understand. Not so much the words, as the feelings behind them. The strangeness of a mother and father talking like this, back to back. It was so different from what I was used to at home.

'No. That's not fair,' Uncle Oliver protested, as he lifted the teapot. His brow was moist with sweat, his hand jerky as he poured. 'Some of these girls have their heads firmly on their shoulders. They're efficient. Positive, happy sort of people. Good company, in fact.'

'Like faithful, sweet little spaniels?' Anna supplied, tartly.

'Say what you like. You usually do,' Uncle Oliver said, trying to sound nonchalant. He took a gulp of tea and set his cup down abruptly, clamping a hand over his mouth. 'Far too hot, eh, Rebecca? Anyway, welcome to your new home, Jacques!'

Anna was still facing the window. She ignored Uncle Oliver and her tea. Her hands were pushing deep into her coat pockets. 'I've discovered, Jacques, that it's impossible for Oliver and me to maintain a family and two careers unless I run a tight ship.

Everyone has to pull their weight. I expect you to do the same. Tomorrow you will ...'

'Perhaps you could wait until another time, Anna? He might be ...' Uncle Oliver tried to interrupt. It was obvious that he wanted to curtail the discussion, I suspected as much for his own need to work as my need for rest.

'No, Oliver. Please. Don't you dare undermine me. This needs to be clearly spelled out. From the beginning!'

Anna had blanched with anger. I noticed for the first time a prominent vein, standing proud, at the side of her forehead. She resumed her talk. 'Tomorrow, Jacques, you will start at Matthew's school. It's an excellent establishment and a superb opportunity for you. Although it's almost the end of the school year, they've agreed that you can spend time with the first year class, familiarising yourself with the layout, adjusting to the language and the school's expectations. Do your best to fit in. The same principle applies at home. Tomorrow evening, after I've taken you through our house rules, you will follow them to the best of your ability. Is that understood?'

I was struggling to keep pace with Anna's rapid English, although I guessed that it was best to pretend otherwise. I had also been wishing that Anna's plain bread and butter were a piece of sweet cake instead. The thought connected in my mind with the cake I'd had for my tenth birthday. I had had a party, just before Maman died. Six of my school friends and I had played football in the park that belonged to the apartments. I loved that park, its broad paths turning, winding round the mounds of the flower beds, its slatted, iron-backed benches where I used to lie on my stomach reading *Tintin*. After the game, Maman sat us at the table in the apartment. Everything was unbelievably and sensationally sweet. There were tartines with strawberry jam, *pains au chocolat*, lemonade. In the centre was the special cake that Maman had ordered from the patisserie. It was shaped like a white castle with turrets flying ribbon flags, forked like snakes' tongues. It had a drawbridge made of a thin biscuit rectangle and a moat of piped blue icing. The thought that it was mine made me feel invincible, noble and strong as a prince.

'Yes, Anna. I understand.'

I nodded and drank the rest of my milk, blinking back the tears, falling back to reality. My king and queen were dead. I was just a helpless little boy, stripped of everything, even his mother tongue.

Shortly afterwards, Anna told Rebecca to take me upstairs. My bedroom was on the top floor, off its own square landing. It was a small, angular space painted in shades of pale blue, with a single skylight in the sloping ceiling. Rebecca's and Matthew's rooms were on the floor below.

'I'll help you unpack, if you like,' Rebecca offered. 'You could show me some of your things from Neuilly.' I felt awkward initially, not wanting an older girl to see Mous, protective of my box of private photographs, painfully conscious that I didn't have anything else belonging to my parents, apart from a hairbrush and a tie.

'Please let me see,' Rebecca persisted, playfully flicking the handle of my case with her foot. 'I don't care about what Mum and Dad said. I want to know about Neuilly. What's in that box?'

I took Papa's Cuban cigar box from my case and set it on the bed. I returned to the case immediately and locked it again.

'Just some photographs of our family.'

'Could I see them?' she asked. 'I always love looking at other people's family photographs,' she added persuasively.

Rebecca sat quietly on the bed, untied the ribbon securing the lid and lifted it off with a thoughtful, serious expression. She held the first photograph carefully at the edges, to avoid touching its surface. 'Is this you? With your Mum?'

It was the only photograph in the collection that I couldn't actually remember being taken. Papa had spoken so often about the moment, however, that it felt as if I could. I was about a year old then, Papa said. I was already walking well. My favourite toys were empty matchboxes and bunches of keys. Apart from 'Papa' and 'Maman' I kept saying the word for egg, *oeuf*. In the photograph I was sitting on Maman's knee, on a bench in the park. Maman was pretending to eat my hand, trapping the ends of my tiny fingers in her mouth. I was laughing at her game.

'You look like your mother, Jacques,' Rebecca said, nodding, looking up at me, then back at the photograph, without awkwardness. Her naturalness made me feel less uncomfortable and nervous. 'You have her colouring ... the same dark eyebrows, thick eyelashes and high cheekbones. She's beautiful. She looks so glamorous with her lovely long hair pinned up like that. Her skin's as white as milk. Very French, I think.'

'That is true.'

It was all that I could manage. My whole body ached. My thoughts were muddled with tiredness. But I wanted to talk about Maman and was relieved that I had something familiar to refer to, however much a reminder of the life I had lost.

'Rebecca! What are you doing? Come down now, please.' It was Anna, summoning her insistently.

'I'm sorry, Jacques. I'll have to go,' Rebecca whispered. 'But I really want to see the rest. There'll be plenty of times when my parents are at work. It's different then. Sometimes both of them are out until quite late in the evening. Normally they work a lot of the weekends as well. We have Mrs Chadwick looking after us, but she mostly does housework. We get left to our own devices a lot, especially after school.'

I wished Rebecca could have stayed with me. The room seemed immediately so much colder and emptier without her. As soon as she left, without her interested questions and lively, distracting conversation, I felt frightened and keenly aware of how alone I was.

I was too exhausted to unpack anything else that night. I put the photograph of Maman and me back in the cigar box and bound it with the ribbon. Not knowing what else to do to help myself, I lay down on top of the bedspread and held the box against my chest. I didn't have the energy to undo the tightly tucked, folded over sheet, locking in the blankets underneath. I made myself recall Rebecca's face and her encouraging voice and how she'd handled my photographs with such care. I then fell asleep on the narrow bed, following dark specks of birds flitting across the screen of the skylight above my head.

3

It was as Rebecca had said. After that weekend, when Oliver and Anna Clark returned to their usual work patterns, life took on a different shape, which, to my mind, was much more agreeable. I was woken the following morning by Mrs Chadwick – 'Mrs Chad' the family sometimes called her – the Clarks' housekeeper. There was something about her that reminded me slightly of Madame Dupont. She was probably in her early sixties, rotund, with tightly permed silver hair. She wore a canvas apron smelling faintly of fried food, over a flowery cotton blouse and pleated skirt. She had quite a different accent from the Clarks. When she pronounced her vowels especially, the sounds were fuller and seemed somehow to come from further back in her mouth.

'Time to get up, son. Your uniform's in the cupboard. Wash your hands and face and get dressed. Downstairs for breakfast, soon as you can, young man.'

The drawers and wardrobe of my room were already stocked with meticulously folded and pressed uniforms and other clothes, all 'age 11yrs', labelled with my name, Jacques Lafitte, written on cotton tapes, neatly hand-sewn into collars and hems. My bathroom was also supplied with perfect stacks of packaged soap, flannels and towels. Anna Clark demonstrated her commitment to material organisation. Her home was equipped with almost military precision.

Uncle Oliver and Anna had already left, Mrs Chadwick said, he for London, she for one of her 'Women's Clinics' near Manchester. 'She's supposed to be a very good surgeon, Mrs Clark,' Mrs Chadwick told me downstairs in the kitchen, before Rebecca and Matthew arrived. 'You have to have the right sort of brain for that. She helps lots of young women, you know. With their … problems.' I thought it best to nod to show that I was listening, although I had no idea then what kind of 'problems' Mrs Chadwick was referring to.

'Morning, Mrs Chad.' It was Rebecca, pulling a cardigan on over her school shirt and tie.

'Hello, Rebecca. Sit down and have your breakfast. I was just telling this young man about how good your mother is at her job.'

Rebecca edged in next to me on the bench. She was yawning, still pallid and creased from sleep.

'So. Has Mrs Chad told you what my mother does, Jacques? Bet you'd never guess! She does abortions! You know what an abortion is, don't you, Jacques?'

'No,' I replied.

'And perhaps it's just as well that …' Mrs Chadwick began, lifting a warning finger at Rebecca. Rebecca ignored her.

'It's when a woman or even a teenage girl gets pregnant, and then chooses not to give birth to her child. They operate and take the poor little baby bud out of her womb. Mum won't tell me what they do with them. But they don't have a proper funeral.

I think it's horrible. A baby isn't just a thing you can throw out with the rubbish, is it? A baby's a baby, whatever size it is. I don't know how she does it. I know I couldn't. Could you?'

'No,' I said. I couldn't think of anything else to say.

'That's enough, Rebecca,' Mrs Chadwick intervened. 'Jacques is far too young to understand. And so are you.'

'No I'm not. And I don't see why I can't have my own opinion. I don't have to agree with Mum because I'm her daughter. And anyway, she doesn't have to listen to the comments I get from some of the girls at school.'

'Such as?' Mrs Chadwick asked.

'Such as, "Here comes the murderer's daughter",' Rebecca told her abruptly.

'Oh, just ignore them, Rebecca. Silly little thoughtless girls. What do they understand about anything anyway? Not everyone could help people like your mother does.'

'No, they couldn't. They couldn't be so unfeeling. You have to not feel to throw out a baby bud.'

'That's enough now. Eat your breakfast, Rebecca!' Mrs Chadwick was losing patience.

I picked up my own cutlery and began to eat, aware of Rebecca's restless mood. Her head was low above her plate, her knotty hair falling around her face, almost touching her food, her hands twisting under the table on her lap.

'We'll be late if you don't get eating now,' Mrs Chadwick remarked. 'I'm not driving like a maniac. You know I'm taking Jacques to school as well today.'

'I won't eat the mushrooms,' Rebecca said, petulantly.

'Why ever not?' Mrs Chadwick snapped.

'They're the little button ones. They remind me of baby buds.'

Rebecca was moving the mushrooms one by one, using the side of her fork, making a neat pile of them on the opposite edge of her plate. 'I'm going to keep them. I'll dry them out and put them in a little box. I might decide to bury it.'

'Oh, don't talk such nonsense, Rebecca!' Mrs Chadwick said in exasperation. 'You know very well you can't dry mushrooms like that! They'll just smell and go mouldy. You really are being childish! And I thought you were turning into such a clever young lady. You should be setting a better example for Jacques.'

'Why?' Rebecca answered, irascibly.

'That's enough now, Rebecca! Brush your teeth. Get your school bag. I'll be having a word with your mother about your behaviour at this rate.'

'You keep saying that. But you never do, Mrs Chad, do you?'

Rebecca escaped from the kitchen before Mrs Chadwick could grab hold of her. I was alone again at the table. 'Where is Matthew, Mrs Chadwick?' I asked. The housekeeper's face and neck were flushed. She was bending over, muttering under her breath, scraping Rebecca's mushrooms hurriedly into the bin.

'Matthew always goes ahead. Walks to school with his friends. You'll do the same probably when you're older.'

Mrs Chadwick left me outside the front doors of Chester Prince's School. Prince's was a private boys' school, described by Uncle Oliver as 'very prestigious, with a great reputation for impressive results'. As I stood outside the school buildings, I felt lost, fragile and insignificant. I had been used to my school in Neuilly, the small, child-friendly single-storey building with obscured glass windows, divided into tiny, lead-framed panes. My first little school behind green railings bubbling with rust, with its enclosed playground, where I knew every crack on the tarmac, every mud-floored den in the bushes and almost every adult and child.

I was about to approach the front doors of the school, when a stout young woman, wearing an ankle-length black gown, came out. 'Jacques Lafitte? I'm Miss Jenkins, your form tutor. Also in the Music Department. Welcome to Prince's. Hope you can understand my Welsh accent! So sorry you've had to come to us through difficult circumstances, but … well, I hope you'll be happy here.'

In Miss Jenkins' company, I instantly felt safer and more comfortable. She wore sweet perfume that reminded me of Maman's. Although I didn't understand everything she said, I was charmed by her melodious voice. 'This is the entrance hall, Jacques. I'll be taking you round the school in a minute, but I need to let someone in the office know you're here first,' Miss Jenkins explained. 'Do you play an instrument? You look like the sort of boy who'd play an instrument.'

'Yes,' I replied. 'The piano. I play classical music mostly.'

'Oh, do you? How very impressive! And what would be your favourite piece, Jacques?'

'Beethoven. The *Moonlight Sonata*, probably. I can't play much of it myself, but Maman used to play it to me. She also liked Chopin waltzes and Schubert.'

'Did she, now? How lovely.'

Miss Jenkins seemed to be touched by what I had said. She took a tissue from her sleeve, and wiped her eyes. 'Right then,

Jacques.' She cupped a hand behind my elbow and guided me across the entrance hall.

As we were about to leave on our tour of the classrooms, I caught sight of Matthew Clark, standing with his back against a radiator, shuffling among a group of boys. He saw me too. I waved in his direction but received no acknowledgement. He simply stared back blankly, shook his head so that his fringe fell in front of his narrowed eyes, and looked down at his shoes.

For the first time, it occurred to me that Matthew probably resented my intrusion into his life. We had been forced to live together, through no choice of our own. I wanted him to accept me, but I suspected that there would be little I could do to change his mind. At the same time, I remembered what Mrs Chadwick had said – that perhaps I would behave like Matthew when I was older. I hoped then that I would be different.

I also realised in that moment what it was that I missed most about Neuilly. Maman and Papa had loved me without question. They were naturally interested in everything I said and did. I had never felt that I had to prove my worth or explain myself constantly to strangers before. Suddenly, without a true home and family, it was up to me actively to earn the sympathy of those around me. They couldn't be made to want to know Jacques Lafitte. The thought frightened me. I started to feel nauseous again. I belonged properly to no one. While I immediately liked Rebecca and felt she was on my side, I had no way of knowing how long her interest in me would last. Although Uncle Oliver had been given the task of looking after me, I could tell that he didn't really love me. Anna seemed so distant and sharp compared to my own soft, ever-forgiving Maman.

My thoughts turned back to the source of Rebecca's unhappiness earlier that morning. Her mention of the 'poor little baby bud', unwanted, taken surgically from a woman's womb. The fragile beginnings of a person, destined for some uncertain kind of disposal. I carried an image of the button mushrooms in my mind, all the rest of that day, trying to repress the memory of seeing Mrs Chadwick cursing under her breath as she scraped the curled, half-formed shapes into the kitchen bin.

In those early days of my new life with the Clarks, I often felt as if I had been immersed in an enormous tank, filled with murky water. The sides, top and bottom of the tank were in the background somewhere, but I couldn't reach them. Occasionally, shafts of warmth and light would pierce through, but mostly it felt as if I was surrounded by varied depths of shadow and shifting shapes. My tongue, my brain and the rest of my body, previously so quick and energetic, seemed to be in slow motion. At times I would feel so overwhelmed it was almost as if I was drowning in the strangeness of everything. I had to cling desperately to the memories of what I had once known. Gradually I became more resigned. I learned to adapt. My sadness, together with the new habitat it permeated, forced me to evolve into a different person.

My parents had always encouraged me to paint. They had bought me a portable watercolour set from an old-fashioned art shop in Neuilly – a quaint cupboard of a place, smelling of linseed oil, filled with pencils, charcoals, paints and sketch-books, which were all hoarded in a honeycomb of pigeon-holes and served by a pot-bellied, hirsute Corsican, with bulbous brown eyes. The set came in a slim black box, containing a mixing palette, trays of watercolour bricks and three paintbrushes. I had been a reluctant artist at first. 'I'm not good at copying things, Papa. Especially people. It doesn't look like your face, does it?' I once asked.

'You must practise, of course. But the important thing is to paint what you see, Jacques. We all have different ways of perceiving, our particular view. Paint your feelings, your own impressions.'

As time went on, I began to paint secretly in my room at the Clarks' house. I would lock myself in my bathroom, pretend that I was having a bath. I would set my paints on top of the laundry bin and sit on the toilet seat with my paper block. I knew there wasn't time for detailed representations, and this liberated me to concentrate on simple impressions.

In Neuilly, I had used light, delicate washes of Aurora Yellow and Rose Doré, delighted in the brightness of Vermilion and Cerulean. I took care not to overwork the surface of my paper. In England, my Indigo, Prussian Blue, Sepia and Charcoal Grey quickly developed deep hollows. I used less water, twisted down hard on the brush, as if I was holding a stick or a sturdy mop, turning it mercilessly in the wells of colour.

I worked repetitively on sombre views of the Clarks' garden, the forms of weeping willows plunging down, lengthening out of all proportion, throwing themselves headlong at the ground with the force of waterfalls. I depicted the River Dee – a broad unreflective band of opaque greys and blues, scratched by the lines of fallen branches, dead birds' wings and corners of half-submerged litter. I captured some of my perceptions of Prince's School. The dark tunnels of its corridors, expanses of blackboard scored with monotonous lines, neither figures nor letters, towering skeletons of buildings. I reduced myself to a scarcely noticeable grey dot, on the lower edge of the paper. In another image, as I remembered playing Miss Jenkins' piano, I felt myself expand as I painted a faintly bracketed space, filled with a chaos of musical notes and keyboard blacks and whites, highlighted with yellow lines.

At other times, I recorded my impressions of people. Anna Clark, her face a blank, featureless oval, sitting alone at a sepia desk, in a swirling charcoal cocoon. Matthew, a black stick figure, merging into an equally dark background. Uncle Oliver, a round, cross-hatched ball of a head, attached to an elongated arm, continuous with a brown box of a briefcase. My maths teacher, a descending grey spiral. My English teacher, a face of diluted indigo, top-heavy with thick Prussian Blue frown lines. Like Miss Jenkins and the keys of her piano, I associated Rebecca with the shafts of light piercing the depths of my murky world. I always painted her in lemon yellow. Sometimes as a simple round of colour, sometimes as a circle, filled with curls or five-point stars.

I destroyed a lot of these paintings afterwards. I think at the time it seemed the best way of both expressing and protecting my own secret feelings. I wet each picture, rubbed it with soap and held it under the running hot tap until the paint had washed off. I then tore the saturated paper into small pieces, which I hid in the pocket of my school bag, until I could get rid of them in the playground bin.

I often felt better for a while after painting, as if the process had released something that I couldn't quite sum up in words. I felt lighter, more free. My world seemed less blurred and dark.

As my paintings of that period expressed, I felt closer to Rebecca than to the rest of her family. While we both agreed early on that we would never see each other as brother and sister, we were naturally drawn together as friends, enjoying and seeking each other's company. Anna, Uncle Oliver and Matthew, it seemed, chose, consciously or unconsciously, to keep their distance from me and also from each other. Anna and Uncle Oliver, even when they were under the same roof, generally spent their time apart. I rarely saw them in the morning, only heard their cars, one at seven, the other at seven-thirty, tyres crunching the gravel on the front drive. When they did both return, it was some time after seven-thirty in the evening, after Rebecca, Matthew and I had been fed by Mrs Chadwick and told to finish our home-work. They greeted us briefly and went to their own offices, Anna's on the ground floor and Uncle Oliver's on the second, on the same corridor as his children's bedrooms. I never saw them actually eat together, except whenever the meal had an agenda, in which case it would involve the whole family. Usually they simply lifted their dinner trays prepared by Mrs Chadwick, poured a glass of wine and disappeared in opposite directions. As he was frequently away on business, often Uncle Oliver wouldn't come back for up to a week.

As Anna had told me the evening after I arrived, when she outlined her 'House Rules', the couple were only to be interrupted if it was an emergency, or when it was time to say goodnight. On these occasions we had to come individually to their respective office doors, knock quietly and wait to be invited in. Anna Clark often left her door ajar. She would either be at her desk, writing notes, or reading in an armchair. Her wine-glass always seemed to be empty, the last drop staying, like blood, in the bottom of the glass, leaking, or so it seemed, into the stem below. Anna's armchair was straight-backed with stiff wings, upholstered in buttoned, mahogany-coloured leather. Once, when she was out, I slipped into her room, wondering what it would be like to sit in the chair. In spite of the luxurious appearance of its cushions, I discovered that its surface was completely unyielding. It seemed to tolerate rather than support my weight. When I stood up and looked back at the robust, tightly stuffed seat, I seemed to have left no impression whatsoever.

Anna had a habit of letting me wait every night, after I had knocked, before she acknowledged my presence and then fixed on me unblinkingly over the sharp frames of her half-glasses.

'I hope you've had a productive day, Jacques,' she would finally say. The lines on her lips were stained crimson with wine, her words, usually staccato, more legato. 'It's probably the best some of us can expect. If only we didn't have perpetually dry eyes.' She would sigh, then reach for the miniature bottle she kept on her desk. She would take off her glasses, let her head fall back heavily and deliver a drop of the solution into each eye. 'Age has made me arid, Jacques. Dry as a stone! Though stones have their uses, don't they? We wall places off. Put suffering wretches out of their misery.' The same repeating theme, occasionally slight variations on the words. Then, 'Go to bed, Jacques! If you believe in God, it might be worth asking if you can at least be useful. It really has been my main consolation.'

I didn't believe in God. Like my Papa, I never had. Maman had always whispered that she thought there might be a kind spirit watching over us. She told me that she wanted me to have faith in things that I couldn't see, to go to sleep trusting that a good spirit had me personally in mind. To make her happy, I had reassured her that I would. However, like Papa, I thought that the best that I could probably do was to try and look after myself.

On the way to my bedroom, I would knock on the door of Uncle Oliver's office. It was always kept closed. It sounded as if Uncle Oliver was constantly on the phone or dictating notes briskly into his voice recorder. When he heard my knock, I could hear him tutting impatiently. He unlocked the door and emerged on a warm wave of sweat, aftershave and cigarette smoke, still in his suit jacket, his tie loose, slightly askew. 'Off to bed, are we, Jacques? Great stuff. Good day, was it? That's what I like to hear!' I had said nothing. 'Up you trot.' He closed the door even before I had the chance to turn. As I climbed the stairs to my bedroom, I would overhear him do and say exactly the same things to his own daughter or son.

It was on one such occasion and with equal brevity that Uncle Oliver chose to inform me of the death of my grandmother in France. 'Oh, by the way, Jacques. Got some news for you, I'm afraid. Your grandmother passed away this morning. It was all perfectly peaceful, I gather. She went in her sleep.'

I hadn't known my grandmother very well due to the early onset of her illness. I had gone occasionally with Maman to visit her in the nursing home, had sat in the soft chair covered with cardigans and stockings next to the bedside cabinet, while Maman tried to talk to her. Sometimes she had been in bed, wearing her lace-collared nightdress buttoned right up to the neck, fidgeting, constantly pinching at invisible objects on her bed covers. At other times she had moved restlessly about the room, as if searching for things she never seemed to find. With her trailing white hair held back on either side with small jewel-headed clips, her bulging dark eyes, pale long hands and bare feet below her nightdress, she reminded me of an ethereal dragonfly, flitting around the surface of a pond. Maman had warned me that she was very confused, that she couldn't remember from one minute to the next who we were or where she was, facts that I found strange and at the same time fascinating. I knew that Maman found the visits upsetting. She would cry when she described what had happened later to Papa, recounting how frail her mother had looked, how again she had failed to recognise her.

'So will I be going to France for the funeral, Uncle Oliver?' I asked.

'Oh, don't worry about that, Jacques. Everything is being taken care of. There will be money due to you from her estate when the formalities are settled. No need to disrupt your schooling. Your grandmother was very old. All in the hands of God, as they say. Off to bed now, Jacques!' As I would later come to understand, Uncle Oliver had an occasional, functional and gestural form of Christianity.

I had no choice but to accept that Uncle Oliver had said everything that he wanted to say about my grandmother. I went upstairs that night feeling sad, not as much for her or myself, as for Maman. If I had been able to attend the funeral, it would have been for her sake, to say goodbye on her behalf.

My main source of comfort during those years in the 1980s derived from the times that I had with Rebecca. We spent every afternoon after school together, as well as most of the weekends and school holidays. I could tell that she genuinely liked my company and wanted to help me feel happier and more confident. She would also fiercely come to my defence, even in situations involving her parents.

Rebecca was the sort of person who was naturally fascinated by others. I was relieved that her curiosity about me wasn't just a passing phase. She persisted in asking me about my life in France. We would sit on my bed, spread out all my photographs and I would recount my associations with each one. As she questioned me, I often remembered aspects of incidents I hadn't recalled before.

'So where was this? It looks like you're on holiday?'

'Yes. Les Gorges du Tarn. It was a very hot day. Papa and I played in the river. You can't see Maman. She took the picture. Can you see the little walls of stones at the edge? Papa and I made lots of tiny harbours and filled them with boats we had made out of leaves and twigs.'

'He must have been very patient, your Papa. To play with a child like that, all afternoon.' Rebecca stared hard at the photograph, scrutinising it within inches of her face. 'I don't remember our father ever playing with us like that.'

'How about your mother?'

'No. She never played. She was always too busy. We didn't have holidays like you hear about other families having together. We sometimes went away for a few days and had walks and meals in restaurants, like we do occasionally now in the summer. It's serious and grown-up. Mum and Dad always take work with them. It's not much fun. Especially since Matthew has turned into a teenage zombie. He says I'm infantile. Mrs Chad says it's because of his age, but I don't think he should have an excuse for being nasty. He hasn't exactly been friendly to you, has he?'

'I think that he does not want a French boy living in his house.'

'Oh, just ignore him! He's got about as much brains as a stick insect.'

'A stick insect?'

'Yes! I don't know what it is in French. Those skinny, ugly things like sticks, from tropical places. They spend ages just creeping and lying around, trying to merge into their surroundings. Horrible and boring! Anyway. Let's not talk about Matthew. Tell me about this picture instead. Were these your school friends?'

Rebecca also delighted in 'debriefing' me after my school day, inviting me to relate my feelings about teachers and fellow pupils. She had a knack of helping me to feel better by encouraging me to laugh at people, quickly inventing her own nicknames and eccentric voices for them and making me describe and exaggerate their traits. 'So, how was Poggy Pig today, Jacques?' She would fall about hysterically on the bed and roll off onto the floor holding her stomach, consumed by her own humour. 'Was his poor lickle bwain feeling stodgkins? Was he cwoss because it was too long 'til his dindins?'

'Yes!' I would join in, although I knew that I couldn't do the voices as well as Rebecca. 'He was a very sad little pig. He couldn't wait for the bell.'

Rebecca and I also played outdoors whenever we could. Sometimes her friends, Jennifer and Louise, would join us in the garden. We would devise obstacle courses, running races, versions of ball games, such as rounders and volleyball. We weren't really supposed to play ball games on the lawn – Anna didn't like holes worn in the grass. But as long as we put everything away afterwards, Mrs Chadwick turned a blind eye.

While Rebecca liked spending time with Jennifer and Louise, she also enjoyed sharing her observations of their foibles with me after they'd gone home, knowing that I would take what she said in the right spirit. 'I'm not being horrible, but have you seen the way Louise runs now, Jacques?' she asked me one afternoon. 'All girly tippy-toes! She doesn't like to get dirty or mess her face or her hair up. Especially when you're watching!'

'What do you mean?' I asked, innocently.

'Because you're a boy, of course! And you're French!' she took pleasure in informing me, rolling her eyes. 'She never used to care so much about what she looked like, but she's never her natural self around boys any more. She's always pouting and preening, as if she's posing for a photograph. Jennifer's not much better. They're forever giggling and whispering together at school, talking about boys from Prince's they fancy. They don't really know any of them. They could never have a proper conversation. I mean, what's the point of saying you really like someone, if you can't even talk to them?'

'You're right,' I agreed with her. I found her revelations about the psychology and behaviour of teenage girls intriguing, even if it felt as if I would never properly understand that mysterious other world she described.

As well as playing in the garden, we would explore the city centre, often visiting Chester Cathedral, the Rows and the remains of the Amphitheatre. Rebecca had a remarkable memory for details and a proud manner of telling the city's stories as if they were her own.

What I much preferred were the times when Rebecca and I were together by ourselves. It felt far less complicated. Whether we were talking or quiet, we could relax, without any pressure to compete or try to impress each other. Often we'd just take some food into the garden and sit, or lie on our fronts, side by side on a rug, doing homework, reading or talking.

In the late summer, around a year after I had arrived in England, at the back of the garage we found an old badminton net, two rackets in creaking wooden presses and some yellowed feather shuttlecocks. The net had originally come from Rebecca's grandmother's house in Wales. Her parents had played occasionally when they were younger, Rebecca explained.

We tied the net between two willow trees and Rebecca used lengths of rope to mark out the boundaries of a simple court on the grass. We started to play badminton in the evenings, weather permitting, and continued well into October. I'd played some tennis, but never badminton before. Rebecca taught me the basic rules, although since we were playing outside for fun, she said, we could be quite relaxed. Patiently, she taught me how to serve, dropping the shuttlecock and following through with the racket. It took me some time to connect the two and get the shuttlecock consistently over the high net. 'I'm sorry, Rebecca,' I kept apologising. I was frustrated with my clumsiness, desperate to learn quickly so that the game would be better for her.

'It's fine, Jacques. Don't worry. You'll soon get the hang of it. You mustn't be hard on yourself. I mean, I've been playing for ages. I didn't find serving easy myself to begin with.' I guessed she was underplaying her own ability, but I was grateful for her encouraging words and the way that she allowed me so many extra chances. I felt that I was gradually improving. By October, even if not on an equal footing, we were able to play a good fast game. We both felt sad, knowing that the days were shortening and that soon we wouldn't be able to continue due to the lack of light.

I particularly loved some of our later October games, as the leaves changed colour in the garden. There were windfall apples and pears on the grass, the air was growing damp and cool as autumn edged in. With the dimming light, against the stillness, the sounds of our voices and the shuttlecock buzzing through the air seemed somehow keener.

'Don't you wish we could just go on and on playing like this, Jacques?' I remember Rebecca saying one particular evening. We had finished a game and were just keeping the shuttlecock going easily to and fro over the net as we talked. 'The two of us always have a good time, don't we?'

'Yes, we always do,' I replied. It was heartening hearing her express exactly what I felt myself. 'I love our games. I feel like … it's a bit like I'm a shuttlecock myself … flying.'

'Yes! High up with the wind through your feathers!' Rebecca answered, laughing. 'I know what you mean. Oh Jacques! I like the way we can talk to each other. However stupid or crazy I am, you don't mind. We can just say things, can't we?'

'Of course!' I agreed.

'You know, I can't imagine ever having a better friend than you,' Rebecca then said, as she returned my shot. I was so touched by her compliment that I lost concentration and hit it into the net. 'Oh sorry, Jacques. That was my fault for talking to you.' She screwed up her eyes, smiled slightly awkwardly at me, then looked down at her hand pressed flat against the strings of her racket.

'No. It was my fault,' I told her, approaching the net to collect the shuttlecock. 'And … what you said … it's the same for me, Rebecca. I've never had a friend like you before.'

We both stood still where we were, saying nothing, just smiling, looking each other in the eyes. I wasn't quite sure what to do next, although I was completely sure that I meant what I'd said.

'It's getting a bit dark to play, but it's still so nice out here, isn't it? I don't really want to go in yet. Do you, Jacques?' Rebecca said after a while.

'No, I don't. Although I'm not sure what else we can do. It's getting cold for sitting around.'

'Why don't we go for a walk? Down by the river? We needn't be long. Just to the edge of the Meadows? My parents aren't going to worry. It's nowhere near properly dark yet. And they'll think we're still in the garden.'

It was only a short walk to the path by the River Dee, in the direction of the Meadows. We'd sometimes go there earlier in the day with Jennifer and Louise. They would chatter incessantly. The girls would take turns to hold Jennifer's irritable Yorkshire terrier, Jippy, sharing school stories and crumpled paper bags of sweets. I would wander dreamily at a distance behind them. Although not far from the city centre, I enjoyed the relative wildness of the place. The expanses of open, riverside ground, ruffled by summer wind, reminded me of the broad back of a gentle animal, drying its matted pelt in the sun. I would imagine myself sometimes, grasping the strong tussocks of the beast's hair, feeling it breathing underneath my stomach. In my fantasies, the whole back would gradually lift up. I would be lying snug against its warm spine and be carried upwards into clear turquoise sky. The beast would then transform into a magic carpet, ready to take me anywhere I wanted to go. In many ways, while moving towards adolescence, my imagination was still very childlike.

That evening, when Rebecca and I walked close together on the narrowing path in the half-light, the river was hushed and calm.

'So different from during the day here, isn't it?' Rebecca said.

'Yes. I think I prefer it. The river has a thoughtful, secret feeling,' I replied.

'And it feels exciting. Doing something you've not done before ... just you and me ... in the evening. Doing what we want to do, without other people making us follow their rules.'

I was walking with my hands in my pockets as she slipped her arm through mine and pulled me in against her side to keep warm. I had started to shiver a bit myself and it felt natural to be close to her, sharing our body heat.

'Yes it is,' I acknowledged, finding it hard to think about anything but Rebecca's closeness to me, the soft bare skin of her arm touching mine, but trusting that it didn't matter whether I spoke or not. As we returned along the path, still linked in the same way, and through the quiet streets to the house, I felt happy, knowing that I was appreciated, just for being myself. It meant so much that we had spoken of our mutual affection and it made our bond feel even stronger. Even if I couldn't have verbalised it all, somewhere inside I knew then that with Rebecca I belonged; however distant from my own *terroir*, I was at home.

4

The Clarks' 'family lounge', as it was called by Mrs Chadwick, was a relatively small room on the ground floor. The label 'family' didn't really apply to it at that time, as it was only mainly used by Rebecca and me. Occasionally, when he had invited some friends and we were elsewhere, Matthew would watch television there, although generally he preferred to stay in his bedroom.

On the other side of the house, there was a long room divided by French doors. At one end there was a formal dining area, floored in thick carpet with bold blue and red swirling patterns, dominated by a polished rectangular table and eight throne-like chairs. Above the table was the antique crystal chandelier that I saw Mrs Chadwick dusting regularly. The light was hardly ever switched on. Anna and Uncle Oliver rarely entertained. 'If I had a beautiful light like this I'd have it on all the time,' Mrs Chadwick would confide in me. 'I'd lead my whole life under that light and think I was already in heaven!'

On the other side of the French doors was an equally formal sitting-room, with a stiff chaise-longue and a selection of antique chairs with pert, fringed cushions. Dark green ivies trailed down from wrought iron stands. There was a black marble fire-place, where I had never seen the fire lit, the grate concealed behind a funereal metal screen decorated with a relief of what looked like brooding pods or buds, destined never to come into flower. I gathered from Mrs Chadwick that some of the Clarks' furniture had been inherited from Anna's deceased mother, a wealthy woman with a penchant for antiques, who had lived on her own until she had died, five years previously, in a grand house in North Wales.

In the corner of the sitting-room, however, there was something that made me keep coming back. It was Anna's mother's upright Bechstein piano. Most of the time it would be hidden under a Welsh lace shawl, its tapestry-covered stool tucked underneath, until Mrs Chadwick came to dust it. She would lift down the solemn pewter box and the metronome from the top, fold the shawl and dust the piano thoroughly, outside and inside. Before closing its lid, she would run her duster from the top to the bottom of the keyboard, playfully press down a few keys, then assiduously rub away her fingerprints. I liked to observe her secretly from behind the French doors. I couldn't understand why someone would have a piano and never play it. One day, Mrs Chadwick caught me watching her.

'You can come and take a proper look if you like, Jacques.'

I was at her side instantly, stroking the smooth, polished white keys.

'Have you ever played yourself, son?' Mrs Chadwick had reverted to the rhythm of her cleaning ritual, following my fingers with her duster.

'Yes. My mother had a Bechstein too. She taught me. Maman was very gifted, I think. Papa said that she was.'

'Did he now? And I'm sure he was right. Could you play without music?'

She pulled out the piano stool and motioned for me to sit down. 'Why don't you play something for us?'

I sat down and rested my right hand, as my mother had taught me, over the keys, thumb at Middle C. I remembered sitting at Maman's beautiful piano, her warm breath at my cheek. My fingers sitting on top of her own fingers as she played chords. The jaunty ticking of the metronome, Maman clapping to its time. My pleasure growing as I felt more and more fluent with the music, as I absorbed Maman's tender words of praise. The memory of her encouraging, gentle voice made my eyes start to fill with tears.

'Play something, Jacques.' This time it was Mrs Chadwick. 'It doesn't matter if you make mistakes. Try and remember a tune.'

I started to play, my mind struggling, having to trust my fingers' memory, the beginning of an arrangement of Tchaikovsky's 'Dance of the Sugar Plum Fairy'. 'Oh, how lovely.' I was aware of Mrs Chadwick sighing, murmuring in the background, but I was mostly with Maman, my eyes pricking with her compliments, the bright enchantment of the little piece. 'Play something else now, Jacques.' I played an arrangement of Beethoven's 'Ode to Joy'. Maman had bought me a book of pieces by classical composers, simplified versions for children, which she had encouraged me to learn by heart. Papa had often amused his business guests by telling them that I was fully fluent in the works of all the greats.

'You're very clever, Jacques. I'm sorry to have to stop you, but I have to finish cleaning now. Pity no one else plays. Neither Matthew nor Rebecca seem interested. Mrs Clark's mother played a lot apparently, but she never opens it herself. Always insists it stays covered up.'

It wasn't until 1986, when I was in my second year at Prince's, that Anna gave me permission to play her mother's piano. She had been approached by Miss Jenkins, who suggested that I take piano lessons with her at school. Ideally, I would need to practise at home, if that was at all possible.

Anna asked me to accompany her into the sitting-room. She carefully unveiled the piano and told me to sit on the chaise-longue. 'You will practise twice a day, without fail, Jacques. In the morning before breakfast and in the evening, after homework. I expect you to treat my piano with the utmost respect. Privilege always comes with responsibility. If I am in any doubt, I will cancel your lessons immediately. You will wipe the keys after each use, and replace the cover and stool. Is that clear?'

'Yes, Anna. I am very happy. Thank you so much.' I could barely control my excitement. Although Mrs Chadwick had continued to ask me to play each time she dusted the piano, I had longed to be able to use it more openly and frequently.

I enjoyed my evening practices best. Occasionally Rebecca would sit on the floor close to the piano stool and listen to me play. She knew that I preferred not to talk when I was playing. At first I would be slightly self-conscious, aware of her being there, until I became absorbed. I would then start to concentrate more on keeping time, on the movement and conversations between my hands, the effects of the pedals. The phrases of sound would connect with something inside me, my feelings recognising, identifying instinctively with the rise and fall, the shifting moods. Images would come flooding into my mind. Pictures from memory. Others pure fantasies, summoned, created by the music's magical force. 'You look like you go into another world when you play the piano, Jacques,' Rebecca told me. 'It's so … I mean, it suits you, the way you start to move. The kinds of faces that you make, the way your fingers lift up, touching the keys, but above them, gathering the notes. You're so clever! Much more musical than I am. I've never been very good. I wanted to join the school choir but they said that I sang flat. I don't mind, I suppose. Luckily I'm quite good at science and sport. But I wish I could be really talented like you.'

I was extremely surprised when Anna started to make a habit of coming into the room about halfway through my practice. The first time I heard her, I turned round and stopped playing at once. 'Carry on, will you, Jacques? I'm just reading in the other room.' She had a glass of wine in one hand and a handful of papers in the other. From the corner of my eye, I was aware of her going into the dining-room, leaving one of the French doors open and sitting down at the far end of the table. When I finished my practice she would still be there, no longer reading but drinking her wine, staring at a picture on the wall, her chair pushed back from the table. I would say goodnight and she would usually acknowledge me briefly and continue staring in the same direction.

I had been playing for about six months when one evening, instead of dismissing me, Anna asked me to step into the dining-room.

'You play well, Jacques. You obviously … have a talent for this.' Anna's frank words of approval were completely unexpected. I was embarrassed and confused, but at the same time overwhelmed with gratitude. Her voice had lost its abrasive edge – it had a hesitant, fragile quality that I didn't associate with Anna.

'Thank you, Anna. I like to play. I always …'

'I can tell. You're very connected with the music. Not everyone feels that.'

Anna had been looking at me directly. She turned back to the picture on the wall and contemplated it in silence. I had asked Mrs Chadwick about the painting. It had belonged to Anna's mother and was the work of a Welsh artist, an old friend of Anna's mother's parents. It was a depiction of a mountain landscape in oils – somewhere in Snowdonia, Mrs Chadwick thought – a dusky rendering of hills and stone walls, with a mood of impending storm.

'Music is important, Jacques.' Anna kept her eyes on the painting. 'For reasons that you can't possibly understand yet. There are things that can't be said. Things music speaks to that … my mother wanted me to learn to play. I didn't have the patience and then I didn't have the time. I had so many other, better things to do – at least, so I thought. She told me that I would always regret it. My mother was good at that. Although this time she really was right. I do regret it. So many regrets, Jacques. And now … it's too late.'

'Maman wanted me to play the piano too. She would often stay to keep me company while I was practising. When I play I remember the happy times when we sat together, listening to each other, or learning duets,' I said quietly.

Nothing had prepared me for Anna's sadness. She had been angry, bitter, generally imperiously in command and I had learned to be comfortable with that. Yet I still found myself wanting to try and console her. 'I am certain that you could have piano lessons, if you would like to,' I suggested, nervously, as cheerfully as I could. I felt too bold and out of my depth, but was intent upon saying something. 'Perhaps a teacher could come and teach you here in the evening. I think that an adult would learn very quickly. Especially an intelligent person, like you.'

Anna turned back towards me and toasted me with her wineglass. 'You're right, Jacques. In theory I could. If only it were all so simple. For some of us, unfortunately, there's no going back. Our hearts are no longer so open and innocent. Our hands are heavy and irrevocably stained. I have too much blood on my hands, Jacques. Even for a surgeon. No amount of piano lessons would take that away.'

I didn't know what to say. Everything about Anna seemed different and unpredictable in those moments. The only thing I knew was that the answer was beyond me. I looked down awkwardly, making my eyes swirl with the red and blue shapes on the carpet. Anna suddenly stood up and set down her glass. She put her hands into her skirt pockets and looked down at her black patent shoes. 'I'm sorry, Jacques. I don't expect you to say anything, of course. The main thing is that you continue to practise your piano. Time for bed now. See you tomorrow.'

'Goodnight, Anna.'

I went upstairs to say goodnight to Uncle Oliver before I went to bed, still struggling to make sense of what Anna had said. I also had in my mind the things that Rebecca kept repeating resentfully about her mother's work, the 'horrible' abortions that happened every day of the week in those remote, unseen places where 'baby buds', as Rebecca described them, were taken from wombs. Anna's words and behaviour towards me that evening had challenged the view that I had held of her since I had arrived. It would have been simpler for me to side with Rebecca and to keep believing in a simplified account of Anna's character, which didn't include any hints of such feelings as sadness, guilt or regret. However, even at thirteen, I suspected that the most accurate version of the truth was the less simplified one, despite the unsettling feeling that it generated.

Outside Uncle Oliver's office, I stood quietly for a moment. It sounded as if he was on the phone. Normally I didn't bother tuning into what he was saying. It would inevitably be about things I had no interest or understanding of, always loaded with technical jargon and numbers. That night, however, Uncle Oliver's voice sounded markedly different. 'So, are you really alright?' I heard him asking. 'I'm sorry I couldn't have stayed any longer. Only … it's difficult. I'll try and think up an excuse tomorrow. We could go for dinner in that little Italian place in Manchester you like. I'll say I have to stay away overnight. Anna won't question it.' I began to feel uncomfortable again. I guessed that it wasn't a conversation that I was meant to hear. I knocked loudly on Uncle Oliver's door.

'Sorry. Listen, I'll have to phone you back again later. Is that OK? Bye for now.' I could hear him slamming the phone down, fumbling with the key in the lock.

'You don't need to knock so hard, Jacques! I'm only a few yards from the door! Not on the other side of the universe.' I felt unwelcome and embarrassed. He was obviously annoyed with me, and couldn't banish me quickly enough. 'Off you go, then. All ready for tomorrow are we?'

'Yes. I'm very sorry, Uncle Oliver. Excuse me, please.'

I went up to my bedroom, wishing that I hadn't listened outside Uncle Oliver's office. I had stumbled into a secret part of his adult world. It was an accident, but I still felt ashamed, burdened with information that I didn't want or fully understand. Information I already knew that I shouldn't share with Rebecca or anyone else.

From that evening, Uncle Oliver was more often absent from home. As well as his business trips abroad, he began to stay overnight more frequently at hotels. When he was at home, he and Anna fought, with increasing intensity and regularity. While they were fractious with each other all the time, Anna and Uncle Oliver would wait until we had gone to bed to quarrel in earnest. Even in my bedroom, I could hear the force of their complaining, accusing voices gathering as the night went on. Occasionally there would be a sudden thud or what sounded like something breaking on the kitchen floor. Mostly the episode would end with the front door banging and Uncle Oliver's car driving off.

One night, as I was forced to lie awake again listening, I felt acutely claustrophobic. It seemed as if the walls of my room were constricting, threatening to crush me. I jumped out of bed, opened my bedroom door and stood on the landing, trying to catch my breath.

'Jacques?' It was Rebecca. She was sitting at the top of the stairs, on the edge of her own landing. I could tell by the thick quality of her voice that she had been crying. 'Are you alright, Jacques?'

'I just needed some air. What are you doing?'

Rebecca lifted her arms and leant her forehead against the banisters, as if peering through the bars of a prison. 'I can't sleep when they're arguing like that,' she whispered. 'I feel trapped in my room. It seems better out here. Even if I can't do anything. Come and sit beside me, Jacques.'

I squashed onto the stair next to her and she immediately slipped her arm through mine.

'I feel better now you're here, Jacques. Can't you hear them in your room too?'

'Yes.'

'I suppose the thing is ... I know what's it's about, and you don't, do you?'

I was trying to think how best to respond honestly as Rebecca carried on.

'I listen to them all the time. I quite often go further downstairs. You can hear everything down there. They haven't caught me yet, but actually, I don't care if they do.' Rebecca stopped, looked me straight in the eyes and took a deep breath. 'Dad's been having affairs. With women he meets at work. It's been going on

for ages. On and off. Mum always finds out. Tells him to make
sure it doesn't happen again. He says he's so, so sorry. Their marriage and his family life are so important to him, he tells Mum.
So important that he lets the same thing happen all over again! It
seems more serious this time. Mum keeps telling him she wants a
divorce, but he won't accept it. He says he doesn't want to leave us.'

'So ... what do you think, Rebecca? What you want?'

'I honestly think it might be better if he just moved out. It
sounds cruel maybe, but we don't see that much of him anyway.
There wouldn't be any more of this horrible bickering. We could
still go and visit him in another house and ...'

Rebecca began to sob. She unhooked her arm from mine,
curled forward and buried her head in her lap.

'Rebecca, Rebecca, it's alright. Please try not to cry.'

I hated it when Rebecca cried. She was generally so buoyant and
unshakeable. She could be moody and preoccupied, but I had
never seen her so distressed. Eventually she sat upright again,
wiping her eyes and nose on her pyjama sleeves. 'But it isn't
right, Jacques. Why should we have to suffer because Dad needs
his ego stroking? That's what Mum calls it. She keeps telling him
he's such a weak, spineless person.'

Instinctively I put an arm around Rebecca's shoulders. I pulled
her towards me. I had to try and comfort her somehow. She
hugged me back, her warm heaviness resting for a while on my
chest. We hadn't held each other quite that way before. I could
smell her hair's scent of lemon shampoo, her girl's faint sweat,
different from a boy's. The heat and moisture of her breath

through my pyjama top. I felt a bit awkward when I began to think that I was holding her, a girl, like that, but I desperately wanted to make Rebecca feel better. And holding her felt right.

After a minute or so, Rebecca let go of my neck and moved away suddenly. She rubbed her nose vigorously again against her cuff, more as if it was itchy than anything else. Her voice was firmer when she spoke, although she didn't look at me. 'You'd better go to bed, Jacques. I'm sure everything will work out for the best. Thank you. You've made me feel better.'

'Goodnight, Rebecca.' I went to my room and tried to settle back to sleep.

Anna and Uncle Oliver were still arguing downstairs but the noise seemed more distant. I was distracted by other thoughts. The memory of holding Rebecca, knowing that I could make her feel better. The comfort of her body heat, like a soft animal's. The tickling sensations as her hair brushed my face. A warm tingling that began somewhere low in my belly, which became a sort of buzz through my body. The smell of another person: real, distinctive, up close.

While I know now that I was shifting towards adolescence, at the time I felt confused by how I was changing. Since that evening when Rebecca and I had played badminton and confirmed how much we valued each other as friends, then walked arm-in-arm by the river, I noticed that I was thinking more and more about how pleasurable it was, sharing ideas we would share with no one else, as well as being physically close. I never doubted that it felt right; at the same time, everything was seeming less simple when I thought about it. My mind was becoming a more elaborate, potentially entangling web. Rebecca and I were special friends, soul mates. And also, we were a girl and boy growing up, on our way to being a man and woman. Something told me that Rebecca had quickly moved away, and spoken more firmly to me because things were becoming less simple for her too.

Shortly after I had turned fourteen and Rebecca was fifteen, the summer before Matthew left home to study chemistry at Cambridge, Anna announced that she and Uncle Oliver would be getting divorced. As for many of her previous announcements, that evening Anna gathered us around the table in the kitchen, while she stood with her back to the sink. Uncle Oliver was already seated, wearing his work suit, his tie tightly knotted, his mouth set in a tense smile that obviously had nothing to do with any immediate pleasure.

'I'm sure you already have some idea about what I'm going to say,' Anna began flatly, peering over her glasses. 'There's absolutely no point in making a meal of this. Your father and I – Oliver and I, Jacques – are getting divorced. He has fallen in love again! This time it's madly and deeply, isn't that right, Oliver? He's going to live with Amanda and I have given them my permission and blessing. Over to you now, Oliver.'

'Yes. Although it isn't all as cynical and flimsy as you're making out, Anna,' Uncle Oliver protested, defensively. His mouth began to pout, his lower lip trembled. 'Amanda and I really are in love. We make each other happy. I'm happier than I've been for a long time. That isn't anything to do with any of you children, of course!'

'Oh, no! Of course it has nothing to do with them!' Anna remarked, scornfully. 'That's pretty obvious, Oliver. Percentage-wise, I'd say it has to do with you, ninety-nine per cent. Amanda might just sneak in there at one per cent if she's lucky!'

'Oh, come on, Anna. That's not fair! I thought we'd agreed not to subject the children to any more of this? As you will all find out very soon, Amanda is a lovely, giving person. Just because she's caring, it doesn't mean that she's a doormat!'

'So, will this affect me going to Cambridge?' Matthew asked his father, blinking anxiously, pushing his steel-rimmed glasses further back on his nose, as he did habitually. He had been one of the privileged few in his year to obtain a scholarship to the university.

'No, not at all, Matthew. Cambridge will run as per plan,' Uncle Oliver confirmed quickly, as if his efficient tone could somehow recompense his son. 'Your education won't be affected. Your mother and I will still take care of everything financially. You will have your room to come back to, here, if you want, during the holidays and suchlike. Any other questions, Matthew?'

'No. None.' Matthew stood up and left the kitchen as quickly as he could, without looking back.

'See you later, Dad,' Uncle Oliver said to himself, rhetorically, wistfully, assuming the part of the rejected father.

'But what about us?' Rebecca ignored his remark. Her tone was sharp, unforgiving. 'What's going to happen to me and Jacques? We're not going to be made to live separately, are we? That wouldn't be right. Why should our lives be spoiled, just because you want someone else instead of Mum?'

'It's not quite as simple as that, Rebecca.' Uncle Oliver looked intensely irritated, wincing as if he had been stung. His ever positive, future-facing stance was being severely tested. He began to make neat pointing movements with his pinched forefinger and thumb. 'It turns out that your mother doesn't really want me either, in fact. She probably hasn't wanted me for a very long time, if the truth be known. Not all of us can run on empty, I'm afraid.'

'Poor little hurt victim Oliver,' Anna pronounced, letting her lower lip protrude, making a dramatic, ironic pretence of sympathy. 'Isn't he lucky to have a sweet adoring soul like Amanda to make him feel so much better and snug again? Don't be so bloody self-centred, Oliver! Rebecca's asking about herself and Jacques! It isn't all about your deep wallow of emotional need.'

'At least I know I've got needs!' Uncle Oliver declared, dramatically.

Anna had already turned away from him. She was the cool, unwavering surgeon again, her hands still, her words composed. 'Don't worry, Rebecca and Jacques. We've already arranged that you will stay here with me. Your Uncle Oliver will still have financial responsibilities for you as a guardian, Jacques, and you and Rebecca will be free to visit him in his new abode as and when it suits him and Amanda. We do at least both agree that it is better to make as few changes to your school and home lives as possible. When you're eighteen you can choose to do as you like, of course. I wouldn't blame you if you wanted to cut loose. I imagine that's probably what Matthew has in mind. So . . . that's about it. Why don't you both go to bed early tonight? If you have any other questions, we can deal with them tomorrow.'

As far as I was concerned, Uncle Oliver and Anna's divorce didn't make a huge difference. Uncle Oliver would still be my guardian, no more or less connected with me than he had been before. I was glad that I didn't have to move again, and especially relieved that I was able to stay with Rebecca and could carry on playing Anna's piano. I never knew exactly how Matthew felt about his parents' separation, in the same way that I didn't know what so many other things meant to him. As Anna had anticipated, as soon as he left home for Cambridge, he would rarely return to Chester. Occasionally he would inform us, in a factual, brief paragraph of a letter, about his academic progress and results. Matthew would never disclose how he felt, never speak of any new interests, friends or girlfriends. Rightly or wrongly, I pictured him continuing to lead a silent, hermetically sealed sort of life, poring over formulae, his main relationships with substances and test tubes.

Rebecca undoubtedly suffered. Not so much because she missed her father's company or friendship – which she knew she had always lacked – but more because she resented the way that he had had the power to unsettle her mind, to confront her with the fact that security and happiness were not entirely hers to command.

'Why should I have to come from a broken home?' Rebecca often complained to me, galled that her life could be labelled without her agreement. 'It isn't my fault they decided to get divorced.'

'No, of course it isn't,' I would tell her, wishing I could some-how soften the blow.

As soon as Anna had agreed to their divorce, Uncle Oliver moved into Amanda's home, a detached house on a new hous-ing development close to Altrincham. She had lived there with her teenage daughter, Julie, for about three years, since her own divorce. Once a month on a Saturday, Uncle Oliver would collect Rebecca and me from Chester and drive us over to Altrincham. Everything about the house seemed new, to the point where anything with a history – including people – seemed almost out of place. In contrast to our apartment in Neuilly and the Clarks' Chester home, there was virtually nothing old in Amanda's house. There were very few books, only modern ornaments and furniture, silk flowers and plastic ferns.

We would talk or watch television in the stiflingly hot cen-trally heated lounge until Amanda made lunch. It was usually a sandwich or a salad. She had never been a very confident cook, Amanda confessed, apologetically. She was also very conscious of her weight and had to be careful about what she ate, although we were to make a point of telling her, she insisted, if we ever wanted her to prepare any more food for us. From when we first met, I felt there was something poignant about Amanda, about her painstaking grooming, the fact that she always wore make-up and meticulously painted her nails. She waited on us anxiously and pecked, in a nervous, bird-like manner, at her own small portion of food. In my sketch-book, she appeared occasionally in lightly pencilled bird shapes, with twig-like legs and faint suggestions of tiny folded wings.

Invariably Uncle Oliver would then take us all into Manchester, where Amanda and Julie were eager to shop for the rest of the afternoon. Rather than taking the opportunity to spend time doing something different with Rebecca and me, he insisted that it would work best if we all stayed together.

'Everyone can get to know each other better. And I know you appreciate a little hand with your bags, girls, don't you? I'm sure that Jacques will be gentlemanly enough to offer as well, eh, Jacques?' Uncle Oliver suggested.

'Yes.' I remembered that Maman had often told me how important it was to be a gentleman.

'Amanda isn't a girl, Dad!' Rebecca corrected. 'She must be at least as old as Mum! Mum always says it's patronising to call a grown woman a girl. Don't you think it's patronising, Amanda?'

'Oh, no! I don't mind, Rebecca. Your dad meant it nicely, I'm sure. Didn't you, Oliver?'

'Of course, darling. A compliment if anything. There's no need to be nasty, Rebecca.'

Amanda coughed nervously and combed her lacquered nails through her bleached blonde hair, as if removing non-existent tangles. She reminded me of the perfectly groomed, doll-like women selling perfume and make-up, the ones I used to stare at, when Maman occasionally took me with her to the Galeries Lafayette department store in Paris.

Rebecca actively made herself dislike Amanda and Julie by constantly dwelling on their habits and weaknesses. Each time that Uncle Oliver drove us back to Chester, she launched into a tirade about that day's visit. 'Why do we always have to go shopping with them, Dad? They're so boring. Julie, do I, or don't I, look fat in this thkirt?' Rebecca had spotted Amanda's slight lisp immediately. 'You could take Jacques and me to the museum, or a gallery, or a film or something else instead. You know we don't like shopping. Why don't you do that, instead of trailing round after them like a bleating little lamb the whole time? Amanda had a little lamb, little lamb, little lamb ... you're so pathetic!'

'That's enough Rebecca!' Uncle Oliver answered peevishly. 'I've told you already. I want us all to get to know each other. And anyway, I like to spend my time off with Julie and Amanda too.'

'Well, I don't want to get to know them. I've told you already I'll never want to know them. I'm sure Jacques doesn't feel that he needs to either. They aren't people I'd ever choose to want to know. Anyway, you only see us once a month. Isn't this supposed to be our time together? Don't you love us enough to be interested in our lives?'

I would sit in the back of the car, saying nothing. Personally I thought that Rebecca was being overly critical of Amanda and Julie, but I tried to imagine how I might have felt in her position, if Uncle Oliver had been my father. I could feel the deep hurt and anger behind her unrestrained remarks. While Uncle Oliver had no hesitation in identifying his own emotional needs, he seemed incapable of selflessly acknowledging his daughter's uncomfortable feelings, let alone offering her comfort. 'Life isn't always as simple as you seem to think, Rebecca,' he would repeat, sighing wearily. 'Surely you can't blame me for wanting a little happiness of my own? When a person feels properly appreciated and good about themselves, then they have more to offer other people, haven't they? How can I give you what I haven't got?'

'But that's not my problem, is it? A parent can't be like that, can they? They always have to have something for their child, even if they feel they haven't got anything. You have to follow through on your choices, Mum says.'

'Your mother's hardly perfect herself.'

'But she's there, isn't she? At least she doesn't go on about what she needs all the time. It's like she says. Your life is just all about you. And you never even ask Jacques about what he's doing. His own parents are dead. He was only eleven and he lost so much. You agreed to be his guardian. His parents must be turning in their graves.'

'Leave it, Rebecca. That's quite enough.'

I counted the minutes until we could be back in Chester, when Mrs Chadwick would be there to open the door, when Rebecca and I could be our more relaxed selves, when I would find myself again at the piano. Even if most of the time in those days it still felt as if Anna was a fairly distant presence, I grew to prefer her detachment to days with Uncle Oliver – fractious, soul-destroying occasions, that seemed to have nothing whatsoever to do with what Rebecca and I wanted or needed.

5

Although Rebecca and I continued to spend most of our time outside school together, as we grew older, things inevitably changed. It was as if we were playing in the same river, but while I was still content to paddle at the edge, in the shallows, endlessly floating leaf boats in stone harbours, Rebecca was increasingly drawn to a deeper, faster-moving flow.

I was fourteen when I really began puberty. Although just a year older, at fifteen Rebecca was already in a woman's body, a fact that she disguised initially by wearing loose sweaters and jeans, but gradually felt more confident to reveal. She preferred clothes that I could only describe as romantic – pastel-coloured dresses and skirts that accentuated her waist and closely fitted her bust, which also complied with her strong sense of propriety. A style of femininity that set her apart, she felt, from people like Amanda and Julie. 'I'm not being prudish, Jacques. But they don't leave much to the imagination, do they? Those dresses that Julie wears are virtually see-through! And you can see the tops of her thighs and knickers when she bends over sometimes in those skimpy mini-skirts. Well, you can, can't you?'

'Well, I suppose you could be right, perhaps, but I ...' It was territory in which I felt distinctly uneasy and had no considered, ready opinion. I also suspected that it wouldn't be difficult to say the wrong thing.

'You must have noticed, Jacques! Why Amanda thinks she suits those clingy tops, I don't know! It looks cheap and nasty. I'm surprised Dad lets her go out like that. When a woman's her age, I think she should wear classic clothes and keep things covered up more. Otherwise she's mutton dressed as lamb. That's what Mum says.'

'Mutton dressed as ... ?'

'It's when an older woman dresses in clothes really designed for younger women. Amanda's a good example. She can't let herself grow old gracefully or enjoy dressing up just for herself. It's like she still wants to attract men. It's tarty and tacky.'

I would have been lying if I had told Rebecca that I hadn't noticed the way Amanda and Julie dressed. I had, but it wasn't something that I felt comfortable to share with her. I was acutely aware that I had begun more and more to observe girls and the shapes of their developing bodies – an increasingly regular preoccupation accompanied by a wash of mixed feelings – guilt, warm, stirring pleasure and curiosity. I saw them as more aesthetic than boys' bodies, particularly my own gangling assembly of erupting, stretching skin, bone and muscle, which at times seemed like a strange mutation of my compact, hairless prepubertal form. The sight of Julie's curvaceous bottom and the way that her tiny shirt lapped the tops of her plump, pink thighs fascinated me. I was also becoming fixated on the vast array of sizes and sculpting of women's breasts and felt excited to envisage what they would look like unwrapped, what it might feel like to hold one secretly in my hand. How I would actually manage the whole situation to include the rest of the woman, I still couldn't quite imagine.

My growing interest in girls' bodies extended to Rebecca's. I couldn't help stealing a glance now and again at her small conical breasts, the S-shape of her spine, the suggestion of her broadening hips under the folds of her skirt. I still regarded her as my best friend and had found no one I could talk to in the way I could talk to her. And yet now, I also couldn't forget how it had felt walking with her in the half-light by the river, how I had felt holding her that night on the stairs. I couldn't deny to myself the warm buzz through my body, the same feeling consistently stirred by her lightest touch. It was becoming clearer to me that I was romantically and physically attracted to Rebecca. I was developing the same kinds of feelings I heard other boys talk about at school when they discussed the girls they 'fancied'. What I had begun to wish for with her went beyond simple friendship. I had liked her from the beginning, but I think it was around this time that I was starting to fall in love with her.

I told myself that I had no reason to expect that Rebecca would ever feel the same way about me. The fact that I could no longer be completely honest made me feel as if I was deceiving her. But I still didn't think then that it would be fair to ask her directly if she felt attracted to me. I think I understood instinctively that we were beginning a different kind of game, with new, unfamiliar rules. As well as contending with other people's expectations of our age and gender, we would have to work out for ourselves what felt necessary or appropriate. I started to feel more and more guarded about what I said, and especially about any physical contact with Rebecca. I shrank from the thought that I could offend her by making her uncomfortable. I couldn't risk spoiling our special friendship. In many ways, my awkwardness and uncertainty were no different from that of any developing teenage boy, even if it was obviously compounded by the unusual context of our relationship, Rebecca's parents being my guardians.

Rebecca had always been an energetic, outgoing person. As her adolescence progressed, she became even more restless, both mentally and physically. She took up rowing with a club on the River Dee, played hockey, swam regularly, pleaded with her mother to pay for dancing and horse-riding lessons. She often refused to go to Altrincham to spend time with her father. When she did go, she would usually end up getting angry, even flying at him with her fists. He would catch her wrists and hold her locked at arm's length, sometimes trying to make out that it was all just a joke. At other times, he would attempt to devise an effective sanction and fail miserably. He lacked the imagination to know what really motivated Rebecca, or what to deprive her of to impose his authority.

Rebecca went into Chester more often without me, in the company of Louise and Jennifer, and other girls. She also insisted that we meet up with larger groups of friends. Gone were the days when we'd spend hours playing badminton in the evenings or just lying around in the garden together. Louise and Jennifer both had older brothers, David and Sam, whom I recognised from the sixth form at Prince's. They started to come to our house at the weekends and after school, along with a few of my own friends from my year. We would all stand around talking in the garden, or half-talk and half-watch television in the lounge, until Mrs Chadwick called Rebecca and me for dinner and waved everyone else home.

By this stage, in spite of my reservations about school, I had developed a small group of close friends with whom I felt I had more in common. We would meet regularly at break-times, share food, sometimes kick a ball around a corner of the school field, talk about what had happened in our classes, analyse teachers and share our impressions about other boys. Having them around made days at Prince's much more congenial. Among these, my best friends were Daniel Mitchell, 'Mitch', Adrian Wheeler, 'Wheelie', and Stephen Reid, a newcomer to the school.

Their characters, I often thought, were reflected in their physical appearances. Wheelie was big and bold, with dark, wavy hair. Mitch was tall and fair, his fine-boned features camouflaged under a thick cover of freckles. Stephen was smaller in height and build than I was, had pale skin, short fair hair and the beginnings of a slight moustache. In my drawings, Wheelie was a thick black wheel with wide spokes, carrying a bold red *W*. Stephen was a blue spiral, tightly curling round on its own pale gold centre. Mitch made me think of a fine sable-tipped paintbrush.

Mitch and Wheelie were unquestionably more worldly-wise and socially adaptable than I was. They were both good at sport but didn't regard their achievements as bestowing any superior status and certainly were never against playing purely for fun with less competent players. They were also academically capable, without being obsessed with results or driven to study too much. Stephen had started that year at Prince's, after his parents moved from London. We would sit together in a lot of our classes. We understood that we were both, in our own ways, outsiders. Stephen, affectionately nicknamed 'Brain' by Wheelie and Mitch, was picked on by other boys for his seriousness, his extensive vocabulary and passion for chess. He was a quiet, neat, considerate and intelligent sort of boy, who shared my love of classical music and art. He read avidly and had a sensitive imagination that made him both sympathetic and prone to being anxious.

'Come on, Brain! Don't be frightened of the ball. Get yourself over here!' Mitch would shout over at Stephen when we played our own games of football, changing the rules as it suited us. 'Trust me, it's full of air, not lead. Let your legs do the thinking for a change. I need you! Come on! Even Jacques is going to slaughter us the way things are going.'

'Even Jacques?' I threw back, winking at Mitch. He knew I didn't mind the joke, especially given that his intention was to include Stephen. I was quite happy to admit that though I could run fast, when it came to managing a ball, my skills were at best only average. Whatever the result, I enjoyed our games, which brought back fond memories of playing with my friends in Neuilly on long summer evenings in the park. Papa and Maman would sometimes come with a simple picnic – usually *pain de campagne* with ham or cheese and pears or peaches – for us all to share. They would watch and cheer us on. Occasionally Papa would join in, even if he could only manage a short stint as goal-keeper before starting to cough and get breathless. He always made light of it, telling us that players of our talent were better off without a clumsy father holding them back. It was much better that he watched and learned from us all instead.

At break-times when Wheelie unveiled one of his mother's cream and jam-filled egg sponges, which he had been instructed to share with his friends, Stephen would wait nervously, while the rest of us needed no invitation to help ourselves to large slices.

'What are you waiting for Brain?' Wheelie would quickly ask. 'We depend on your support as a consumer for continuing supplies. It would offend my mother deeply if I had to return her sumptuous offerings uneaten. Get stuck in! The brain, above all other organs, must be well fed.'

'Thank you, Adrian. You're very generous. And so is your mother. Although ... only if you're sure you don't need any more yourself?' Stephen moved forward tentatively.

'My name is Wheelie, Brain. I've told you, please call me Wheelie. Look at me, Brain. Objectively. Do you really believe I need more cake? Want, perhaps, but need?'

With his humorously self-deprecating, robust manner, Wheelie had a rare ability to make the shyest person relax.

'Thank you, Wheelie. Yes, I'd love some,' Stephen eventually agreed, his hand still shaking as Wheelie served him a slice.

'Brain, you know, you could sweat the small stuff less,' Wheelie observed, pointing to Stephen's head. 'You've got a lot more going on up there already than the rest of us put together. You could afford to rest back a bit on your laurels. Why not? Perhaps allow yourself to just indulge in the jam and the cream?'

Some time after Rebecca had turned sixteen, I noticed that she had obviously taken a liking to Jennifer's brother, Sam. He would be the one she chose to talk to and sit beside. She touched him frequently, playfully smacked his arm or his hand when he said something amusing or contentious, squashed in next to him roughly on the sofa. Sam clearly enjoyed the attention, pushed and rapped her back, met her eyes when she looked up at him. Sam was at least six foot, solidly built with sandy hair, brown eyes and tanned, relatively acne-free skin. He played for the first rugby team at Prince's. He appeared self-assured, as confident, I thought, as a lot of older men. I admired and envied him simultaneously, especially when Rebecca started to change her allegiances from me to him.

'Want to dance, Sam?' I remember Rebecca asking him coyly, on one occasion in the lounge. She had brought her CD player downstairs and she, Louise and Jennifer were dancing giddily in the middle of the room, taking it in turns to put on their own choices of music. Louise and Jennifer were particularly obsessed with songs from the soundtrack of the film *Dirty Dancing*. It irritated me the way that Rebecca joined in when they drooled over their idol Patrick Swayze.

'Oh, come on, Sam!' Rebecca continued to entreat him, grabbing his hands and trying to pull him up onto his feet. Even self-assured Sam wasn't immune to having moments of embarrassment, I was pleased to observe.

'No. Not now, Rebecca,' he told her, his face flushing as he refused to be moved from the sofa. 'You girls just dance by yourselves. I can't dance anyway!'

'Yes you can, Sam!' Jennifer contradicted her brother. 'Don't be shy! *I've had the time of my life ...*' she sang stridently, wrapping her arms around her body. 'Wouldn't mind being with Patrick for this one, would you, Lou? Think we could get up to a lot more than dancing! Come on, Sam! On your feet!'

'No, I don't want to. Leave me alone, will you, Jen?' Sam answered. 'Nothing personal, Rebecca, but ...'

'I think you should take no for an answer, Rebecca,' I intervened. 'Sam obviously doesn't want to dance, does he?' If I was honest, I knew that I was speaking less on Sam's behalf than on my own. I really didn't like the idea of watching Sam and Rebecca together.

'Mind your own business, Jacques! Sam can decide for himself. He doesn't need you chiming in!' Rebecca snapped, still tugging at Sam's hands.

'Actually, he's right,' Sam said, giving me a grateful look. 'Maybe another time, though, Rebecca?'

Rebecca let go of Sam's hands abruptly. 'I was only having a bit of fun. Thanks for that, Jacques,' she finished curtly, without looking at me. She turned back to dance with Louise and Jennifer. They started behaving even more hysterically, hugging cushions, pretending to slow-dance with each other, making a show of messing up their hair.

Rebecca and I spoke less and less alone. She very rarely came to my room any more. I really missed her company. Even if I knew, in theory, that what was happening was part of the process of us both growing up, I couldn't help feeling hurt.

I was surprised one evening when she knocked on my door. I had completed my piano practice and was locked in the bathroom with my sketch-book and charcoals. While I still painted in watercolour, faithfully restocking the trays of my childhood set, I enjoyed experimenting with charcoal. The soft blackness of the medium and its potential for varied degrees of light and shade suited the range of my teenage moods. I was beginning another sketch of Rebecca. She had let me attempt her portrait twice and then refused to sit for me again. She didn't like the idea of being studied in such detail, she said. She found it boring and uncomfortable having to stay so still, waiting for me to finish. I had started to work from memory instead, which made the studies more impressionistic.

My book was filled with profiles, heads and shoulders, drawings of Rebecca's whole figure, including all her curves. As usually happened when I painted or sketched from my imagination,

I would drift into a trance-like state of mind, entering a realm where anything seemed possible, where the boundaries of everyday life dissolved. In one drawing, I had even tried to imagine what Rebecca might look like without her clothes. The drawing was predictably quite abstract. It was based on a strange amalgam of the brief glimpses I had had of naked women in life and art. As I had worked on it, I remembered a surreal labelled image of what lay below the skin of a breast in one of my science books, a structure of knotty strands like seaweeds and another diagram of a woman's uterus and fallopian tubes curling like antennae. I also recalled the flashes of nakedness I had seen on television. Snatched sights of things I suspected that I shouldn't have seen. Half-lit shapes and breast silhouettes against a soundtrack of heavy, animal-like breathing and sounds. The time when Rebecca had switched on the set and we had been confronted with a couple making love, when she had joked that it was too 'steamy' for someone of my age and had quickly changed the channel, clearly embarrassed herself.

My fantasy nude of Rebecca remained one of my favourite pieces of work, even if I couldn't completely make sense of my attachment to it. I found it difficult to know what to do with it and my other drawings of Rebecca. It would have felt wrong to have destroyed them, as if I was being hurtful and disrespectful somehow to Rebecca herself. At the same time, I dreaded the thought that she would discover them and be forever shocked by my confusing persisting preoccupation. Until I was able to think of a better solution, I pushed the sketch-book under the rug below my bed.

'Jacques? Can I come in? Are you there, Jacques?'

'Yes! One minute! I'm just in the bathroom,' I shouted back, closing the sketch-book and quickly gathering up my charcoals. Returning the book to its usual place, I rushed over to unlock the door. Rebecca was waiting in her dressing-gown, cheeks pink and hair damp from showering.

'Well, can I come in?' she asked, reminding me that I was barring the doorway.

'Yes, of course. I thought you were in bed already.' Rebecca made her way straight to my bed as she used to and sat down. I took the chair from my desk and pulled it up opposite her. The fluffy yellow towelling of her over-sized dressing-gown overwhelmed her figure and made her look much larger than she actually was. I was relieved on this occasion to be spared the precise lines of her body.

'So, what have you been doing, Jacques? What's that black stuff on your hands? You've got some on your forehead as well.' Rebecca had the perceptive powers of a bird of prey. I cursed myself inwardly for having forgotten to wash my hands.

'It's just a bit of charcoal from my art homework. I'll go and wash it off.'

I went to the bathroom, lathered my hands and scrubbed my nails with the thoroughness of a surgeon. When I looked in the mirror I saw that my forehead was darkly smudged too, as Rebecca had said. I rubbed the mark roughly with a flannel, in a strange attempt to rub away my feelings of guilt.

'Can I see what you've done?' Rebecca called through to me. 'Where is it?'

'Oh, you wouldn't like it,' I answered, as casually as I could. 'It's only a boring thing from a photograph.'

'You know I like drawings. As long as I don't have to sit for them. Please let me see, Jacques?'

'Trust me. It's not your type of thing. So ... have you had a good day?' I returned to my chair, desperately racking my brains for a way to distract Rebecca from the drawing. Fortunately she was easily persuaded to go in the direction of her own agenda.

'Yes, I did. Actually, that's partly why I ...' Rebecca was rarely hesitant. In that respect she resembled her mother. I sensed she was slightly nervous from the way that she was fiddling with the ends of her dressing-gown belt. 'I walked home from school with Sam today. He'd asked if we could meet at the gate. He's really, really nice ...'

The word 'nice' wasn't a word that featured often in Rebecca's vocabulary. She was more a person of superlatives – she would say 'fantastic' or 'incredible' or 'great'. Her moderation seemed to verge on a lie. I felt irritated, although I didn't say anything. I could tell that Rebecca wanted me to encourage her to say more about Sam, but I deliberately held back. It felt mean, but I just didn't want her to talk about him.

'So ... what do you think of Sam, Jacques? You like him too, don't you?' She lifted her eyes from her dressing-gown belt and looked up at me. I could read her earnest appeal, the way it made her vulnerable.

'He's OK.' I shrugged, pretending indifference, crossing my arms over my chest. 'I don't know him very well, I suppose.'

'But you've met him quite a few times here, haven't you? He's spoken to you quite a lot. And you know him from school as well?' Rebecca was obviously frustrated by my lack of enthusiasm and acknowledgement of her new hero.

'I don't know him from school really. You don't usually know people from other years, do you?' I was picturing Sam's smug smile, his virtually flawless complexion. In my sketch-book I drew Sam as an unoriginal stick man, with a simple smile on his circle face and no other features. I didn't like talking about him. I found myself incredibly jealous of the attention he was getting. I just wanted Rebecca and me to talk about ourselves and other things.

'Well, anyway,' Rebecca carried on. 'He's asked me to go into Chester with him at the weekend. So it's like we're officially going out.'

'Officially going out?' I repeated instead, critically.

'You know what I mean!'

'I do?'

'I mean … well, we haven't kissed or anything like that yet, but, well, everyone knows I'm his girlfriend!'

'Have you told Anna?'

'Not yet. But that won't be a problem. She won't mind. As long as I don't end up getting pregnant or something! And she knows I wouldn't.'

I was fairly sure that Rebecca's seemingly nonchalant reference to a potential pregnancy involving Sam was her own way of getting back at me for my lack of enthusiasm over her news, by implying that the two of them belonged together in an adult world from which I was excluded. It certainly had the desired effect. I felt cold in the pit of my stomach. 'Well ... I suppose that makes everything alright then.' I acted the line to the best of my ability. The thought that Sam had apparently so effortlessly become Rebecca's boyfriend didn't seem at all right to me. 'So, if there's nothing else? Sorry, but I need to get my things ready for tomorrow, Rebecca.'

'Oh, come on, Jacques! Don't be so grumpy!' Rebecca threw herself back on the bed and hinged forward again immediately. 'I was going to tell you something else as well, in fact. But I don't know if you really deserve it now.'

'Oh well, perhaps you don't need to bother then,' I responded churlishly, although I was immediately curious. Rebecca continued undeterred, intent on imparting her information.

'Well, it's just that ... Louise still fancies you. She always goes on about your 'gorgeous dark hair and moody eyes'. She keeps saying she wishes you'd ask her out. I said I'd have a word with you, see if I could talk you into it.'

I had never particularly warmed to Louise. She rarely had anything interesting to say and was slow to understand jokes or irony. Perhaps if she had been more physically appealing to me I could have overlooked her lack of personality. Unfortunately, though, I pitied her for the way her top teeth protruded and for the disconcertingly sour odour of her sweat, unmasked by her cloying chemical cocktails of perfume and deodorant. 'No. Sorry, Rebecca. Nothing against Louise,' I started, 'but I think you know already that I don't fancy her. I can't ask her out. Tell her what you like. Make something up. I'm sure you can think of something.'

I didn't get to sleep for a long time after Rebecca had left that night. I got up in the early hours of the morning and hurriedly completed the sketch of her that she had interrupted me working on.

It wasn't as good as I wanted it to be. It solved nothing, made my thoughts turn faster around our unsettling conversation and the feeling that everything was changing. I hated myself for wanting to punish Rebecca. Never usually a person to cry, I began to sob fitfully, helplessly, not exactly understanding why, my tears running down into the charcoal, spoiling the sketch irreparably.

It seemed hardly any time since Rebecca and I had been so close and open with each other. Now, however, as each day passed between us we seemed bound to ruin the simplicity and integrity of our friendship. And perhaps it didn't matter so much to Rebecca. But it mattered to me.

6

Before long, the general consensus was that Sam and Rebecca were definitely boyfriend and girlfriend. I was probably more uncomfortably aware of the fact than anyone else. Rebecca giggled stupidly when Sam pulled her onto his knee on the sofa. They had prolonged, twisting kisses under the trees in the garden. I was sickened by their lack of restraint and obsession with each other. Rebecca's behaviour struck me as particularly silly and out of character.

Even in his absence, Rebecca always seemed to be listening to Sam's music. '*I still haven't found what I'm looking for ...*' and '*Can't stand losing you ...*' she would sing, over and over again.

'You do realise how inane you sound, don't you?' I would tell her.

'No I don't! They're really good lyrics. You should try listening to them yourself. The Police and U2 are Sam's favourite bands. It's like he says, they have to be some of our best modern poets.'

'Of course! Obvious substitutes for T. S. Eliot and W. H. Auden. Sam says ...'

'Don't be so horrible, Jacques!' Her mouth twitched with suppressed laughter as she said it. I could tell part of her found what I'd said funny, but she forced herself to look cross and serious. 'You're such an intellectual snob sometimes.'

In order to distract myself, I played the piano more and listened to music in my room, often with Stephen Reid. It was undoubtedly simpler and better for my self-esteem than to have to deal with the fraught complexity of situations with Rebecca or other girls. When I had turned fifteen, Anna had bought me a radio CD player similar to Rebecca's and a small collection of classical music, including a selection of works by Chopin and Beethoven. In keeping with Anna's frugal and sensible approach to things, it was a fairly basic, though adequate, piece of equipment compared to the expensive hi-fi tower Stephen's parents had got him. However, while Stephen's parents restricted his use of the hi-fi to weekends, being in an attic room off its own landing, I was allowed to play music at a reasonable volume whenever I liked, as long as it was no later than eleven at night.

Stephen was good company. There was an unspoken trust between us. He was the only other boy in our year who preferred classical music to rock and pop, and had been subjected to the same accusations of being pretentious, effeminate, out-of-date and elitist as I had. Long after I had given up trying to explain myself, Stephen had persisted. 'I'm not trying to be pretentious at all,' I often overheard him saying. 'I'm not being critical of you for liking the stuff that you like. It's just that, well, I don't enjoy it like I do classical music ... it doesn't suit me somehow.'

In spite of his intention to improve communication with the other boys, Stephen's way of articulating his thoughts had, as I anticipated, only made his life more difficult, reinforcing his reputation for being hopelessly intellectual, socially incapable and probably homosexual.

Rejection made Stephen deeply unhappy. He constantly worried, reflecting on how he could have handled an argument better. I identified with his desire to be accepted and his sensitivity to ridicule and tried my best to dissuade him from setting himself up to be hurt. My own experiences had taught me about the importance of self-protection. Still believing in ideals of openness and peace, I could see a place for attack and defence. For the first time, I began to understand the appeal of Wagner and other rallying, martial music.

'There's no point sometimes in trying to explain yourself,' I remember telling him one evening. We had been listening to Stephen's favourite CD of J. S. Bach. If he had his choice, it was usually Bach, Schubert or Chopin. Mine would always be Beethoven. 'They won't respect you for it. They'll actually end up hating you more. They're like dogs. They smell the scent of your fear.'

'Possibly,' Stephen allowed, thoughtfully. 'Though, I don't like feeling cut off from people.'

'I know what you mean. But sometimes you've got to keep yourself to yourself. Why should you have to suffer to win friendship? It's not really friendship then, is it?'

'No, you're right, but ...'

'That's what I think anyway. And Mitch and Wheelie are real friends, aren't they? You can't be everyone's friend. You can't expect the whole form to like you.'

When I first knew Stephen, he had an old dog called Mack. It was a mongrel, part collie, he told me, with a thinning black-and-white coat and stinking breath. Stephen loved Mack in spite of his decrepitude and insisted on bringing him with us whenever we went for a walk. We had to stop regularly along the way so that Mack could rest. The old dog would lie down wearily, rest his chin on his front paws, his breathing laboured, his rheumy eyes closing.

'He's like a kind of Buddha, isn't he?' Stephen once said. He often suggested that the dog was wiser in many ways than a human. 'He doesn't have to prove himself.'

'No,' I replied. 'He knows what he's meant to do. He's content with a simple life.'

'And he doesn't make judgements,' Stephen added. 'He accepts you for who you are. As long as you feed him and take him for a walk, he's always there, without other conditions.'

'You're right,' I agreed, although I knew, as I guessed that Stephen did, that Mack wouldn't be with us for much longer. Stephen's parents had been talking about whether it would be kinder to have Mack put to sleep, but Stephen wouldn't hear of it.

'He still obviously has a good quality of life,' he kept telling me. I suspected that he was trying to convince himself. 'And I can't think about him not being here. I know some people would say he's just a dog, but he's such a good friend to me.'

By Stephen's own admission, his and Mack's quality of life were inextricably bound.

When Mack died naturally in his sleep, Stephen was distraught. He insisted that I accompany him and his father when they buried the dog at the end of their garden. 'Maybe it sounds pathetic, Jacques, but ... I'll never forget him,' Stephen said afterwards, his voice thick with emotion, as we stood over the mound of earth.

'It's not pathetic. He was very important to you.'

'And of course I knew it was his time to go, but it's hard to believe sometimes that that's it ... that your one and only chance of being together for all time has ended.'

'I know what you mean. It's almost too big a thought. Although I suppose the main thing is to remember and to try and make the best of all the other chances that we still have.'

Stephen had an enthusiasm for collecting things. He loved my box of old photographs and often asked to see it, encouraging me, as Rebecca had done, to tell the stories of my childhood in Neuilly. He seemed to understand the real importance of safeguarding personal and meaningful things from the past. The collection of Stephen's that I most admired was his box of fossils, some of which he had inherited, some of which he had gathered with his parents on various holidays.

'This is my favourite one, I think,' he told me, unwrapping the specimen slowly, cupping his hand protectively around the ammonite. The coiled embryonic form seemed at odds, some-how, with the stone in which it was embedded. 'It's beautiful, isn't it? Like a young fern. Though it's so old. Makes you wonder ... do you think, if someone found us ... our skeleton, our spine curled round ... would they think that we were just as beautiful?' It interested me, the way that Stephen's mind would often travel down such unpredictable avenues.

'I don't know,' I said. 'I don't see why not. The human skeleton is incredible, if you think about it.'

'Yes, although ... I'm not so sure,' Stephen said quietly. 'I'm sure I'll never be as perfect as this ammonite.'

Back then I began to think about my music more and more as a kind of lifeline. It linked me like an umbilical cord to my parents, especially to Maman, and to the qualities of grandeur and elegance that I felt had characterised the atmosphere of my past in Neuilly. Sometimes a piece of music had the power to wrap me in a sympathetic cocoon. I had the impression that I was both accompanied and peacefully alone, able simply to be myself, without having to conform to anyone's requirements. At other times, the music and I made mutual emotional journeys, melodies letting me approach and go beyond my particular passing sadness or euphoria, enabling me to acknowledge moods and helping them to move on, in a way that felt humane. It could also allow a general feeling of romance about things that made them more bearable. For that moment it wasn't relevant how irrational, sensible or real that view actually was.

Anna continued to listen to me playing from the dining-room in the evenings. Since she and Uncle Oliver had divorced, I noticed that she was less irritable and would talk to me more after my practice. As I was growing in self-confidence, I had more courage to engage with her and ask questions about her life. One evening, I had been working on my favourite Chopin waltz, the 'Grande Valse Brillante' in E Flat Major. It was a piece that my mother had played beautifully. I had often danced around the room, my head filled with images of giant sparkling crystal chandeliers. My fantasy was that I was in a grand ballroom, surrounded by waltzing aristocratic couples. Maman loved my dancing, she told me. One day, she always said, I would find someone beautiful to dance with, someone who would be the luckiest girl in the world.

Perhaps I felt the contrast to the exuberant quality of the 'Grande Valse'. That evening, when I looked at Anna sitting at the dining-room table, I thought that she seemed particularly tired. Her cheekbones seemed much more severe, her burgundy-stained mouth stark against her anaemic skin. 'Are you not well, Anna? You look very pale,' I observed tentatively.

'Oh, come in, Jacques! Why don't you sit with me for a while at the table? You could have a small glass of wine if you wanted. You're almost sixteen.'

I was startled by Anna's offer. As a child, I had occasionally been allowed a share of Maman or Papa's wine diluted with water. This was the first time that I had been asked if I wanted a glass of my own. 'Yes, thank you. I'd like that,' I agreed, nervously. I didn't want to discourage Anna's gesture towards treating me as an adult, but I also felt wary of the effect that the wine could have on me in her company. Especially after having listened to the accounts of some of the boys who had bragged about their drunken exploits at Prince's.

'That's what I like!' Anna pronounced, bringing the bottle from the sideboard and pouring me a full glass. 'Someone who can make a decision for themselves! So many people can't nowadays, can they, Jacques?'

'It's true.' I wasn't at all sure what Anna's remark referred to specifically, but I had a hunch that she was about to inform me. I sat down at the table opposite her and reached quickly for the cut-glass goblet she had placed on the highly polished surface – for once, I noticed, without one of her ubiquitous coasters.

'I've had a dreadful day today, Jacques. You could probably never imagine how completely and utterly dreadful. You understand what I do, don't you? You must by now. I'm sure Rebecca has you thoroughly briefed. She doesn't approve. I suspect she may not see things quite so much in black and white as her words might suggest, but my daughter is a young woman who needs to assert her own independent opinion, especially with her mother. I can't imagine it's always been easy for her at school either, when friends and their parents enquire about what I do for a living.'

'I'm sure she doesn't mean ... I'm sure ... well, someone has to help ... It's true, isn't it?' I gulped down my wine, groping for words like a blind person fumbling around in an unfamiliar room.

'Yes! Yes, Jacques, they do, in fact. We must have our butcher as well as our baker. And really, when decisions are made in good time, it isn't all that bad. But when they're made late ... It can be awful, Jacques. Even for someone as cold-blooded as me. Confronted with the reality of the little lamb's heart beating, even the most experienced butcher shrinks from … Sorry, Jacques. Shouldn't be inflicting this on you.'

It was one of the rare moments when I saw the beginnings of tears welling in Anna's eyes. She blinked hard, lifted her wine, drained the glass and wiped her mouth with the back of her hand. I knew intuitively that her departure from her usual sense of etiquette followed from an altered mental state.

'Pour me another, will you, Jacques? And help yourself if you want to.'

The warmth of the wine was creeping through me. My head felt light as I stood up and carried the bottle round to Anna's side of the table with deliberate care and concentration.

'Fill her up, Jacques. That's it. Right to the top. The woman herself's empty as hell. Some people might even suggest that she needs psy-cho-therapy! But she prefers to just drown her sorrows like kittens and listen to you playing Chopin waltzes.'

I topped up my own wine and sat down again. Anna unexpectedly changed tack.

'So. What do you make of Rebecca's new boyfriend, Jacques? She seems quite infatuated. A dashing young chap, I have to say.'

'He's OK. Rebecca likes him.' Everything was feeling more and more distant from me the more I had to drink, including Anna's face and my jealousy towards Sam.

'Very diplomatic, Jacques. Although – and you must forgive me for being cynical here – my prediction is that it probably won't last. Don't tell her that, of course. He's very beautiful and charming, but not quite Rebecca's type at the end of the day.

A bit more depth of character will eventually be required, Jacques. Someone with a touch more storm in the soul.'

I found Anna's comments deeply gratifying. The alcohol was gradually releasing me from the fear of saying the wrong thing. 'I think you're right, Anna,' I declared boldly. 'Sam doesn't seem in keeping with her character. She needs someone more intelligent and interesting. Although she'll have to find that out for herself.'

'Well put, Jacques. I certainly couldn't tell her! We have to stumble across our own paths, I suppose. Even if it would be good to spare a person some of the pain.'

'Yes,' I agreed, confidently, not quite knowing at that stage what I was agreeing with.

'And the heart is a stupid old thing, Jacques. Mine certainly was,' Anna carried on.

'In what respect?' I was vaguely aware somewhere in my blurring brain that perhaps I shouldn't have been quite so inquisitive, but the words had already left my mouth. Anna didn't seem to mind.

'I was impulsive, I suppose. Like most younger people are. Quickly and easily impressed, Jacques. Open to flattery. You probably wouldn't think it, looking at me now, but I can assure you that I was. I was always incredibly decisive. I also didn't believe that I could simply change my course of action. In spite of what I said before, that isn't necessarily a good quality. Sometimes if we would allow ourselves to take more time over our judgements, they might be better ones, Jacques.'

'So ... they aren't the choices you'd make now?' My inhibitions were dissolving, I was talking the way that I was thinking.

'No. What I would choose I don't quite know but ... sometimes Life happens, Jacques, no matter how determined we might be to control it. I did things. Before I had time to realise that they weren't what I really wanted. I mean, this will probably strike you as very odd, Jacques, but looking back, I probably wasn't the sort of person who should have had a husband and children. I wasn't suited to that kind of life, the way some women are. I'm reliable. Responsible, but not deeply maternal.'

'But, you love your children?'

'Yes, I do. In the way that I would always want to do the right thing by them, because I had brought them into the world.'

'And Uncle Oliver?'

'Not for very long. Not in the same way. That's what I was saying before. I was initially flattered, taken in. Although it wasn't too long before he ... but I'm boring you now, Jacques. I must be?'

'No. Not at all.' I was being honest. The alcohol was making me feel more confident. It was also making possible a level of conversation that I was hungry for and reluctant to give up. 'Tell me about when you were younger. Before you lived in Chester. About why you became a surgeon.'

Anna smiled slowly. It seemed that she had slowed down in every way. My suggestion appeared to please her.

'That's a very long story, Jacques.' Anna shifted her chair, turning slightly so that she could look at her mother's painting. 'I was brought up in North Wales, not far from those mountains. My mother's family were pretty well-heeled. And Father was a doctor. We had a grand house, a materially comfortable, privileged sort of existence. Apart from the fact that Mother was a manipulative, discontented woman, who slowly drove my poor father round the bend. He started drinking, became a resigned alcoholic. It made him increasingly forgetful, duller mentally. Irritable sometimes, but rarely aggressive, never physically. I idolised him, totally adored him. It made me feel sad and powerless, seeing him slowly but surely drink himself to death.'

'So he died very young?'

'In his sixties. Mother was determined to carry on fairly seamlessly with her own life afterwards. Her endless socialising, her resilient little bridge parties appeared to be all the comfort she needed.'

'And what about you?'

'I had to take comfort where I could find it. I studied harder. I had wanted to be a doctor like Father since I was about five. I also met this older Welsh man, who was pretty quick to offer me his own kind of comfort.'

'He became a good friend?'

'No. Not at all! He was trying to be, maybe. He certainly left me with his own legacy.'

'Legacy?'

'He got me pregnant and didn't hang around to face the consequences. I ended up having to come clean with my mother. At least it was all in the early stages, she said. She arranged for me to have an abortion straightaway. If Mother wanted something, she knew how to get it. She was one of the Welsh elite, had connections in all kinds of places.'

'So ... is that why you decided to do abortions yourself?' I wondered if I was risking too much. Anna didn't flinch.

'I think that came into it. I never forgot the feeling I had of being taken over by something I didn't want and had no control over, the relief when it was all 'put right' by someone else, no matter how painful and wrong it seemed. I trained as a doctor, went into obstetrics and gynaecology, expecting I'd eventually become a G.P. or something. But I developed a fascination with surgery. Ironically I only decided to do what I do now after I'd had the children. It paid well, I had reasonable hours, a specialism I could gain some mastery of ... I found that I could do something some of my colleagues couldn't. Perhaps a kind of atonement for my past crime? Someone had to help them and so why not me? I could hardly sit in judgement ... Anyway, on that note, I think you've listened to me for more than long enough, Jacques, don't you?'

My thoughts were swimming. I knew that I needed to go to the toilet, but I didn't know if I could stand up. 'I'm sorry, Anna. I think I need to go to the bathroom.'

'Of course! You're probably ready for bed now anyway. Oh, listen! Sounds like Rebecca and Sam at the door. Fond goodnights and all that.'

'Thank you for the conversation, Anna,' I made myself say as I stood up.

Rebecca and Sam's voices fortunately seemed far away. For once I had no interest in trying to hear what they were saying, my only aim being to get upstairs to my bedroom. 'My pleasure, Jacques. Sleep well. Hope you don't have too much of a headache in the morning.' Hoping that my actions didn't appear altered, I deliberately pushed my chair right in against the dining table, steered a course around Anna's chair, in the direction of the French doors, and began my ascent of the stairs, desperate to get to my own bathroom.

I was just in time. I went straight to the toilet and peed like an endless waterfall, not caring that I had left the doors of my room and the bathroom wide open. Intensely relieved, I threw myself down on my bed, my whole head and body turning, words from my conversation with Anna mingling with the distant murmur of Rebecca and Sam's voices and phrases remembered from the 'Grande Valse'.

In Neuilly, I had loved the exhilaration of spinning on the roundabout in the park, jumping off when it was moving fast, the odd sensations of still being in motion as I lay safe on the short grass, the moments of sickness only transient. This time, however, the sickness didn't pass. I had to get up, lurch back towards the toilet, vomit repeatedly. Eventually, when my stomach was empty, I fell asleep with an aching, pulsing forehead, the same sort of headache that I woke with in the morning.

As Anna had predicted, Rebecca's relationship with Sam was relatively short-lived.

'Sam's been really irritating me recently, Jacques,' Rebecca announced one day, without preamble. It was the summer term of her lower sixth year. Sam would soon be leaving school. It was one of the rare afternoons when we found ourselves alone together after school in the lounge, watching television. 'He only seems interested in one thing.'

'What do you mean?' I asked, trying to sound calm, staring ahead at the screen. I knew exactly what she was referring to. But the thought of Sam moving in on Rebecca and the unwanted images that went with it in my head made me feel intensely uneasy. Surely she was bound to sense that?

'Oh, you know!' As I looked towards her, she looked down. She was playing with a broken elastic band, winding it round one of her fingers, making it look like a beef joint, bound with string. 'He never leaves me alone.'

'But ... I thought you liked that?'

'I used to. Until recently. It's starting to really annoy me. Like all his other habits. Ouch! That hurt!' She had over-tightened the elastic band.

'It would. Don't know why you keep doing that,' I commented, unhelpfully. 'So, you were saying ... other habits ... such as?'

'Such as always breathing heavily through his mouth, tearing his finger-nails off rather than cutting them, nose-picking, having nothing to say, asking too many inane questions.'

'So what are you going to do?' I was privately delighted by Rebecca's dissatisfaction and the way she had offered me an open-ended list of Sam's faults.

'I've decided I'm going to split up with him, actually. I'm telling him tomorrow, after school. I'll feel better when it's over and done with. I suppose the least I can do is to tell him to his face. Unless ... unless you could tell him for me, Jacques? That way I wouldn't have to see him again.'

'No,' I said. 'You can't just use me like that, Rebecca. And anyway, it wouldn't be fair on him.'

'You're right,' Rebecca admitted. She looked genuinely ashamed, which made me feel more sympathetic towards her again. 'Look... I'm sorry, Jacques. I shouldn't have said that. You're right. It would be mean. I owe him more than that, don't I?'

After she had broken up with Sam, although we couldn't return to how things were between us when we were younger, Rebecca and I did spend more time together talking. She grew more serious and fixated on doing well at school. 'I can't be bothered with relationships any more,' she told me solemnly. 'I don't want to make the mistake that some people do, of being distracted from their careers.' Rebecca was going to become a doctor, 'a totally different kind of doctor from her mum, of course'. She would specialise in something like treating cancer medically and would object on the grounds of conscience to be involved in abortion. Her heart was set on going to Edinburgh University.

I was disheartened by the thought of Rebecca leaving home and deliberately tried not to think about the future. Rebecca, on the other hand, kept insisting that I should. 'So, what are you thinking of doing at university, Jacques? Or would you think of going to music college instead?'

'What makes you think that I want to study music like that? Not everyone goes to university anyway. A lot of people prefer to get a job.' I still wasn't sure at all what I wanted to do, but I was becoming strongly resistant to other people's attempts to manage me. Rebecca tended to assume that she knew what I needed better than I did myself.

'But you're quite an academic sort of person, Jacques. It'd be a waste if you didn't do something with your intelligence. If anyone was meant to go to university, I'm sure it's you. You're very good at debating, for instance. You'd probably make a great lawyer. Or how about something like architecture? You've got the drawing skills and the creative ideas.'

'Do you know what I am really thinking of doing?'

'What?'

'Buying a ticket.'

'A ticket? What do you mean?'

'A lottery ticket.'

'Oh, don't be so daft, Jacques! You'll have to start really thinking about it. I can't keep trying to help you if you don't take it seriously yourself.'

'I don't expect you to. You know, you're going to love being a doctor. So many people to look after, everyone wanting your advice. The opportunity to be a very important person...' I teased her, anticipating the effect my humour would have. Endearingly, she became even more determined to rally me.

'At least I've got some kind of ambition! You've got such a lot of potential, Jacques! Don't you want to be really happy? Don't you want to do something with your life that would make your parents proud?'

'*Eh bien ... À quoi bon?* What would be the point? I mean ... they'll never know, will they?' In spite of my increasing confidence and fluency in English, I couldn't help reverting to French occasionally, particularly with Rebecca, when I felt annoyed or moved.

'Well, yes, I know, but it was only a way of asking you to think about what you really wanted. It's important. You're … I really want you to be happy. But it's up to you, Jacques.'

'That's true.' I shrugged, with apparent carelessness, although I was actually very touched by her saying that my happiness was important to her. 'Rebecca … I know you want to help. But don't worry about me, please? I'll do my best to do my best.'

Rebecca did well in her A-levels and was accepted to study medicine at Edinburgh. Although we had in some ways grown apart as we got older, I was still closer to her than I was to anyone else and hated the thought that she would be living at a distance. She would return for holidays, of course, but things would never be the same again. A whole new world was about to open up for her that I knew nothing about.

'It'll be fine, Jacques,' Rebecca told me that September in 1991, just before she left. She was dressed in jeans and her new skiing jacket, holding a small rucksack over one shoulder. We were alone together in the hall. Anna was outside, packing the last things into the car. It had been arranged that I would stay behind with Mrs Chadwick, while Anna had decided to take two days off work to drive Rebecca to Edinburgh to help her settle into her halls of residence. 'And you'll write to me, won't you?' asked Rebecca. 'I promise I'll write to you, and phone as well so we won't lose touch. Give me a hug?'

I hugged Rebecca hard. I wanted to more than anything, although I still found physical contact with her unsettling.

I had made up my mind not to show that I was upset, but the smell and feel of her instantly summoned a train of memories, reminding me that her presence had always brought me comfort and strength. She was wearing a new perfume. It wasn't the sweet flowery sort that I associated with Maman, but a sharper, cooler scent of green leaves and lemons.

'Of course I'll write. And you should study as hard as you can. Be the best doctor that you can be,' I tried to say matter-of-factly, although I knew that my voice sounded choked. I hugged Rebecca harder, desperately hoping that she wouldn't notice, but she did.

'Oh, you're upset, Jacques! Let me see you.'

She loosened my arms. I stood back, wiped my eyes briskly on the side of my hand and shoved my hands into my pockets. I could hardly bear to look at her.

'Jacques! You're not usually like this.'

'No.' I bit my lip, determined not to make even more of a fool of myself yet unable to stop myself thinking about how much I would miss Rebecca.

'Look at me, Jacques.'

It had been a long time since we had really looked each other in the eyes. At first only acutely conscious of how my own vulnerability would be read, as I looked at Rebecca I sensed that she too felt unable to completely control her responses. Whether she was reacting to me or to something within herself, I didn't know. 'I wasn't sure if you still cared about me, Jacques. We always used to get on so well, didn't we? And then we started to drift apart. But I want you to know that I do really care about you as well. I always have, Jacques. We'll always be friends, won't we?'

'As long as we want to be.'

Rebecca's eyes, often sardonic, sharpened usually by her habit of narrowing them, now appeared wider, softer, receiving rather than resisting. I could feel that warm buzz again in my body, even more so when she lifted her hand quickly to my cheek and brought it down again with a single, barely perceptible stroke. I felt at once that I wanted to touch her partly open mouth in return, but forced myself to keep my hands in my pockets. I wondered if Rebecca was feeling the same way, if she'd wanted me to reach out to her too. Something about the way she was looking at me without stepping back made me think that she did, even if it was just my wishful interpretation.

'You're handsome, Jacques. You must know that. A lot of girls think you are as well. Lots of people would go out with you if you wanted.'

Rebecca hardly blinked as she spoke. Her tone was utterly serious. As soon as she was finished she broke eye contact with me. There was no doubt that she had wanted to give me a sincere compliment. I was flattered in spite of my embarrassment, but the way that she had included other nameless girls in the equation irritated me. I didn't want to talk about other girls. I just wanted it to be about Rebecca and me, about what was happening in that moment.

'And?'

'Well, all I was meaning was that you should believe in yourself.' I could sense that Rebecca was already needing to move away from what she had said. 'There's no reason why you shouldn't have a girlfriend. I'm sure it would do you good. I mean ... what I mean is ... Jacques, I'm sorry. There isn't time to talk properly. That's

Mum calling. She must have finished packing the car. I'd better go. Look after yourself, won't you?'

'You too.'

My stomach was churning. I was sad and deeply frustrated, I didn't want her to leave. It seemed as if we'd been turning closer to each other again, towards what we genuinely felt. If I had touched her back at that moment as I'd wanted to, would she have still retreated into talking about me going out with other girls? If Rebecca hadn't been on the point of leaving for university and we'd had time to carry on the conversation, what would have happened then? I was tormented by the question. Everything felt unfinished, hanging in the air.

7

I remained good friends with Stephen Reid. While many criticised his nervousness and saw it as a sign of weakness, I felt privileged to know someone of Stephen's intelligence, intuition and intense, compassionate imagination. He wanted to hear about what was difficult for me and learn all about my past life in Neuilly with my parents, the grief I had suffered, as well as the strength I could draw from particular memories. He listened sympathetically when I spoke about Rebecca and I trusted completely that he would never discuss what I'd said with anyone else. What others judged as a lack of confidence, I saw as a respectful, mature and gentle tentativeness. Something about his readiness to admit his own vulnerability allowed me to express mine. Stephen wanted to help and empathise with my problems.

In contrast to me, Stephen was very clear about his future plans. He had a passion for the ancient Egyptians, especially their beliefs about the afterlife and their funerary customs. He would pour over photographs of the pyramids, royal artefacts, mummified animals. On his bedroom wall, facing the window, he had a sun-bleached map of Egypt, showing the main archaeological sites, covered with pencilled notes in his own neat, intense handwriting. His ambition was to win a scholarship to study ancient history at Oxford.

Although Stephen was obviously a very intelligent and conscientious person, he had never coped very well under pressure. The mere thought of an exam or any kind of competition caused him acute anxiety. The idea that he would have to give an account of himself, in the presence of what he saw as a panel of academic gods, produced ripples of fear that affected him in everything he did. He lost his appetite, his hands shook uncontrollably, lack of sleep gave him an otherworldly, ghostly appearance. 'I don't think I can go through with it, Jacques,' he confided in me, as we listened to Mozart's 'Requiem' one evening in my bedroom, the week before he was due to go for his exam and interview at Oxford. 'My mind keeps going blank, even about things I know that I know. I'll just go to pieces like an idiot in front of them. I know I will. I'm going to let Mum and Dad down. They'll say it doesn't matter, but they won't get over it.'

'Oh, don't worry about it!' I told him. 'You can go to Manchester instead. I'll even come with you if you like. I have no idea what I want to do yet, so it could be fun.'

The Friday after Stephen had returned from Oxford with his parents, I phoned to find out if he had been successful. His mother answered, explaining that Stephen was too upset to speak to me. He felt that he had made a complete fool of himself and had been so nervous at the interview that he had hardly been able to speak. He was utterly convinced that he had no chance of being accepted. 'I'm very sorry, Jacques. Stephen doesn't want to talk to anyone he says. Not even you. We're sure he's done so much better than he thinks he has, but he feels terribly ashamed. He has his heart set on the idea. Though we keep telling him that there are plenty of other universities, of course. Do you want me to give him a message, Jacques?'

'Just tell him that I called and we can talk about things on Monday.'

The following Monday, when Stephen didn't join me first thing in the morning at Prince's, as he usually did, I assumed that he was so embarrassed about his performance at Oxford that he had decided to hide at home for a few days, in order to avoid questioning.

When I saw the vice-principal, Mr Morgan, waiting at the front of our classroom alongside our maths teacher, Mr Astbury, I had no idea why he was there. Both men seemed tense and stood in silence as we filed into the room.

'We have some difficult news, I'm afraid,' Mr Morgan announced. He was standing over Mr Astbury's low, Formica-topped desk, his long purplish fingers whitening as he leant forward. 'We've just learned this morning that Stephen Reid died suddenly on Friday night. It's very sad and hard to believe, but it would appear that he meant to take his own life. We will be having a special assembly later this week in his memory. If anyone would like to say something or do a reading, please let me know. We can also arrange to send any messages of condolence to Stephen's parents. I appreciate that some of you will find this upsetting, but I would ask you to carry on as well as you can at school.'

'Yes,' Mr Astbury added. 'I would be grateful if you could continue working through the questions we began on Friday. Mr Morgan and I have a few matters that we need to discuss outside the classroom.'

Mr Morgan's appearance and speech had the quality of a peculiar dream, its contents unrelated to the happenings of ordinary life. I knew that I had heard what he said, had automatically registered the fact that my friend Stephen Reid was dead, but it was as if the usual mechanisms of my thoughts and feelings had been suddenly immobilised. Apart from a niggling apprehension that I should be feeling a great deal more than I actually was, the rest of me seemed to have entered a kind of ghastly state of paralysis.

It was a feeling that I recognised from the time when I had been given the news at school of Papa's death, by the policeman who had been waiting for me with my headmistress, Madame Harel, in her neatly organised office that always smelled of lavender air freshener. After hearing that Papa had died in that accident *mortel et effroyable* – fatal and horrific – as the policeman described it, I was allowed to sit quietly reading *Tintin* and drinking hot chocolate, not knowing what to think or feel, aware that the privilege of sitting in my headmistress's office was an unreal kind of advantage, whose dreadful cost far outweighed any momentary pleasure.

By break-time on the morning of Mr Morgan's announcement, news of Stephen's death had spread throughout Prince's and was being discussed in murmurs by groups of boys clustered along corridors and around radiators in the entrance hall. I stood at the back of the cloakrooms with Mitch and Wheelie.

'You can't really believe it, can you?' Wheelie started. 'You just keep thinking he's going to come along the corridor at any minute.'

'You never would've thought he'd do something like that,' Mitch said. 'I mean, he never gave you the impression that he was desperately unhappy or anything, did he?'

'He was really worked up about the whole Oxford thing,' I explained. 'I can imagine he felt terrible about not doing as well as he wanted to at the interview. He would have seen it as letting his parents down. Although, I never thought that he'd feel that bad.'

The numbness began partially to thaw as the three of us spoke. The idea that I might have helped Stephen more by showing more seriously that I had understood his feeling that he had made a complete fool of himself was almost unthinkable, but I forced myself to think about it. Somehow I wanted to make myself suffer. If I had said something different, even if it was only through his mother that evening, could I have changed his mind? Could a few more wisely chosen words from me have prevented Stephen's suicide? It was such a terrible, unbearably tormenting question.

'I wonder what he did exactly? There's a rumour going round that he hung himself in his room, but ...' Wheelie shrugged awkwardly.

Wheelie was only voicing what many of us were thinking, alongside similar discomfort and self-censorship. Certainly, amid all the other more socially acceptable questions in my own mind, there were others that seemed much less decent. I too wanted to know precisely how Stephen had killed himself. However morbid it might have been considered, I wanted to envisage the whole terrible chain of small actions and thoughts that had led to his end.

I think now that part of what lay behind my desire for knowledge came down to a boy's innate, unflinching curiosity about the realities of life and death, including the truth about the impact of physical violence. At the same time, I had a genuine wish to suffer along with my friend, to accompany Stephen in imagination in a way that I hadn't been able to do in life. I wanted to know what it had felt like to be in his shoes, to grasp the minutiae of his experience. The facts of his death needed to gain their full weight, so that I could accept that they were indisputable. I had an urge to see him dead, so that I could personally lay my hands on the body of evidence – in the most literal sense.

Later the same day, we were informed that Stephen's memorial assembly would take place that Friday. There wasn't yet a definite date for his funeral, but it was expected to be arranged the following week. I was asked if I would like to say a few words on either or both occasions. Mr and Mrs Reid had told the school that they had considered me their son's closest friend. Their generosity made me feel more guilty and I committed myself to giving a short speech at the funeral.

On the way home that afternoon, I made myself call at Stephen's house. Although I was reluctant to disturb or inconvenience his parents, I felt compelled to see them and to convince myself that Stephen was no longer there. I hadn't thought clearly about what

I would say. If I was made to feel unwelcome or uncomfortable, I thought, it would simply be what I deserved.

It was Mr Reid who answered the door. He looked tired, but otherwise exactly as he always did, his side-parted hair smoothed, his glasses highly polished, shirt and black tie smart under a navy buttoned cardigan. 'Oh, hello, Jacques. I hoped we might see you. I was going to call you this evening. I wanted to speak to you before school today, but we've had so much to ... Anyway, come in, won't you? Mrs Reid's upstairs having a lie-down at the moment. Mike and Jane are at their grandmother's.'

The Reids' house was Edwardian like the Clarks', although it had a different, more informal atmosphere, thick carpets everywhere and homelier, less grand furnishings. The sitting-room was dimly lit by two brass-stemmed table lamps – the blinds, usually left open during the day, were virtually closed. There was a used tea tray with a plate of biscuits and three cups and saucers on the coffee table.

'The police have just been here again,' Mr Reid explained, as he lifted the tray. 'I'll just put this in the kitchen. Have a seat, will you?'

For a moment it was as if I was in some kind of waiting room instead of at my friend's house. I had never been in Stephen's home without him and had never had reason particularly to notice what the rooms contained.

I knew there had been family photographs on the walls, but it was the first time that I had actually studied them. Stephen figured in most of them, dependably serious, with his parents, his old dog Mack, his younger sister Jane, and his older brother Michael. Two-dimensional versions of Stephen, still watching from a distance. When Mr Reid returned and stood with his back to the mantelpiece, Stephen's multiplied face seemed to be staring down at me over his shoulders.

'I wanted to say ... how sorry I was ... am ... to hear about Stephen,' I began, not knowing what I was going to say next. 'I can't believe it, almost. It was a real shock. It must have been even more so for you and Mrs Reid ... and everyone.'

'It was, Jacques. None of us saw this coming, I'm afraid. His mother and I knew that he was very upset about Oxford and, well, Stephen's always been a very sensitive sort of boy, but you never expect anything like this. We just wanted him to be happy. But it seems that it got to him more than we imagined.'

'So ... did he ... do you know for certain that that was what it was about?' I needed to know, then immediately felt as if I shouldn't have pried.

'Well, yes, Jacques. Stephen did leave a short note to us. He said that ...' Initially extremely composed, Mr Reid suddenly was struggling to speak. The whites of his eyes were quite bloodshot, he held the end of his nose, and had to keep swallowing. 'He said that he was sorry. That he was too disappointed with himself, that he couldn't see a time when he wouldn't feel disappointed. He wanted to thank us for everything we had done for him ... wanted us to pass on thanks to everyone he knew as well ... told us not to think that it was our fault ... it was his own decision ...'

'So there was no doubt that ...'

'No. The police don't suspect any kind of foul play. I suppose they could still want to talk to you or some of his other friends in relation to the inquest, but probably not. I shouldn't think there would be anything that could be added. They think it was obvious that he meant to hang himself.'

'So, that's what he did?' I still felt driven to pin down the details, however ashamed I was of my question. Fortunately, Mr Reid didn't seem offended. He wearily issued me with the facts.

'Yes. In his bedroom. Used his leather school belt ... sorry, Jacques. I'm sure you don't want to know any more.'

'It's alright, Mr Reid. I don't mind. Stephen was my friend. It's the least ...'

I couldn't help feeling the contradictions in Stephen's attitude to his own life and the attachment he had had to the life of his old dog, Mack. He had been so adamant that Mack shouldn't be put to sleep, and yet he had chosen deliberately to cut short the time that his family and I had to enjoy being with him. I was angry at times that Stephen had only partially revealed his despair to me, that he seemed to have made the choice to surrender because he had failed to meet his own standards for perfection, while I had to persevere in an imperfect life.

Although I felt that it was important for Stephen's death to be acknowledged at school, I was reluctant to be a part of any gesture towards mourning him in that context. There had been many people there who had made Stephen feel vulnerable and unworthy. I despised them for their shallowness and lack of compassion. The way that they were automatically given permission to be involved in such a sad and deeply personal moment and could somehow be absolved from their guilt by going through the motions of a public ceremony disgusted me.

Throughout the memorial assembly, I stood with my head down between Mitch and Wheelie, painfully aware of Stephen's absence, telling myself that I would keep all my words about Stephen for his family funeral, deliberately detaching myself from the Head Boy's perfectly composed and rehearsed reading of Psalm 23. I could tell that some of the other boys were looking at me occasionally, nudging each other as we stood in rows across the school hall, in the same way that they had been staring and nudging each other since the news of Stephen's death.

At break-time after the assembly, when Mitch, Wheelie and I had withdrawn to our usual meeting place against the coats at the back of the cloakrooms, we were approached by Robert Smith, who was surrounded as usual by his faithful entourage. Robert was one of the boys in our form who had been particularly spiteful towards Stephen about his chess and music. He was a fairly clever boy, good at sciences and maths. He especially prided himself on his excellence at sport. Although he never would have admitted it, I guessed that he was painfully aware of not having the looks to complement his prowess on the field, a realisation that undermined his self-confidence. His face, chest and back were constantly covered in outcrops of resurgent yellow pimples.

'Really awful about Stephen, Jacques,' Robert said quietly. He stood opposite me with his hands in his pockets, ignoring Mitch and Wheelie. I became uneasy immediately, distrustful of what appeared to be a simple show of sympathy.

'Yes, it is. Obviously,' I replied, bitterly.

'You must be really missing him,' Robert continued. 'Especially with you two being so close.'

'Of course.'

'I mean, I suppose it's hard for some of us to imagine. If he'd been a girl ... well, I ...'

I instantly felt defensive.

'What's that meant to mean, Robert? Jacques, Mitch and I all really liked Stephen, so ...' Wheelie had stepped forward in front of me, his face close to Robert's.

'Yes, but don't pretend you don't know what I mean. Everyone knows that Stephen and Jacques were doing each other.'

'Stephen and I were very good friends, Robert. No less, no more. We liked the same things. We could have an intelligent conversation, although I don't suppose you would –' I only managed to say before Wheelie took over.

'You stupid little bigoted shit!' Wheelie attacked Robert like an animal, grabbing him by the collar, swinging him round towards the back of the cloakroom, pushing him backwards. Wheelie was heftily built, even if he didn't have Robert's agility. They fell down on the ground together, Wheelie on top, Robert kicking and biting, clawing at his face, attempting to squirm free.

'Don't bother with him, Wheelie!' I shouted. Robert had the reputation for being a sharp, devious fighter. However admirable Wheelie's intentions, I didn't want him getting blinded. 'He's just a stupid half-witted bastard! He isn't worth it!' Absorbed by his rage and the effort of holding Robert pinned down, Wheelie seemed to be oblivious to what I was saying. His neck twisted from side to side to avoid Robert's poking fingers; his cheeks had turned flaming red; saliva poured from his open mouth onto Robert's face.

The commotion, fortunately or not, attracted the attention of Mr Morgan, who appeared abruptly at the edge of the cloakroom, clutching his gown imperiously at his chest. 'What's going on here? Stop this at once! On your feet now, Wheeler!' Startled by Mr Morgan's booming voice, Wheelie sprang away like a guilty dog and got to his feet, Robert scrambling up behind him.

'So, is someone going to explain to me exactly what's going on here?' Mr Morgan demanded. 'This is a total disgrace. We've only just had the memorial service, for Christ's sake! And you animals can't restrain your basest instincts! Lafitte? Can you tell me what's happening?'

We declined to commit ourselves. Mr Morgan dismissed us with instructions that we were all to attend his detention group after school. As far as I was concerned, Robert's nasty stupidity, driven by the insecurity deriving from his sense of his own ugliness, didn't even deserve the attention of a complaint. I didn't want his lies to have another airing, even if it did mean that Mr Morgan might punish him and be more sympathetic towards me. The incident only affirmed my decision not to give a speech at the memorial assembly.

I was given the afternoon off school to attend Stephen's funeral. Anna had initially offered to come home early from work and take me there herself, but Mr and Mrs Reid asked specifically if

I would like to go with them and the rest of the family instead. Anna told me that she had gathered that they were concerned about how I was coping and had regretted being unable to inform me personally of Stephen's death before I went to school that Monday. I was willing to agree to anything that might help Stephen's parents in some small way.

In contrast to my previous experiences of funeral processions, with darkly clad men and women sitting straight-backed and isolated in formal, pristine cars following a hearse, we all sat squashed together in the Reids' old red Volvo. Stephen's parents were both in black suits, but Michael, Jane and Stephen's grandmother Rose were dressed quite casually in pale colours. Under a blue cardigan, Jane was wearing a pink top with her name printed beside a red flower. Stephen had particularly liked it, she told me, and had once made a joke of trying it on himself.

In spite of the fact that none of Stephen's family was particularly religious, an Anglican vicar had been asked to lead the short service at the cemetery chapel. He stood at a simple wooden lectern between us and Stephen's coffin, which was decorated with two bouquets of white lilies. I was seated three rows back, with the rest of Stephen's family, next to Jane, on the aisle end of the pew. As the vicar's anodyne tones led us into the ceremony, my eyes wandered to the lilies behind him, their tall waxen heads breathless and still against the flat backs of dark leaves. I tried to imagine how Stephen looked as he lay beneath them, separated from their elegance and fragrance by so much more than his coffin's lid.

Stephen had loved flowers, something else some people had thought strange for a person of his age, and another reason to mock him. I admired him for openly enjoying them, lifting them to his nose, commenting on their scents. I liked them myself, but always felt more inhibited, anticipating the inevitable suggestion that having such a conventionally feminine taste had to mean that I was gay.

The question of whether or not Stephen had been homosexual flickered momentarily into my mind again, followed at once by a sense of guilt. I didn't want the question to be a part of me. Especially since it happened to be provoked by some very limited ideas about defining what it meant to be a man. There was no rational reason why it should have bothered me. Wouldn't I have been his close friend whether or not he was gay? Stephen had never talked about girls with me, but perhaps that was because it was something he felt shy about. I hadn't confided in him on the subject either. I had tended to reserve an occasional comment about a particularly attractive girl for Mitch and Wheelie, who would share equally brief confidences of their own. The fact was that Stephen and I had chosen to talk about other things. Whatever the case, he had certainly never made any kind of approach towards me sexually, however much others had decided to assume that we were 'lovers'. It was just one of a list of things that I would never know for sure about Stephen. Still, even if I had been given the opportunity to ask him one further question, there were so many others that I would have wanted the answers to first.

'And now, one of Stephen's school friends, Jacques Lafitte, would like to say a few words. He is also, I understand, going to play something on the piano afterwards. Jacques?' The vicar was looking at me, nodding his head meaningfully, indicating that I come to the front and stand beside him. I had been so caught up in thinking about the bouquets on Stephen's coffin, I hadn't been concentrating on what he had been saying. I was holding my handwritten speech folded on top of my music, behind the Order of Service. My palms were saturated with sweat.

Noticing that I was looking bewildered, Jane nudged my elbow encouragingly. 'I'll hold your Order of Service if you like, Jacques. Go on up. You'll be fine.' I made my way to the front and the vicar moved to allow me to use the lectern. I stood to one side of it and unfolded my paper, my hands trembling. The thought of reading from the lectern made me feel uncomfortable. It seemed too formal a place from which to deliver the personal words I had written for Stephen and his family. I kept looking down, staying deliberately focused on my paper. As I cleared my throat and started to read, I suddenly felt calmer.

'I liked Stephen from the first time that we met at Prince's. I knew at once that he was a good person. Although we were different in many ways, I felt that Stephen and I were the same. Coming from London, Stephen understood, as I did, how it felt to be an outsider. We were interested in the same sort of things. Stephen was much better than me at chess! We appreciated the same kind of music. Stephen loved Chopin, Beethoven, Bach, Mozart and Schubert. Stephen wasn't ashamed of the emotional part of himself. He told me that he loved the music's romance. I admired him for being able to be honest, in a way that not many other people can. He seemed much older and more mature sometimes than me and the other boys.

'Stephen was a caring person. Sometimes I wonder if he cared too much. I know that he would want me to say how much he loved his family and he knew that they loved him too. Most of all he didn't want them to worry about him. He hated the idea of them being upset on his behalf.

'It's difficult for me to say this, but I think we have to respect Stephen's decision. Though his life was shorter than it should have been, it was a good life. Much better than some people who have lived to be ninety. Of course, like everyone here, I wanted him to live for longer, but I know that that was, as they say, up to him. There are so many other things to say, but I am going to stop now. I hope that it is enough.'

When I looked up at the end of my speech, I made eye contact with Mr Reid. He nodded, managed a trace of a smile, mouthed, 'Thank you, Jacques.' Beside him, Mrs Reid was sobbing silently, her hand over a tissue covering her nose and mouth. In spite of what I had just said, I immediately began to question my choice of the word 'respect'. Stephen's actions had caused such intense pain. However ideal it might be to respect his freedom, might it not be more realistic to simply aim towards tolerating it?

'I wanted to play something for Stephen,' I announced. 'I've chosen part of Beethoven's Piano Sonata No. 8 in C Minor, the Adagio Cantabile of the "Pathétique".'

I made my way quickly to the chapel piano. My legs were shaking. I hoped that the nervousness would leave my hands when I started to play. I settled on the old piano stool, sat quietly for a moment, then began.

I had always thought of the Adagio Cantabile as the most compassionate, experienced listening ear and empathic voice at the same time. Within it, I felt so many echoes of Papa and Maman. As I played, I felt surrounded immediately by an atmosphere of sympathy. As I thought of Stephen, I had an image of him, holding his carefully wrapped ammonite, cupped protectively in his hand.

After the service, I went with the Reids to the burial ground. We all stood, watching as the bouquets of lilies were set on the freshly mown grass of the cemetery and Stephen's coffin was slowly lowered into the grave against the backdrop of an otherwise ordinary, warm autumn afternoon. Part of me wished that it had been a bitterly cold, wet, day, more congruent with the harsh truths of sudden death and separation that we were being forced to come to terms with. It seemed wrong in a way to bury Stephen on an afternoon when we could have been walking in sunshine on the path across the Meadows. The kind heat, the vicar's droning blessings above the grave, the softly murmured conversations about weather and flowers, all seemed too easily friendly, as if Nature was gently firm in its intention to keep us in unison and moving steadily on.

Knowing that it would have been selfish and totally in-appropriate, I still felt a momentary urge to scream in protest and anger. Anger at Stephen for doing this to us, but also anger at the world. Jarring, profane words that I couldn't precisely think of, to express a moment that connected in my mind with an image of the jagged edges of a broken bottle emerging from beneath the apparently smooth, sun-warmed surface of the River Dee.

As the moment passed, I suspected then, as I know much more certainly now, that more than at any other time, we needed that light and heat. We needed to distract ourselves in whatever way we could from grief. Even if we were unable immediately to accept Stephen's suicide ourselves, Nature seemed to be accept-ing it non-judgementally on our behalf, making it favourable even for him to return to where he came from.

I looked back at the bouquets of lilies that had decorated Stephen's coffin, now on the grass, close to the mound of soil that would eventually fill in his grave. Unlike him, they would escape the darkness, if only for a few more days. They would lie on guard, above him, like some loyal, graceful dogs with their chins against the earth, pining, eventually dying, realising their wish to be with him again. Later, when I was finally alone in my bedroom that evening, I worked into the early hours of the morning sketching a series of lily heads, progressing from tightly closed buds to fully open flowers. Those of us who wished Stephen could have stayed with us were left feeling that his full promise had been far from fulfilled. As time passed, I came to accept more that, however short, he had had his own complete lifetime.

8

When Matthew had left for Cambridge, as far as I was concerned, his absence had made little difference. However vivid his life might have been to him – and I found it difficult to imagine that possibility – he had chosen to share so little of himself with me that his reality had been shadowy, to say the least. In contrast, Rebecca's presence had always been a strong, vibrant statement, in sound and colour. The Clarks' house, like my inner world, often seemed empty without her. My awareness of the arbitrary quality of my own existence, strongly intimated at the time of Papa's death and heightened after Stephen's suicide, seemed keener after Rebecca left. Although I had needed to see myself as a self-sufficient kind of person, I was struck by how dependent on others I could feel, an ambivalence created and compounded by my survival of grief. While I knew that I was capable of being alone, I recognised that solitude was always better when it included the possibility of its opposite.

Two recurring images from my life in Neuilly kept coming into my thoughts at that time: suggestions, perhaps, of my attempt to make sense of my life and to connect it with my past. One was the cotton reel topped with short nails with which my mother had taught me how to make lengths of woollen rope. As you wound the wool around the heads of the nails and 'knitted' each new row, a tail of rope appeared from the hole in the bottom of the reel. It was nothing compared to the huge expanses of knitting that used to grow from Maman's needles, but I still thought that it was magical how something could be created from such basic equipment.

I also thought about the plastic pot of cloves that Maman had given me to play with when I was smaller. Every clove was precious, Maman told me, and I would only be allowed to continue having the pot on the condition that I looked after it. I could take off the lid to smell the cloves, but I had to be careful not to lose a single one. I used to imagine that they were small fragrant people with little round heads, often apart, sometimes falling against each other as they rattled around in their tall-sided home.

Initially, the thought that I would be living on my own with Anna and Mrs Chadwick made me feel uncomfortable. Fortunately, I discovered that the reality was something different entirely. Both Anna and Mrs Chadwick had a tendency to distance themselves from me, but for different reasons. Anna, by her own admission, was responsible but 'not deeply maternal'. And Mrs Chadwick, in spite of her nurturing instincts, had a staunch sense of professionalism that made it almost impossible for her to apply herself any less thoroughly to her practical housekeeping duties whatever the circumstances. While she undoubtedly cared and felt responsible for looking after me, attention to my needs had to be fitted in among her other tasks.

I had also come to accept over the years that the particular kind of mothering that I lacked and craved wouldn't come from either woman, through no act of ill will on their part. Still, while I continued to mourn the loss of the deep, joyful love I had felt from my parents, I recognised that there was an integrity and consistency in my relationships with Anna and Mrs Chadwick that allowed me a separate space in which to develop a sense of my own identity.

I understood that each woman did her best to respect me and to give me what she could. While their connection to me lacked the delight and depth of natural warmth that I had had from my parents, I think that Anna and Mrs Chadwick created an environment characterised by principle and truth, which approached an unconditional form of love.

Mrs Chadwick saw to my practical needs meticulously and reliably. While occasionally, as I had already discovered, Anna would converse with me as if I was an adult, and in ways that I didn't expect, most of the time she maintained very clear boundaries and didn't make a habit of discussing her own problems or dilemmas. However, she listened to me playing the piano regularly, seemed genuinely interested in my opinions and ideas and invited me to have an occasional glass of wine with her in the dining-room.

One evening after my piano practice, Anna asked me directly if I had decided upon what I wanted to do after I left Prince's.

I had taken art, music and history for my A-levels, simply because I enjoyed the subjects, without any precise long-term ambition.

'You will have to decide what you want to do soon, Jacques, although I have to say I feel increasingly that seventeen is far too young to make a significant decision about anything. Unfortunately we are forced to work within the present system. You have ample finance from your parents' estate to do what you want. And Oliver and I are willing, of course, to support you as well. Have you had any particular thoughts?'

'I was thinking I might do history, possibly. At Manchester.'

'So, you wouldn't want to study music or art? What I've seen of your artwork is exceptionally well-executed and original, and you're clearly a talented musician. Aren't those the things you enjoy most?'

'Yes. But I don't think I want to study them in that way. I mean, I want to carry on playing and with my own art, but ...'

'And you would be taking history with what end in mind?'

'I'm not sure exactly. I could teach perhaps.'

'You could indeed. If that was what you really wanted. It has to be your call, Jacques.'

Although every now and then Anna would ask me to reflect upon my rationale for not pursuing a career in music or art, otherwise she seemed prepared to accept my decisions, however insubstantial the reasoning behind them. The truth was that I didn't truly know what I wanted to do. Particularly since Stephen's tragic death so young, I had felt even less motivated to think about it.

I couldn't help feeling sometimes that the relatively insignificant details of my future plans were almost irrelevant. Did it really matter whether I chose to study history, art or music, when Stephen's whole life was over, when such a good friend was already becoming inseparable from earth?

In spite of my struggle to come to terms with Stephen and Rebecca's absences, I was consoled by my continuing friendship with Wheelie and Mitch. They hadn't been as close to Stephen as I had, but they had enjoyed his company and could identify in some ways with my feelings.

We started to spend more time together around Chester and in each other's houses. I could tell they were deliberately trying to think of ways to help me feel better. At school we came to be known as 'The Three Musketeers'.

Both boys lived within easy walking distance, on the same side of the River Dee as the Clarks' house, also in large houses with big gardens. We developed a habit of meeting at weekends in Mitch's back garden, in a dilapidated summer-house, filled with flowerpots and damp conservatory furniture.

Sometimes Mitch would steal some bottles of his father's potent home-brewed beer. Wheelie would always have a packet of cigarettes. I was sick when I first tried one but I quickly came to enjoy the effect and the taste. We talked about incidents at school, made fun of teachers, teased Wheelie about his attempts to learn to drive, discussed our personal tastes in books, art, actors, films.

'Favourite ... book, Mitchie! What's your favourite book?' I remember Wheelie beginning on one such evening, as he sat, dreamily blowing smoke rings.

'That's difficult ... I mean, there's lots of books I like,' Mitch answered, thoughtfully, extracting the last precious chemicals from his cigarette stub.

'Oh, come on, Mitchie! You gotta make a decision,' Wheelie said, lapsing into his practised fusion of American accents. 'A man's gotta have an opinion. He's gotta have somethin' just a-trippin' off his tongue.' It was something that Wheelie genuinely believed. Even if you changed your mind in the next hour or the next day, you had to be able to give a definite view in a conversation.

'Well, probably a Hemingway or a Steinbeck, or perhaps a Graham Greene. I like *The Quiet American*.'

'Good choice, Mitchie! Great book! On my own list, as it happens. And what about you, Jacques? Though, let me think, let me think ... I asked you this one recently ... Monsieur Camus, wasn't it? *L'Étranger*? Bit of an outsider, eh, Jacques?'

'Yes. Or possibly Kafka ... *The Trial*. A sensitive mind, bewildered by incomprehensible experiences.'

'Yes, Jacques! All a bit too torturous and profound for me, but you got it!'

'So what about you, Wheelie? What's your favourite?' I asked. Wheelie loved to be the interviewer, but he especially relished being interviewed.

'As always, I prefer to have a full hand, Jacques!' Wheelie sat back, savouring the moment when he would reveal his own choices. 'Salinger's *The Catcher in the Rye* ... an absolute gem of a book. Love the dark humour, the whole American adolescent theme. *Lord of the Flies*. A masterpiece. Next has to be ... a bit of ... D.H.! Every man has to have some of his own *Lady Chatterley*! And then, perhaps some Conrad, though have to confess the film *Apocalypse Now* grabbed me as much as the book. Couldn't do better than old mad Marlon, could you? A monument of a man! I've got the video. We could all watch it sometime if you like? Now, Jacques. Quick-fire, individual round! Favourite ... piece of art?'

'Rodin's sculpture, *The Kiss*.'

'Yes, Jacques! Favourite ... composer?'

'Ludwig van Beethoven.'

'Of course! Favourite ... actor?'

'Pacino ... De Niro.'

'A man after my own heart. Favourite ... actress?'

'Catherine Deneuve. Isabelle Huppert. Juliette Binoche. Yours?'

'Marilyn Monroe. Meg Ryan. Kim Basinger ...'

At other times we talked about girls, or in Wheelie's case, older women. Wheelie was especially obsessed with his geography teacher, Miss Warburton, a dark-haired, buxom young woman with pointed eye-teeth, reminiscent of a vampire's. Most of the boys found her presence pleasantly overwhelming, but Wheelie admitted that he had persistent and elaborate fantasies. He also liked to hear repeated accounts of her from other people's perspectives. 'So, tell me again, Jacques,' he began slowly, sprawling across the old wicker-backed couch, lighting another cigarette and inhaling deeply with his eyes closed. 'You saw her in the hall, talking to The Stud?' Mr Parry was one of the P.E. teachers, a short, muscular bully of a man whom Wheelie had sneeringly dubbed 'The Stud'.

'Yes. I was on my way to music. They were alone in the middle of the hall.'

'Which means that I must have been on my way to English. Wonder why I didn't see them myself. So, was she still wearing her academic gown, or had she taken it off?'

I tried my best to rewind the scenario, realising that I hadn't really paid much attention, or at least insufficient attention to answer the intensity of Wheelie's interest.

'She had taken it off.' I was really only groping towards the memory.

'And what was she wearing underneath? A buttoned shirt? One of her ribbed jumpers?'

'It was a shirt. Pink, I think.'

'With white round buttons?'

'Most buttons are round, I think.'

'So, how far up, I mean, down, was the shirt buttoned, Jacques?'

'I'm not sure. I don't know if I noticed.'

'Oh, come on, Jacques! You must remember!'

'I think it had one or two buttons undone at the top.'

'And what else was she wearing?'

'A grey skirt.'

'Long or short?'

'Quite short.'

'Knee-length or higher, Jacques?'

'Knee-length, I think.'

'Tight or loose?'

'I can't remember.'

'You're killing me, Jacques! How close was she standing to The Stud? A foot away? Six inches?'

'No, I think they were closer.'

'Close enough to be touching?'

'Perhaps, I mean, yes, I think they were.'

'Are you sure about that, Jacques?'

'I think so. Yes, I'm pretty sure their arms and shoulders were together.'

'So, did she look as if she was enjoying it? The fact that they were touching, I mean?'

'How would I know? I'm not a mind-reader, am I?'

'Well no, but you can tell the signs. She might've looked a little flushed. Perhaps her breathing was faster or she had a suggestion of pleasure about her open mouth ... or she was staring at him, like she didn't want to look away ...'

'Like you wished she'd stare at you?' Mitch enquired, highly amused by Wheelie's preoccupation.

'Of course. I'm not ashamed. She is pretty amazing. Don't pretend you wouldn't like some private time with her yourself.'

'She must be almost thirty, Wheelie!'

'And?'

'It'd almost be like doing it with one of your mother's friends. She'd eat you for breakfast!'

Wheelie lay where he was and took a long draw on his cigarette. He narrowed his eyes and shifted his neck with the smoothness of a snake. 'Never underestimate me, Mitch. I have skills you can only dream of. Think I can't handle an older woman? Watch this space.'

Wheelie's lust for Miss Warburton was destined never to be fulfilled outside his fantasies. It wasn't long, however, before he set his sights more realistically on a younger woman. The new object of his desire was sixteen-year-old Sandra Worthington.

Sandra went to St Hilda's, Rebecca's old school. She was in the same year as Stephen's sister, Jane. As Wheelie began to organise small parties in Mitch's summer-house with Sandra and her school friends, I came to know Jane better and found that we got along really well, independent of any associations I had had with her family.

Since Stephen had died, I briefly visited his parents now and then. As I grew more friendly with Jane, my visits gradually became longer and more frequent. Jane was quite different from Rebecca in both looks and personality. She had straight, shoulder-length whitish-blonde hair and remarkably smooth skin. There was something ethereal about the quiet way she moved and spoke. While I thought that Rebecca was beautiful in a strong, uncomplicated way that was inseparable from her state of radiant physical health, Jane's beauty was more subtle and fey. It was an inspiring kind of beauty that made me idealise more than lust. Jane was also an exceptional singer and had

had lessons from an early age. I had once seen her perform a solo of 'Nymphs and Shepherds' at a concert at Prince's. She had a tremulous soprano voice that prompted me to paint her as a scattering of delicate powder blue butterflies across page after page of my watercolour block.

I was intrigued by Jane's deceptive quality of lightness. Her mind, like her voice, could flutter along with humour and apparent nonchalance, but she had an intellect that many people overlooked. Inevitably, Jane and I would often talk about Stephen, what he might have said and done in particular situations, how we both missed him. At other times, we would talk about ourselves, especially about what we were doing musically. I didn't feel that I could quite be myself and communicate as directly with her as I could with Rebecca, but still, in time I came to acknowledge the truth of Wheelie's observation that I had 'developed feelings' for Jane.

'There comes a point when you gotta make your move, Jacques,' Wheelie counselled me one weekend, when it was just him, Mitch and me in the summer-house. 'She obviously likes you. You should get there before Scav jumps in. She'd go for you first anyway.'

'Scav', short for 'Scavenger', was Wheelie's name for Alex King. When it came to girls, behind an apparently charming façade, lurked Alex's predatory nature. While the thought of Alex exploiting Jane Reid certainly gave me more incentive to act swiftly, I was still feeling inhibited by the fact that Jane was Stephen's sister.

'So what's holding you back, Jacques?' Mitch asked me directly. Although Wheelie was never ill-intentioned towards me, he was more extrovert, straightforwardly pragmatic and less thought-ful than Mitch. Mitch's style was often to observe silently for a long time, reserving judgement until he had had enough time for careful consideration.

'The thought that Jane is connected to Stephen and his fam-ily. I can't help feeling a bit guilty, I suppose. That I could think about enjoying myself with Stephen's sister when he's ... and I might not get everything right.'

'So? Who does?'

'I know, but imagine if, after everything, I upset ...'

'No one should expect anyone else to be perfect,' Wheelie declared. 'Of course you could get it wrong and you're still young and it's unlikely to last forever but you can't not take a risk. Why feel guilty about being attracted to a girl? Even if it's just good for a while, at least you've both had that.'

A fortnight later, Wheelie decided that we should have a party and invite some girls, including Sandra and Jane. Mitch's par-ents were going out and they gave us permission on the condi-tion that we kept it to a small group of friends. It was the end of April 1992 and we had been feeling the pressure of our impend-ing A-levels. 'Wine, women and song would do us all good,' Wheelie pronounced. He would make sure that he had plenty of cigarettes. Mitch had succeeded in accumulating a sizeable secret store of alcohol, including a few bottles of wine sneaked from his parents' cellar.

I felt apprehensive when the night of the party finally arrived. I had almost resolved to ask Jane out at some point during the evening, although had told myself that I didn't have to, if I felt that I didn't have the courage. Paradoxically the tension resulting from giving myself this option made me feel worse. Every time I looked at Jane, I was reminded of my impending task. 'Go on! Have another beer, Jacques!' Wheelie encouraged, throwing me a can from the door of the summer-house. '*Bonne chance!*'

Jane looked even more appealing that evening than usual. Her hair fell loose around her shoulders, apart from two thin plaits close to her face, which were pinned back with silver clips. She was wearing a long pink dress and a white lacy cardigan that reminded me of a silk cocoon. The fact that Jane's clothes weren't quite suitable for an April evening gave me the opportunity to be chivalrous and to initiate physical contact with her.

'You can have my jacket, if you like,' I offered, as Jane stood shivering beside me. Most of us were standing close to the old brick barbecue at the end of Mitch's garden. Mitch had started to cook some sausages. It relieved some of our general awkwardness to watch and pretend to criticise him.

'Thank you, Jacques. I will, if you don't mind. But aren't you cold yourself?'

'No. Not at all, in fact.' I wasn't lying. The sight of Jane and the anticipation of my oncoming task was making me sweat. I didn't feel the cold. '*Eh bien* ... here. Let me help you.'

I took off my jacket and carefully put it around Jane's shoulders. Taking a deep breath, I stood beside her again, decisively extended my arm and laid it across the shoulders of my own jacket. With the other arm I fortified myself with another drink of beer. I hardly dared look at Jane, though I could tell from the corner of my eye that she was looking at me and slightly smiling. She certainly didn't make any effort to remove my arm.

Wheelie was standing further back on our left, his arm around Sandra Worthington. As I turned in his direction, he lifted his beer at me, in what I assumed had to be a congratulatory gesture.

Wheelie had been showing off since the beginning of the party, throwing all the boys cans of beer, smoothly offering the girls cider and wine. He was wearing what he referred to as his 'smoking jacket', looked extremely debonair and equally aware of the fact. While he looked confident, I could tell by his twitchiness that he was nervous. He had told Mitch and me that he had already gone 'pretty far' with Sandra sexually and intended to go further as soon as he could, that evening if possible. He couldn't wait, he said, to be more of a man.

We all ate Mitch's sausages. I wasn't feeling hungry but attempted to eat greedily like the rest of the boys while the girls picked over their food. Afterwards some of us sat around talking in the summer-house while Wheelie held a bit of an audience with Sandra and a few of the other girls outside.

Mitch hadn't declared an interest in any particular girl. I envied him having no agenda for the evening, being simply able to eat, drink and joke. After a few beers he was a natural storyteller and had the ability to entertain everyone in the summer-house with his wry humour. The girls couldn't get enough of Mitch's recounting of school anecdotes, particularly his meticulously observed impressions of our teachers and their tics. However violent or cruel a teacher's behaviour, Mitch managed to transmute their actions into comedy.

'You're a most peculiar little person, Mitchell,' Mitch often began with the strangulated voice of his personal tormentor and French teacher, Mr Holmes, known generally as 'Sherlock'. Unlike his literary counterpart, Fred Holmes lacked any powers of empathy or imagination and had a mechanical, robotic kind of intelligence. 'I mean, you seem to think that I can teach you nothing. That you know everything there is to know about the French language already! Your stupidity never ceases to surprise me, Mitchell. I feel it is my duty to guide you. To teach you in a way that you can't so easily ignore!' Mitch's face contorted as he acted out the moment when Sherlock took hold of the short hairs of his own side-burns and twisted them upwards mercilessly. He stood up to try to loosen the power of the pull, following the movement of the teacher's arm.

The girls squealed with delight as Mitch recalled countless similar episodes, each one with its own unique twist of cruelty.

'You're so funny, Mitch!' Jane kept saying as she recovered from laughter. 'Tell us about something else.' I was jealous of the way that Mitch had so effortlessly delighted her while I was inwardly suffering over my imminent decision to ask her out. I could feel myself taking a back seat in Mitch's audience, a fact that he eventually picked up on. 'That's it for now!' he suddenly announced. 'Someone else's turn – Jacques? Or are you perhaps thinking of going outside instead? It's not a bad night?' Mitch was usually more subtle. While he might have simply justified it to himself as offering me an opportunity, he was also quietly retaliating against my withdrawal of support as an admiring member of his audience.

'You're right. I was thinking of going out,' I replied, trying to sound casual, my heart thumping in my chest, knowing it was time to act. 'Want to come outside with me, Jane?'

'Yes, why not?' Jane laughed nervously. The other girls were staring at her fixedly, widening their eyes meaningfully. Mitch lifted his thumb almost imperceptibly at the side of his beer can.

It was dark outside. Wheelie and Sandra were nowhere to be seen. A few girls were still chatting over the glowing embers of the barbecue. I didn't want us to get involved in a conversation with them. The beer had taken the edge off my anxiety, and I knew that I would have to act soon, before nerves took over again. I walked deliberately towards the trees on the other side of the garden, hoping that Jane would follow me. Fortunately she did.

'Mitch is funny, isn't he?' I hadn't intended giving Jane any more reason to think of Mitch, but they were the words that came out of my mouth and I was grateful for them.

'Yes. He has such a talent for impressions,' Jane agreed.

She had taken off my jacket in the summer-house and now started to put it around her shoulders again. She didn't need any help, but I offered, taking advantage of the moment to put my arm around her shoulders. As we reached the deeper darkness under the trees, she rested her head on my shoulder. For a moment I felt as if I could hardly breathe. The weight of Jane's light head seemed to remind me even more that the onus was on me to change the course of our relationship. If I didn't do it then, I probably never would.

We stood quietly together for some time, our eyes adjusting to the darkness, the shadowy presence of apple trees above the long grass. I noticed Jane's faint sweet smell, felt her hair tickling the side of my chin. 'I was wondering ...' I started, hesitantly. Each blurted word seemed to crash headlong into the silence. 'Perhaps you might like to go somewhere with me. I mean ... on our own?' I waited for Jane's reply, cringing inwardly.

'Yes,' she said, without lifting her head. 'You mean the cinema, or something?'

'*Exactement*! Sorry, I meant yes! That was the kind of thing I was thinking of. Only if you wanted to, of course. There is no obligation.'

'Yes, alright. That'd be great, Jacques.'

I felt relief wash over me, although I knew that I couldn't completely relax yet. I had to kiss Jane to seal the transition. I wanted to, desperately, but I had never kissed a girl before and feared my own clumsiness. In spite of all the kisses I had observed on films and Wheelie's unforgettable coaching words which rang in my ears – 'When the moment is right, move in, tease her lips, nibble, then go straight in' – when it came down to it, I knew that I was on my own with Jane.

Jane lifted her head and looked up at me. I could tell by the speed at which she was blinking that she was feeling awkward too. Before I could think any more, I swooped down, angled my neck and caught the top of Jane's upper lip between my own lips.

As soon as I was there, tasting her mouth and the delicious strangeness of her sweet breath, feeling her holding me and murmuring my name, I felt as if I wanted the achingly pleasurable moment to go on forever. I was able to affirm the truth of one of Wheelie's favourite sayings, 'Making love is so much less complicated than making conversation.' When Jane broke away to draw breath, I pressed my face into the curve of her neck and kept kissing her lightly, telling her how beautiful she was. While I knew that I had heard similar clichés repeatedly on films, it didn't detract from my own tenderness and enjoyment.

We stood holding each other, hearing the others' voices in the background, the doors of the summer-house opening and closing, the occasional movement of a bird. Then suddenly we heard voices that were much closer, that seemed to be coming from the depths of the trees and shrubs next to where we were standing. I realised that it was Wheelie and Sandra.

'Cut it out will you, Wheelie?' Sandra's tone was sharp and irritable. 'I told you I didn't want to do that!'

'But you said ... you said next time I could ...' Wheelie followed, pleadingly.

'Well, I've changed my mind. I don't want to any more. Let's go back to the others. You can't force me, Wheelie.'

'I wasn't going to. I just thought that you wanted ...'

'You were wrong. OK?'

'It'll have to be, won't it? Come on. Let's go.'

Jane and I stood completely still, listening to the sounds of leaves rustling and twigs snapping as Sandra and Wheelie stumbled hurriedly unseen back towards the summer-house. 'Sandra and Wheelie,' Jane whispered, when they had gone. 'Sounds like he didn't get what he wanted.'

She covered her mouth with her hand, muffling spasms of laughter. I couldn't help laughing too, although I also felt sorry for Wheelie, knowing how difficult he would have found the rejection, especially in a situation in which he invested so much personal pride. 'No. I don't think he did. Poor Wheelie.'

Later, when all the girls had left and Mitch, Wheelie and I were having a last cigarette in the summer-house before Mitch's parents returned, I was amused to hear Wheelie's reframing of his experience that evening. 'So, looked like you were having a good night, Jacques?' Wheelie commented, unwrapping a single fat cigar that he had bought himself and saved in his pocket for the end of the night. 'Get on OK, did you? Successful first kiss and all that?'

Although Wheelie liked details, compared to some of the boys at Prince's, he was actually quite restrained and respectful of other people's privacy.

'Yes,' I said, as casually as I could. 'I asked Jane out and she said yes.'

'That's what we like to hear, isn't it, Mitchie?'

'Certainly is. Good for you, Jacques! Hopefully I'll not be too long behind you.'

'Meaning what exactly?' Wheelie asked immediately, eyes keen as a fat rat's.

'Meaning I'm getting on pretty well with Samantha Bishop.'

'Go for it, Mitchie! Right, Jacques?'

In spite of Wheelie's suave performance, I knew that his lack of success that evening was eating away at him. He was talking even faster than usual, probably in an attempt, I thought, to distract himself from his hurt pride, as well as to avoid being interrogated on the subject of his progress with Sandra. 'Yes, Samantha's nice. Your type of person, Mitch.'

'So what about you, Wheelie? How did things go with Sandra?' Mitch asked straightforwardly. I would have felt cruel asking Wheelie myself, after what Jane and I had overheard.

Wheelie pulled hard on his cigar. He coughed and spluttered for a while afterwards. I guessed that he was buying time to mentally compose his lines.

'Fine. Fine, actually. Chugging along nicely thanks. Getting there, slowly but surely. Three beers left in the crate, Mitchie. I think we should finish them up, don't you?'

I decided not to pursue Wheelie further on the matter. He had an irresistible tendency to brag and assume an air of worldly wisdom and was bound sometimes to be hoist by his own petard. So saying, I had a fondness for him because of the same qualities. Even if he was driven to lie to his friends to protect himself, he was a person who genuinely liked to see me happy, whose advice, however overdone, was usually given with good intentions.

9

Mitch and I were accepted to study history at Manchester, pending reasonable grades. Wheelie had decided to do English at Bristol. He was interested in being a journalist eventually, he told us confidently. A degree in English would provide him with a good 'springboard' for his future.

I still wasn't completely convinced that I had made the right choice, although Mitch's enthusiasm and evocation of possible scenarios, featuring us both enjoying all aspects of university life, helped to carry me along.

Rebecca meanwhile had almost finished her first year of medicine at Edinburgh. At the beginning of her course, she had written regularly and phoned for brief conversations with her mother and longer talks with me. As the year went on she made less contact. It wasn't that she didn't want to talk, she explained. It was just that she was extremely busy. The work wasn't really difficult, but there was almost too much to learn. She was otherwise happy, enjoying her new social life and friends. She had had a couple of dates with fellow medical students, she said. Now, she 'had her eye on' one of the junior doctors at the hospital and was sure that he was on the brink of asking her out.

I always felt uncomfortable when I heard Rebecca discussing her feelings for other people, even more so since she was starting to talk about men rather than boys. I tried to ignore how it increasingly bothered me, although deep down, I actually knew that I was seriously jealous. I had to keep reminding myself that I was involved with Jane, a fact that I made myself admit to Rebecca during one of our phone calls that June.

'Oh, you might be interested to know something,' I said quickly, towards the end of the call. As usual when I was talking, I was doodling patterns in black ink on the block Anna kept by the phone. I noticed when I spoke to Rebecca, without thinking, I often drew figures of eight, going over and over the lines heavily. At the end of a call, I would tear the top sheet off the block, noticing that the pressure of my pen had marked several sheets underneath.

'What?'

'I'm going out with Stephen Reid's sister, Jane. It's almost two months now, I think.'

'Oh, Jacques! I'm so … I'm really pleased for you. I knew it wouldn't be long before you had a girlfriend. I remember Jane. About sixteen or so, isn't she? Very sweet!' I was grateful to Rebecca for saying something to keep the conversation moving. Even so, her reaction, however kind it was intended to be, felt a bit exaggerated. There was something slightly forced in her voice that made me wonder if she really was as pleased about me going out with Jane as she said she was. Could she be feeling, even if only slightly, the same way as I did when she spoke of having other relationships? I just wished that we could relate to each other honestly about what we really thought and felt. Even if I knew I was hardly being entirely honest myself.

Rebecca's habit of suggesting sometimes that she had special knowledge about me and the course of my life could annoy me. Usually I wouldn't say anything, but this time I was in an impatient mood and I couldn't help challenging her. In retrospect, I think I was feeling as impatient with myself as I was with her.

'You knew?'

'It was bound to happen. Someone was going to snaffle you up eventually!'

'Snaffle me up? That might be your style, Rebecca. But … some of us take a pride in having a bit of self-control and dignity.' As soon as I'd said it, I hated the self-righteous tone of my own voice. It wasn't really the way I wanted to be with Rebecca. Actually, underneath my haughty exterior I was feeling frustrated and vulnerable.

'Oh, don't be so touchy, Jacques! Where's your old sense of humour? Lost that to Jane as well as your … you know what I mean! Or actually, perhaps you don't?'

Rebecca's insulting joke over whether or not I had lost my virginity hurt and angered me intensely. It didn't seem in keeping with the Rebecca I knew. It felt as if we were pushing ourselves and each other into playing defensive word games disconnected from our real selves.

'At least I'm not forever throwing myself at different people!' I snapped back, determined not to let her know how much she had upset me. My hand was working faster, pressing harder, covering the top sheet of the telephone memo pad with bold figures of eight. 'Actually, I think we should stop talking now, don't you? We could both be doing something more enjoyable. I've certainly got better things to do than being insulted and made fun of. Let's be honest, we could have a better conversation when I was twelve and you were thirteen.'

'No, Jacques! Please? I'm really sorry. I didn't mean to upset you, I honestly didn't. I shouldn't have said what I did. It was heartless. Please stay on the phone. Tell me more about you and Jane.'

Although I knew that Rebecca was trying to apologise, I felt that any pleasant atmosphere between us was irredeemable at that moment. 'No, Rebecca. You've pushed me too far. I think we should just leave it.'

'But, I mean … you were hardly perfect to me either, were you?' Rebecca had to persist. 'If you want to talk about insulting. That was really nasty … what you said about me forever "throwing" myself at different people. You know I'm not like that. And yes, maybe it was easier when we were younger, but we can't be twelve and thirteen for the rest of our lives, Jacques. This isn't *Peter Pan*. Things have to change, however difficult it is. You have to move on. You have to … grow up!'

'Yes, thanks, I think I know that, Rebecca,' I answered her curtly. 'Actually, I think it's better if we just stop talking altogether for a while. Maybe after a few years' silence we'll both have grown up enough to have a decent conversation again.'

As soon as I put the phone down, I felt dreadful. However annoyed I was with her, I actually knew that my reaction had been totally out of proportion. I could only keep imagining how churned up Rebecca would be feeling afterwards too, guessing that she would analyse what she had said for hours. But at the time my suggestion that we stop speaking to each other altogether seemed irreversible.

Again, things were hanging in the air between us. Rather than using my decisiveness to move forward for our good, I had closed down communication, leaving us both in limbo as to when we would be reconciled. Rebecca had been right. Neither of us had been perfect. If we had kept talking, we could have agreed to compromise. Instead, in all my stupidity, I made sure that we both had to suffer the consequences of what I would now describe as the simple hot-headed clumsiness of inexperience.

Moving away from the phone, I sharply ripped the top pages off the memo pad and crumpled them into a ball in my hand. I could see there were still deep imprints of the figure of eights on the new top blank sheet. I didn't think too much about what it meant then, though now on reflection, I think my subconscious knew, that for better or worse, Rebecca's life and mine had already become deeply entwined. No longer two separate figures, we were two parts of one.

I continued to go out with Jane Reid during the summer after I left Prince's. We still spent time with Wheelie, Mitch, Sandra and Samantha, but I enjoyed being alone with Jane as often as possible. I tried not to think about the prospect of going to university, leaving her and my friends and the things I had become familiar with.

We went for walks over the Meadows, occasionally saw a film, or took a bus on a Saturday to Wrexham. We also still listened to a lot of music. Jane's tastes were much more diverse than her brother's had been, more varied than mine. She enjoyed Italian opera, jazz, songs from shows. I teased her about what I described as her 'irrational' liking for female artistes such as Whitney Houston and Diana Ross. Often we would sit in the Reids' lounge and play CDs on Stephen's hi-fi tower. If we went back to the Clarks' house, Mrs Chadwick always made us bring my CD player downstairs, insisting that it wasn't 'proper' as she put it, for us to be alone at our age in my room. She still made sure that Jane always felt welcome by bringing us cups of tea and cakes, sitting briefly beside her on the sofa while I played the piano.

I could find very little to criticise about Jane. If anything she was almost too agreeable. She seemed generally to want what I wanted, to say what I needed to hear, to concur with my opinions on most things. In so many ways, she was Rebecca's opposite. I was confused sometimes to find myself wishing that Jane had a little of Rebecca's fiery and argumentative temperament. I found myself irritated by her tendency to submit and desperately wanted her to challenge me or take an opposing view.

When it came to what Wheelie referred to as my 'physical progress' with Jane, I had gone as far as stroking Jane's breast outside her clothes and putting my hand on her bottom when we were kissing. While she didn't move away, I could feel her tensing when I touched her and she made no attempt to return my advances herself. I guessed she still felt shy about it. Increasingly I could foresee the time when, given any encouragement, my growing physical desire could completely overwhelm my own nervousness, but I was reluctant to lead us both into new territory when Jane seemed less than ready to go there. Wheelie, so he informed me, had 'gone all the way', but my past observations reassured me that it was quite possible that even he hadn't yet managed to enter the doors of adult sexuality.

I did much better in my A-levels than I thought I would, with B grades in history and art and an A grade in music. Mitch was pleased to get an A in history. Wheelie was unhappy with his C in English, but characteristically made light of it, arguing that the grade made no difference whatsoever to his acceptance at Bristol or to his long-term plans. In contrast to the sensitive, poignant melody of Stephen Reid, it struck me that Wheelie's way of being was closer to a steady, persistent accompaniment. Wheelie had a wilful, strong personality, a method of integrating difficult experiences, including his failures, as if he never had the choice to give up. He didn't always feel good about his mistakes, but he appeared to force himself to shrug them off and move on, a quality I had to admire, even if I wasn't quite as capable of it myself. I guessed that I was probably somewhere in-between Wheelie and Stephen: not as shaken by my failures as Stephen, but less robust than Wheelie.

I suspected that some of the explanation for Wheelie's attitude lay in his background. His father had separated from his mother when Wheelie and his brother and sister were young. He had a violent streak and Wheelie had witnessed him beating his mother on several occasions. From then on, Wheelie had vowed that he would always protect his family and keep going, whatever he was feeling, for their sake. 'I have to try and be tough, Jacques. You might think I don't care now and then, but sometimes you've got to sort of ignore yourself when you're fed up. Not give in. Pretend you're not thinking the way you are. Pick yourself back up, scrape the mud off your knees before it gets the chance to dry. You've got to survive, Jacques, even if you start questioning yourself: keep overriding any other impulses.'

In some ways I knew that what Wheelie said made a lot of sense, although I thought personally that he was oversimplifying. I also guessed that sometimes he was thinking about Stephen. Wheelie still couldn't understand why Stephen had felt compelled to act as he did, possibly because it didn't suit Wheelie to stretch his imagination in certain directions. Survival, he had convinced himself, should always come first, above the need for a quality of emotional life. He never blamed Stephen outright, but I wondered if occasionally he did privately.

The weekend after the A-level results, I got a card from Rebecca in the post, with a picture of a piano on the front and simply 'Congratulations, Jacques. Rebecca x' written inside. I tried to ignore my sadness as I read her words. We hadn't spoken since our argument on the phone and I didn't know when we would.

Otherwise, I had four celebrations involving different people. Mrs Chadwick presented me with one of her homemade cakes with the words 'Congratulations to you Jacques' piped in blue icing. She hugged me hard against her apron afterwards, albeit only briefly. She was on the point of tears, and whispered 'Well done, lad!' quickly, alongside my ear.

That evening we had another garden party at Mitch's house. Mitch's parents, both solicitors working in Chester, greeted us at the beginning of the evening and offered us all a glass of pink champagne. They also provided beer and wine for the rest of the evening, a buffet and a small fireworks display. The party inevitably had a different feel from our usual unsupervised gatherings, but the luxuriousness of the occasion made us all feel more sophisticated and euphoric. It was a balmy night following a hot summer's day. The girls were in their best dresses, we boys were in ties and jackets. Wheelie pronounced that he was in the 'mood for love'. Judging by the way Sandra was constantly throwing her arms around his neck, I wondered if he might manage to receive some of the kind of love he craved most of all.

On the Saturday evening, Anna asked me to have dinner with her in the dining-room. It was the first time we had ever eaten at the table under the light of the chandelier. It was also the first time since I had known her that she had prepared more than a snack for us. It was a meal that reminded me of special dinners with Papa and Maman, a roast leg of lamb with green beans and potatoes with mint.

'Well done, Jacques!' Anna said, as she toasted me with red wine. She never drank anything else. I couldn't have imagined her drinking white wine, let alone champagne.

'Thank you!' I replied proudly, my self-assurance growing with the knowledge that my success was the reason for the treat. Since I was also more accustomed to the effects of alcohol since drinking with my friends, I felt more comfortable drinking with Anna.

'So, are you still convinced about your decision not to continue with music, Jacques? You did get an A grade after all. I'm sure we could arrange for you to change tack ... if you really wanted to.'

I remembered what Anna had said about her mother being among the Welsh elite, able to arrange anything that she wanted. However much Anna liked to believe that she was different, I couldn't help thinking that she had inherited some of her mother's feeling of omnipotence.

'Yes, I mean, I am sure about not studying music. Though I do intend to keep playing the piano.'

'You must, Jacques. Never give that up. I've noticed that you're making great progress, particularly with Beethoven's sonatas.'

'It's because that's what I want most to play. They're my favourite pieces.'

'I can tell. Old Ludwig appeals to our vital passions, doesn't he, Jacques? And the piano ... personally I've always felt that it was the instrument closest to the human voice. I'm sure some would disagree, but ... So, are you looking forward to Manchester? You will be missed. And I can imagine the prospect of leaving Jane behind will be difficult for you, even if you can easily return regularly at weekends if you want to.'

I was surprised that Anna chose to mention Jane. I had never been particularly aware of her observing our relationship, though I knew from the past that I couldn't always predict what Anna was thinking or would see fit to comment on. 'Well, no ... but ... yes, I think I'm looking forward to going to university. I'm glad I've left school.'

'Oh, I am sorry, Jacques. I've embarrassed you, haven't I? Your relationship with Jane is entirely your own business, of course! Pass me your glass and I'll pour you some more wine. I've just heard from Rebecca, by the way.'

Anna filled my glass to the brim. Some of the wine spilled onto the table as I lifted it towards me. Anna quickly came to my rescue with her own serviette.

'Never fear, Jacques. I've got it. You can always rely on me to mop up!'

Anna laughed darkly at her own joke and folded the stained cloth neatly as she returned to her chair. When she was seated she placed it carefully down on the table next to her. I immediately imagined that she would manage blood-stained swabs at her operating table in the same calm manner.

'So, what did Rebecca say?' I asked, keen to hear about her, in spite of our argument and the fact we weren't speaking to each other. I didn't get the impression that Anna had picked up that there was anything amiss between us.

'She said she's off on a holiday to Greece! With this new junior doctor of hers. She was all set to go to France with some of her other friends, but Ben suggested Greece right at the last minute, so Greece it is. Not like her to let someone else call the tune! Let's just hope she doesn't do something stupid.'

'Like ...?'

'Like getting all bowled over and neglecting her own dream of being an excellent doctor. Don't get me wrong, Jacques, I want her to enjoy herself, but I do know that my daughter is the kind of person who won't be content unless she cuts a dash. Still, she certainly won't thank me for my advice. That would just make her dig her heels in even deeper.'

'That's true.' I gulped down my wine, determined not to allow myself to imagine anything about Rebecca and her new boyfriend in Greece, the two of them alone, talking, exploring a new place together. Ben having Rebecca, all to himself. I couldn't bear to think about it. I was grateful when Anna changed the subject.

'So, Oliver's taking you over to Altrincham for lunch tomorrow, Jacques?' Anna's tone always became more clinical when she had to mention Uncle Oliver.

'Yes. Amanda's cooking something special for me, apparently,' I replied, slightly awkwardly. I usually kept any discussion of what happened at Altrincham to a minimum. I had actually warmed to Amanda as time went on. Since Rebecca had left for Edinburgh, she had been much more relaxed about talking to me and had started confiding in me about Julie and problems she was having with her relatives.

'Oh good! I hope you enjoy yourself, Jacques. Right, time for the pavlova now. I have to confess, not mine. Mrs Chad, I'm sure you'll agree, has done us proud.'

As Uncle Oliver had promised, Amanda cooked a celebratory lunch. Julie was away with her boyfriend, so it was just the three of us. While Amanda's idea of a gastronomic treat was undeniably less satisfying than Anna's, I was touched by her sincere efforts to congratulate me.

Although I still could not entirely understand why Uncle Oliver had made the decision to leave his family, I was beginning to see why perhaps Amanda might suit him better than Anna. She looked after him more attentively, had a way of soothing him when he was enervated, was prepared to constantly make small sacrifices so that his home life could be restful and comfortable.

Whatever Rebecca had said about her style of dress being 'tarty and tacky', I could see that Amanda made an effort to look glamorous in a way that Anna never did. Her desire to be attractive to men was perhaps a kind of weakness, but I couldn't really blame her for it.

I could tell that Uncle Oliver approved of how Amanda titivated herself for him, even if he made a show of being annoyed with her, as in his view, she wasted so much time doing it.

At the end of the meal, Amanda went to make coffee in the kitchen. I stayed at the table with Uncle Oliver, who seemed intent upon offering his opinion on my future career. While I had become more sympathetic towards Amanda, I was finding Uncle Oliver more difficult to bear. As time passed, no longer challenged as he had once been by Anna, he seemed more deeply entrenched in his own materialistic values. He was increasingly judgemental of others who failed to share his belief in the importance of keeping up appearances. I resented his assumption that he was entitled to impose his ideas, given his lack of commitment to developing a genuine relationship with me over the years.

'So, it's history at Manchester then, Jacques?' he began, opening his box of cigars. He lit one, ostentatiously, with his silver cigarette lighter. It had been a gift from Amanda, he had told me repeatedly. She had even thought to have his initials engraved on it, at the centre of two overlapping hearts. I felt a sudden craving for a cigar, although I had never smoked in front of Uncle Oliver.

'Yes,' I said simply, leaving him to direct the discussion.

'And what will the degree lead to, do you think?' I sensed that it was a false kind of patience.

'I'm not quite sure yet. I may teach, perhaps.'

'Wouldn't bother with the teaching if I were you, Jacques,' he said scornfully, blowing a cloud of smoke in my direction. 'Bit of a cul-de-sac career-wise, if you don't mind me saying.'

'What would you suggest?' I knew already that I didn't really want to know the answer.

'Business, Jacques. A reputable company! That's where the money is. If you're at all interested in having a decent lifestyle!' The way that Uncle Oliver spoke about a lot of things had always seemed foreign to me. It appeared that he was more intent on selling his own proposition than on engaging in a dialogue.

'I'd like to have a job that I enjoy.'

'Of course! And there's no reason why you couldn't enjoy the kind of job that I have in mind for you.' Uncle Oliver pushed his chair back slightly from the dining table, stretched out and crossed his legs before continuing with the next stage of his speech. 'OK. Look, Jacques. By all means go ahead and get your history degree. There's no doubt that you can use it as a bit of a stepping-stone. I know our firm's always on the lookout for good competent people, people we can develop and train up. Just say the word, I'd be more than willing to put out a few feelers for you, Jacques. I've said the same to Matthew, you know. Though he seems content to live indefinitely in his own little academic bubble. With today's climate it doesn't pay to be too proud.'

'You're right.'

'So, what do you think, Jacques? Know what I'm getting at?'

'Yes.'

'Excellent! And do you ...'

I was relieved when Amanda appeared at this point with a tray of coffee cups and I immediately offered to help her. Uncle Oliver's blinkered attitude to the possibilities of my future was making me feel increasingly irritated and alienated from him.

'Oh, thank you, Jacques. But don't let me interrupt your chat with your Uncle Oliver. I know he wanted to talk to you about something.'

'It's alright, Amanda. Uncle Oliver and I have finished.'

'We have, have we, Jacques?' The touch-paper of Uncle Oliver's sense of offence was quickly lit.

'Yes. Thank you for your suggestions. I'll keep it all in mind.'

'That's what I like to hear. Though no pressure, of course. You are eighteen now, after all. It's your life, Jacques.'

'Yes. Thank you. I know.'

As time passed I began to feel that Jane was becoming less enthusiastic about our relationship. I couldn't think of anything that I had done to offend her, but she seemed to be pulling away from me. I told myself that her withdrawal was possibly to do with her anticipation of my departure for university. However, as September progressed, Jane returned to school and I had time to kill before starting at Manchester, I became more convinced that Jane was less in love with me. She kept making excuses when I suggested that we meet, sounded almost on the verge of apathy when I spoke to her on the phone.

The change in Jane's attitude saddened me. She had once made me feel proud and privileged to be worthy of her trust, but she no longer opened her heart as she had done. Physically too, she seemed cooler and less spontaneously affectionate. I was puzzled that she offered nothing by way of a straightforward explanation, that every time I asked her if she was happy she either avoided the question or answered me with 'why wouldn't I be?' I was almost relieved, although also shocked, when one night in the summer-house, Wheelie confirmed that there was basis in reality for my uneasiness.

'Don't really want to have to tell you this, Jacques, but if it was the other way round I'd expect you to do the same. I think Scav's after Jane again and she's ... not exactly turning him down. Here. Have the rest of this cig if you want. I haven't got any more with me.'

I accepted the end of Wheelie's cigarette.

'What do you mean, Wheelie?'

'I mean, I saw them together. They didn't know that I saw them, but ... it looked like he was walking her home from school. He was fooling around, putting his arm around her ... kissing her neck ... and she wasn't throwing him off. I'm sorry, Jacques.' Wheelie looked genuinely upset on my behalf. I could tell that he really didn't want to deliver the news, but he felt he had no choice.

'But she hasn't said anything to me.'

'Not always a guarantee, I'm afraid. Some girls are like that. They don't quite have the courage to tell you to your face. Make out to themselves it's kinder if you just sort of find out gradually that they're not so keen. Hope you'll let go of them without a fight.'

'I still can't believe that Jane ... I thought that we'd always be honest with each other.'

'I know but you've got to deal with it somehow. If I were you, I'd get in there first and be the one to end it. That way you'll be in charge. Less humiliation. She can't keep pulling the wool over your eyes.'

I could hardly bear the thought of ending my relationship with Jane. At the same time, I had a feeling that Wheelie was right. Jane wouldn't have allowed Scav to put his arm around her and especially to kiss her on her neck if she wasn't interested. Even the thought that she was involved with him behind my back took away from my dignity. However difficult it would be, I resolved to tell Jane as soon as possible that I no longer wanted to go out with her. The following afternoon, I phoned her after she returned from school. It wouldn't have been the way I'd naturally think it right to end a relationship, but given the circumstances, I thought I would spare myself the pain of meeting her face to face.

'I've made a decision, Jane,' I said straightaway. There was no point, I felt, in prolonging the agony by pretending that it was going to be an ordinary conversation.

'Oh?' Jane seemed genuinely surprised by my tone.

'Yes. I don't want to go out with you any more. I think we both know why, don't we?'

'I'm not sure I know what you mean, Jacques ...' The energy had drained out of her voice.

'Oh, come on, Jane! Found someone new to walk you home from school, have you?'

Any apprehensiveness I had had at the beginning of the conversation completely left me. I felt righteous in my anger. Jane didn't say anything immediately.

'I'm sorry, Jacques,' she said. 'I've been meaning to say something for a while.'

'A while?'

'Yes. Alex kept asking me out and I wanted to tell you myself that ... how did you find out?'

'I think that's irrelevant, Jane. Don't you? The fact is I found out. The fact is you didn't have the basic honesty to tell me yourself.'

'Oh, I am sorry, Jacques.' Jane's voice was trembling, but I suddenly didn't care. Everything she was saying left me detached and cold. 'Maybe we could meet up or something ... talk about it ... maybe we could become friends ... it would be a pity if we couldn't still ... we've known each other for a while.'

'Perhaps you should've thought about that before, Jane. A friend is someone you trust, isn't it? It may come as a surprise to you, Jane, but I don't trust you any more.'

I could hear Jane sobbing on the end of the phone. Just one day earlier, the sound would have made me want to be with her instantly, to hold her tightly in my arms. But she had hurt me too much. The only word I could attach to her then was Rebecca's word 'pathetic'. I wanted to punish her, to make her feel as rejected as I felt myself.

'Jacques ... please! Just stay on the phone at least! I mean ...'

'Yes?'

'Well ... I always really liked you, Jacques. For ages, before we started going out. But I never completely felt that you ever thought of me as much as I thought of you. It was as if ... it felt as if at times, even when you were with me you were somewhere else. And you never stopped talking about Rebecca, about what she might do and say, as if she was always on your mind ... and we'd never quite get on as well as you got on with her.'

What Jane said took me completely by surprise. I needed to reply quickly somehow, but I was struggling to bring my words together. I think if I'd been entirely sure that there was no truth in what she said and that she was only saying it to justify her behaviour with Scav, it would have been much easier. Her observation about Rebecca always being on my mind struck a chord with me. Whatever was happening now between Rebecca and me, it had become almost second nature for me to refer to what she would say, which I could see might have been difficult for Jane. At the same time, I couldn't let go of my anger towards Jane and the way she had fallen in with Scav without telling me.

'So, if that's what you felt, why didn't you talk to me about it? I'm sorry if you felt you didn't have my full attention. But I've never been disloyal to you, Jane.'

'Yes, I know, Jacques. And I shouldn't have ... but ... I mean, I know you don't think that much of Alex, but he really likes me and he makes me laugh and ... maybe we could still be friends, Jacques?'

'No, Jane. I don't think we can. Anyway, you're free to do what you like now, aren't you? It doesn't matter what I think of Alex, does it? You obviously like each other. I hope it all works out for you. Have a good time, Jane. Goodbye.'

Later that evening, I went up to my bedroom and worked for hours in charcoal. Melodramatic black heart after black heart. Some haphazardly, carelessly outlined. Some heavily, deliberately drawn, savagely pierced by arrows. Others completely blocked in, becoming thick with dust. Finally, I tore each image in half and set light to the pieces individually over my bin, feeling the connection between the tearing and my hurt, the affinity of fire with my anger.

PART 2

10

Some experiences bring us awareness we can't ignore. They become touchstones, deeply embedded in the valleys of our psyche. Whether we want to or not, we can't help measuring everything else in our subsequent life against them. Such knowledge has the potential to lead us to despair, as well as to the path of authenticity.

The deaths of my parents and Stephen Reid formed the foundations for two such touchstones in my own mind. Although I tried to distract myself, I knew that these realities and their layers of meaning would always remain with me. Their presence kept me constantly on edge. The fact that I had known great happiness, love and sincere friendship, seemed both an advantage and a torment to me. The loss of these people who had been so important, and continued to be so important, had brought suffering as well as the most significant learning.

What I had experienced sharpened my perspective. Although I actually quite admired people who could allow themselves to be 'drifters', I found it impossible to drift myself, perhaps because it painfully reinforced my impression of how I was already cut loose in a universe where I could wander aimlessly indefinitely, unless I deliberately strove to set my own course and make life meaningful.

While I was still struggling to be certain what direction to take, I knew that I was responsible for my future happiness. I had to make choices based on what I had learned about what really mattered. As well as searching for satisfying, motivating work, life was about making room for relationships and other anchoring experiences of pleasure and belonging.

I studied at Manchester for only two years. My decision to take history had never been one driven by passion for the subject, although I had hoped that, once at university, my enthusiasm would build. Instead, life as a student made me even more unsettled. I found it increasingly hard to apply myself to assignments and private study and repeatedly did much worse than I should have done in exams. My memory, which had previously been reliably sharp, seemed much duller, I think because I didn't care enough about the things I was trying to remember.

Mitch, in contrast, seemed to thrive in his new life, socially and academically. In the absence of Wheelie, who had tended, however unintentionally, to overshadow him, Mitch grew in confidence and gathered a large group of friends. The charm that he held for women, in its embryonic form at school, matured immeasurably.

At the same time, he still continued to do his best to include me in his plans. Occasionally he would drive us out to the Peak District at the weekend. We would spend the day walking in the hills. It suited us both simply to walk for hours without saying much.

'Walking's good, I think,' Mitch would say. 'You don't always know what's changed exactly at the end of it, but something changes. You often sort things out more easily afterwards, without paying attention to them directly.'

'You're right, Mitch. You move things when you travel, don't you? You're less likely to get stuck. Keep going and you carry hope along with you, as well as sadness.'

Mitch knew that I wasn't enjoying my course as much as I had hoped I would. He tried to encourage me to persevere, but also respected that I had my own reasons for things that were just as valid as his own.

I had a string of transient relationships over those two years. While I knew such a pattern was hardly unusual among male and female students alike, it wasn't something that I felt completely good about, even though I had to acknowledge that I was obviously changing. The temporary and superficial nature of these relationships undoubtedly reflected my restless mind and shifting moods. I still tried my best to be as sensitive and respectful as I could towards the women I was involved with, even if I sensed that my instinct was to keep moving on. In fact, it seemed to suit some of them as well as it suited me.

The moment of the loss of my virginity, which at one point I had elevated and anticipated apprehensively, came and went fairly quickly and painlessly. It occurred with the help of Caroline Ainsworth, a jocular, big-boned Lancastrian girl, who was studying geography. Caroline was, by her own admission, already well seasoned when it came to sex. After a few drinks one night in one of the student bars, she literally took me by the hand, in haste, back to her room in halls and invited me to enjoy her body and my own. I had the amusing feeling that we were like pebbles, tumbling around each other harmlessly in a stream. She rolled underneath me, helped me enter her, easily murmured her approval, told me later that I was a 'rather good lover'. For Caroline, a few similar nights were enough. She seemed quite happy that we would both enjoy ourselves and, without obligations or guilt, go our separate ways again.

If not deeply and emotionally meaningful, my experience with Caroline certainly empowered me sexually and boosted my confidence in myself as a man. Even if in other respects my two years at Manchester didn't seem to advance my life's purpose, I was given the invaluable gift of the feeling that I could please a woman, that my 'physical performance' was acceptable. From then on, although I would never assume that I knew everything about women, I no longer worried about the sexual dimension of life quite in the way that I had done before.

Since our argument, apart from brief simple messages in birthday and Christmas cards, Rebecca and I still hadn't been in touch. She was never far from my thoughts. I longed to hear her voice again. I was often on the point of lifting the phone and dialling her number, but then changed my mind. She probably wouldn't want to talk to me, I told myself sometimes. At other times I persuaded myself that I was right to be angry because so far Rebecca had made no effort to call and make up with

me herself. When I knew that she was visiting her mother for
a short break or weekend, I stayed away in Manchester. I wondered if she had spoken to Anna about our falling out, although
I imagined not. If Anna was aware of a change or noticed that
our visits no longer coincided, she didn't confront me about
it, but simply updated me on Rebecca's news. It seemed that
Rebecca was doing well in her studies and was looking forward
to being 'set loose' as she put it, on some 'real patients'. She was
continuing her relationship with Ben, although Rebecca had
said that he was extremely busy all the time and 'probably even
more ambitious' than she was. Ben had a particular ambition to
be a private cosmetic surgeon, a dream that Rebecca apparently
accepted and understood, even if she wouldn't choose to work
in the same field herself. I found it difficult to imagine that she
truly understood such an ambition. It didn't seem in keeping
with her own ideals. She had often made fun of Amanda's obsession with her nose and pleas to Uncle Oliver to encourage her to
have some corrective surgery.

'I mean, it's not as bad as what Mum does, of course,' Rebecca used
to say. 'But I still don't think it's a good use of a surgeon's training
and skill. If someone really needs something done because of a
birth defect, or an accident, or even a serious psychological hang-
up, that's different. But playing around with the shape of your nose
and the size of your lips? That's just silly! Imagine being prepared
to risk a general anaesthetic for something unnecessary!'

Uncle Oliver was furious when I phoned to inform him of my
decision to leave Manchester.

'You're an absolute idiot, Jacques! You need to finish the course at least! Irrespective of whether you like it or not. How do you expect an employer to look upon you favourably when you haven't finished your course?'

'I know it isn't good, but … my heart isn't in it.'

'What's your heart got to do with it, Jacques? Sometimes we've just got to do things. Think about your parents. I can't imagine what they'd think. Think about the money that's been wasted on this already.' I didn't know exactly what Papa and Maman would have said, but I was sure that they would have tried to explore my rationale, instead of instantly blaming me for it.

'So what are you going to do instead? I hope you've thought this through, Jacques,' Uncle Oliver resumed spikily.

'I was thinking I'd get a job in a cafe or a bar or something. There's always plenty of temporary work in Chester. Until I can make other plans.'

'You are joking, aren't you, Jacques? After all this, you're honestly telling me you're going to work in a public house?'

'Yes.'

Uncle Oliver was silent for a moment. When he spoke, he was obviously trying to moderate his tone.

'Look, Jacques. You're intelligent. Bar work may be OK for some people, perhaps. But it's hardly suitable for a person with your education and background. You need something a hell of a lot more stimulating.'

'Possibly, eventually.' I could tell that he was trying a more flattering strategy, although I wasn't convinced that his underlying attitude had changed at all.

'So ... all that I'm saying is ... think about what you're doing, Jacques. If you're completely sure it's the right choice, well, I'll make some enquiries and see what else I can come up with for you. If you change your mind, I'm sure I can have a word with someone at the university and get you back on track.'

Anna, in contrast, accepted my decision more magnanimously than I thought she would.

'At least you've acted sooner rather than later, Jacques. Not completely ideal, perhaps, but ... stay here. Get yourself some kind of a job. Keep up your piano, take some time to think about what you want to do next. You'll come up with something in time.'

Towards the end of that summer of 1994, I got my first job in a bar in Chester called The Narrow Boat, off one of the small streets close to the canal. The owner was a tough little local man called Terry Bostock. The poky interior of Terry's slovenly pub reflected his attitude to life. Terry was definitely mean rather than frugal. Although it was widely known that he had accumulated nothing short of a small fortune from his business, he didn't invest much of it in the comfort of his customers. What Terry did spend his money on, no one seemed to know. He was a bachelor, didn't particularly like women by all accounts and certainly didn't have an interest in clothes or property. He lived in two rooms above his bar, drove a rusting, dented Ford Escort and never seemed to go out socially.

The decor at The Narrow Boat, according to Laura, one of the older barmaids, had altered very little from the late sixties.

Everything, woodwork and wallpaper included, had been repeatedly painted over in thick layers of oxblood and cream paint. The floor, once carpeted, had been stripped back haphazardly to the dirty brown linoleum underneath. The upholstery on the seats and bar stools was stained and threadbare. The television set above the bar had always had poor reception, Laura said. No amount of complaints from Terry's regular customers had persuaded him to do anything about it.

True to Terry's style, he hadn't even been prepared to pay to advertise for bar staff. I had got the job simply by walking into the pub to enquire and being told by Laura that she thought that Terry needed someone regularly. 'It's not a great pub, I'll be honest with you, son,' Laura felt bound to tell me. Her accent reminded me of Mrs Chadwick's. Although she was younger, probably in her mid-fifties, Laura's complexion and faded, dyed-blonde curls bore evidence of countless late nights working in the airless, murky atmosphere of The Narrow Boat. 'But Terry's not as bad as he seems. He always pays you what he agrees and the rest of the staff are friendly. Come in tomorrow evening, around seven. I'll have had a chance to have a word with him. He'll see you then. He says yes or no straightaway. No interview or anything, love. I'm sure he'll give you the job.'

When I returned the following evening, Terry was standing smoking at the end of the bar, dressed in frayed jeans and a shabby T-shirt, watching blurred football on the television. 'Name's Jack, is that right?' Terry began, without taking his eyes off the screen. Terry was like an ignoble, lean rat. He had long yellowing teeth, gaunt half-shaven cheeks and a lick of greasy, greyish brown hair, combed back over his bald head. I would caricature him in drawings of jagged-toothed, narrow-eyed creatures with exaggeratedly long coiled tails, patchy coats and elongated claws.

'It's Jacques, actually. I'm from France, originally.'

'Oh, are we?' he replied mockingly, his tongue flicking momentarily over his thin, dry lips. 'We'll be very privileged to have a posh French boy pulling our pints.' Why my nationality immediately marked me as 'posh' in Terry's mind I wasn't quite sure, but I knew that it wouldn't help my case to say anything. 'Start tomorrow night. We'll have you on evenings to start, to see what we make of you. Laura can break you in.'

'Thank you very much, sir,' I replied quickly.

'Did you hear that, Laura?' Terry immediately piped up. 'I've been promoted to a sir. Remember that for future reference, won't you? I'm not Terry. I'm sir.'

I already suspected that I was going to find Terry's idea of humour tedious. I was delighted, however, that I had managed to get some work. As I made my way back through Chester that evening, I felt quite proud of myself. My employment might be uninspiring and poorly paid, but at least it would help to occupy me while I was thinking about what to do next.

With Laura as my guide and the support of some of the pub's regular customers, I soon settled into my new job. Laura had a skilful way of managing people. She was caring without being overprotective, playfully flirtatious without being inappropriate or manipulative.

'Right, love. Let's keep moving, shall we? Just you and me on the floor tonight. Not much room for tangos behind the bar, but if you take the lead, I'm happy to follow on. Not many women of my age get such a chance with a handsome young French man. Might be the only chance I get. You move right, I move left. Let's not disappoint the audience! That's right, isn't it, Fred?'

'That's right, Laura. You keep the lad on his toes. You've got the legs for the dancing, haven't you, love? If you don't mind me saying.' Fred was one of our most loyal customers. He was recently widowed, round and bristly as a hedgehog, notoriously proud of being eighty-nine. He always occupied the same stool at the bar counter, and could make a pint of beer last for more than an hour. I found it touching that Fred had insisted on hearing me say my name repeatedly and had asked me to listen to him rehearsing it.

'Course I don't mind you saying, Fred,' Laura joked back. 'Don't get so many compliments about my legs these days! Beggars can't be choosers, can they, love?'

'You're right there, Laura!' Fred returned jovially. 'Though what a fine young woman like you's doing without a husband, I don't know.' Laura made a point of talking and laughing quite openly about her divorce.

'You know what, Fred? I can honestly say I've never been happier! Lazy, good-for-nothing sod he was, Fred. Just couldn't keep his hands to himself either. Never thought with his brain. Always thought with his ... pardon me for being crude, Fred, but ...'

'Oh, that sort, was he, Laura?' Fred commented, more seriously. 'You're better off without that sort, love, isn't she, Jacques?'

'Yes. She certainly is,' I replied. 'You deserve a good man, Laura. Someone who respects you.'

I admired Laura for the way she could respond to people, how she could deal with anyone from a grieving elderly man to a belligerent, complaining drunk.

'I think you're very clever, the way you know how to talk to different people, Laura,' I told her at the end of one evening, when we were clearing up behind the bar.

'Oh, I'm not really, love. But you've got to learn somehow in this kind of work. And people teach you, without even knowing it. We're all quite similar in some ways when it comes down to it. I try not to judge. Well, apart from him of course ... my ex, I mean.'

'I think you're allowed to judge him.'

'Yes. And I will. I'm not being ... but some men, Jacques, are ...'

'The word in French is *connard*, Laura. It isn't polite, but they don't deserve courtesy, or happiness either.'

'Yes. That'll do, Jacques. That sounds about right.'

11

Soon after I had got the job at The Narrow Boat, Rebecca arranged to come for a brief visit.

'It's Rebecca, Jacques,' Anna called, after she'd been speaking for a few minutes on the phone. 'She's coming to visit us soon, with Ben. But she'd really like a word with you now, she says.'

I felt suddenly nervous, as well as excited, as Anna passed me the phone and headed humming into the kitchen.

Through Anna, we had both kept up with what the other had been doing, but it was around two years since Rebecca and I had actually spoken. Especially recently, I'd often thought of phoning her, just to break the stupid, unnecessary silence between us.

'Rebecca?'

'Oh Jacques! I can't believe we've not spoken for such a long time. And all because of that stupid childish argument.'

'I know ... I ...'

'I know it's not perfect talking about it over the phone, but I didn't want things going on like this any longer. I know I was horrible to you, Jacques. I don't blame you for not wanting to speak to me but I really want us to be talking again ... please?'

I struggled to answer her at first. I was overcome with the relief of hearing her again.

'Are you alright? Tell me what you're thinking, Jacques?' Rebecca asked, anxiously.

'Yes ... I mean ... I'm so glad, Rebecca. And, I know it wasn't just you. You were right at the time. I was hardly perfect myself. I was stupid cutting you off like that. I got everything out of proportion. I've thought about calling you so many times, but I wasn't sure you'd want to hear from me. I've really missed you ...'

'I wanted to call you as well. I've missed you too. It's so good to hear your voice. I can't wait to see you. I hope we can work things out more, face to face.'

'So ... you're coming to stay?'

'Yes. Actually, maybe it's not ... but ... Ben's arranged to come with me this time. It'll be good for you and Mum to finally meet him.'

Carried away in talking to Rebecca, I had almost forgotten Anna's mention of Ben. It had been difficult for Ben to organise it, but for Rebecca's sake he had eventually managed to get two days' leave. They would arrive on the Saturday morning, and would be leaving again on the Sunday afternoon.

'I can't wait to see you again as well, Rebecca. Thank you for breaking the silence. And don't worry. We're fine now. Everything's alright. See you soon.'

If Rebecca had been coming on her own I might have considered phoning The Narrow Boat with the excuse that I was sick in order to spend more time with her, but the prospect of also spending time with Ben persuaded me to work as usual on the Saturday night.

Rebecca looked beautiful and undeniably older. Her hair was cut shorter, her face seemed paler, more angular; her frame elongated, having lost the roundness of her teenage years. She wore more sophisticated clothes: a skirt instead of jeans, high heels instead of trainers or walking boots. 'How great to see you, Jacques! I'm so sorry. I was very stupid. It's been so long – far too long,' she told me, as she held me tightly on the front drive after hugging Anna. Ben was still climbing down from the driving seat of his Land Rover. Rebecca disengaged from me, turned and linked her arm through his, then formally introduced us, obviously nervous.

'Mum, Jacques, meet Ben. Ben, this is my mother ... and Jacques.'

'Delighted to meet you, Mrs Clark,' Ben said, briefly shaking Anna's hand. His manner reminded me in some ways of Uncle Oliver's. He was undoubtedly a man many people would have described as handsome – tall with tanned skin, sleek, blond streaked hair, a persistent, self-assured smile, southern English accent. But he also had an air of arrogance about him, which immediately put me on my guard.

'And Jacques! Can't tell you how pleased I am to meet Rebecca's stepbrother at last!'

It was almost inevitable that I would object in some way to Rebecca's suitor, but I hadn't anticipated how strongly. The false familiarity of Ben's concluding remark irked me, even before the suggestion that I was Rebecca's 'stepbrother' had time to sink in.

'Pleased to meet you too, Ben,' I stated, mechanically. 'Although, and excuse me for correcting you, I'm not, in fact, Rebecca's stepbrother. We're not actually related at all. Rebecca's mother and father were my legal guardians.'

Rebecca frowned at me, clearly concerned that I had embarrassed her boyfriend. Ben smiled, however, drew his breath deliberately through his teeth and resumed, undeterred.

'Of course, Jacques. Wasn't quite accurate, perhaps, but ... you two were brought up together, weren't you? Amounts to just about the same thing, doesn't it?'

'Actually, I don't think it does, Ben.'

'And can I say how impeccable your English is, considering you're French? I'm right about that at least, *n'est ce pas*?' Ben laughed complacently at his own joke.

'Yes, you are,' I replied as plainly as I could, resolving from then on to invest as little energy as possible in getting to know him further.

Anna was smiling wryly as she observed our exchange.

'Right, boys and girl! Time for a cup of tea, I think. Why don't you come out and get your things later, Rebecca? After you, Ben.'

When Anna asked where we wanted to have tea, Rebecca immediately opted for the sitting-room. 'I haven't heard you play for such a long time, Jacques,' she told me as she slipped her arm through Ben's. 'You must be really fantastic by now! Ben would love to hear you play, wouldn't you, darling?'

I had never heard Rebecca call anyone 'darling' before. It struck me that there was something artificial about the term of endearment, particularly when applied to Ben, that didn't suit Rebecca's personality as I had known it.

I wasn't really in the mood to play, certainly not for Ben's benefit. I begrudged the way that Rebecca was insisting that I perform for the two of them, like an entertaining puppet. 'Sorry, Rebecca. I'm not really in the mood. I'm sure that Ben would rather just have the tea.'

'No, I'm sure he wouldn't, would you, Ben? Please, Jacques! Just until Mum has the tea ready?' Rebecca pleaded, sitting next to Ben on the chaise-longue, placing her hand on his knee. I expected Ben to put his arm around her or place his hand on top of hers, but he didn't. He was obviously otherwise preoccupied, examining the contents of the room. 'What about the beginning of the *Moonlight Sonata*?'

'Great idea!' Ben pronounced brightly. 'It's one of Mozart's best pieces, in my opinion.'

I couldn't help smiling at Ben's mistake, and deliberately didn't correct him.

'Alright then. Mozart's *Moonlight* it is!'

'Oh, Jacques! Don't be so mean,' Rebecca told me, half-smiling, then more stern. 'You know that if it was you, you'd want to be corrected. Mozart didn't compose the *Moonlight Sonata*, darling. It was Beethoven, wasn't it?'

'Of course! Can't take me anywhere, can we, Becca?' In spite of Ben's attempt to make light of his lack of knowledge, I could tell that he felt humiliated.

I uncovered the piano and seated myself on the stool. Playing the piece would provide Ben with a longer pause during which to contemplate his mistake. It was probably not entirely deserved, but for that moment, however unkind, I let myself carry on regardless. I felt myself expand as I began to play the opening of the sonata, leaning into the dramatic accentuations of the melody. As usually happened, I soon found myself taken over by the music, becoming oblivious to my audience, so consumed by its technical and emotional demands that I no longer had energy for pride or self-consciousness.

'Tea, everybody! Rebecca, can you bring the little table for the tray, please?'

I stopped playing when Anna arrived with our tea.

'Must say, I'm impressed, Jacques! Very pretty piece, obviously.' Rebecca had been on the point of saying something, but Ben had clearly needed to have the first word.

'Thanks, Ben.' How anyone could have described the sonata as simply 'pretty' was beyond me. Contemplative, passionate, romantic, dramatic, oppressive perhaps – but hardly 'obviously pretty'.

'You're so good, Jacques!' Rebecca said, while Anna poured the tea. Her eyes had filled with tears. When we were younger, although she enjoyed music, she had found it difficult to concentrate and sit still. Now she was clearly absorbed and deeply affected. 'I mean, you always were, but now ... you're infinitely better, you really are. So passionate! He is, isn't he, Mum?'

'Of course! I still think he could have taken it up professionally, and he still could, of course, but that's not for me to decide.'

'So what is it you're doing now again, Jacques?' Ben seized his opportunity to attempt to deflate me in return. 'I gather you didn't finish your history course at Manchester. Remind me ... did I understand from Rebecca that you've found yourself a job in a bar?'

'That's right, Ben.' I didn't feel I had to explain myself to him.

'Is that not a bit ... below your capabilities, Jacques? Someone with your intelligence and musical gifts could surely ...?' Ben set his cup and saucer down on the table and extended his arm along the back of the chaise-longue, before laying it across Rebecca's shoulders, evidently once more satisfied that he was my superior.

'Although it's only for a while, isn't it, Jacques? The bar job? Just until you know what you really want to do?' While Rebecca leapt to my rescue, I still wasn't sure whether she was feeling more uncomfortable on my account or on her own.

'Possibly. I'll have to see what happens,' I replied, intending to sound non-committal. I was beginning to resent the implication that somehow my value and acceptability depended on my doing something more 'worthy' than being a bartender.

'Still, when push comes to shove, Jacques, we all have to take life deliberately by the horns, don't we?' The combination of Ben's unimaginative clichés, over-familiarity and assumption that he had the right to tell me how to live, again reminded me of what I least liked about Uncle Oliver.

'Couldn't agree with you more, Ben,' I answered, with a false smile. 'I'm sure that's what you're doing yourself, taking it all firmly in hand. Cosmetic surgery – the private, beauty side,

I gather? That's your passion, isn't it? Must be an incredibly exciting prospect ... unimaginably exhilarating ...'

Ben seemed either genuinely unaware of my irony or chose to ignore it. 'Absolutely, Jacques. I'm still in the early stages, serving my stint in surgery first, honing skills, but my intention is to be one of the best, really top-notch. Are you still enjoying your own career in surgery, Anna?'

Anna seemed amused by the question.

'Enjoying is probably not the word that first springs to mind, Ben, if I'm honest. I continue to do what I do, which perhaps says something.'

'And I have to say, I admire you for it. Rebecca objects, of course, on the grounds of conscience, which has to be her prerogative, but if I hadn't been so set on the idea of being a cosmetic surgeon, I might have considered doing something along the same lines myself.'

'Some can ... some can't,' Anna commented, factually.

'You've never said that before, Ben. Not in front of me, anyway,' Rebecca blurted out, before she could tailor her response. I willed her to continue.

'It isn't something that I'd have a problem with,' Ben answered, smiling easily, apparently impervious to the tension behind Rebecca's words. 'It's an essential service, one anyone might have to avail of, whatever their previous principles.'

I kept expecting Rebecca to vehemently correct Ben's assumption. I'm sure Anna did too. Instead Rebecca remained strangely silent, broke eye contact with Ben but kept her hand on his knee.

'So . . . will you be joining us for dinner, Jacques?' Anna asked, filling the silence.

'No thanks, Anna. I'll get a sandwich at the pub. I'm working tonight.'

'Oh, you're not, are you, Jacques? I thought you might have some time off.' Rebecca seemed very disappointed by the news. 'We're not going to have much time to talk, are we? We have to leave tomorrow morning. Ben has to go back earlier than we'd first planned. Why don't you tell the pub you're not well?'

'Oh don't pressurise him, Becca! Jacques has his own commitments,' Ben was quick to assure her smoothly.

Ben's defence of me was so transparently fake that I was tempted to join them after all. In the end, however, I knew that I needed to avoid him, even more than I wanted to punish him. 'Sorry, Rebecca. I do have to go to work. Anyway, I'm sure you and Ben need to have some time on your own and with Anna.'

'What about later this afternoon?' Rebecca persisted. 'Ben wants us to go out for lunch somewhere on our own, but we could do something together later, if you like. I was thinking we could all have a walk round the walls, maybe go to a cafe or something? I'd really like us to catch up more, Jacques.'

'I'm sorry, but I probably need to get a bit of sleep. I've had a lot of late nights at the pub. And I'm sure you and Ben would like to be by yourselves.' If it had been just the two of us meeting, I would have jumped at her suggestion.

'We'd love you to come with us, Jacques! Please, think about it. Tell me later if you change your mind?'

I didn't change my mind. Much as I wanted to talk to Rebecca, to find out how she was really getting on in Edinburgh, I knew that she wouldn't be able to speak freely. It upset me how much she was altered in Ben's company, how she seemed to submit and not assert a view that had once been an irrepressible part of who she was, for as long as I'd known her. I went to my room and lay on my bed for most of the afternoon, listening to music, saddened that Rebecca had chosen to give her heart to someone like Ben, a man who seemed to prefer the surface rather than the depths of things, who could sum up one of Beethoven's sonatas as 'pretty', and seemed not to reciprocate properly her attentive gestures of affection.

As it began to grow dark and I started to get ready for work, I heard Rebecca and Ben's voices as they made their way up to Rebecca's room. 'Nice little city, Chester! Quite a broad range of facilities,' Ben said loudly.

'I'm glad you like it,' Rebecca replied, placidly. 'I'm sure you would've liked the Meadows as well, but ... I know there wasn't quite enough time.'

'As I told you, Becca, I would've got my shoes and trousers dirty. I'm not equipped. Anyway, we saw the most important sights, didn't we?'

'We did.'

'We'd better get ready for dinner, Becca. Don't want to keep your mother waiting.'

'No.'

I had never heard Rebecca sound so devoid of vitality before. It was hardly surprising, given Ben's insipid, clichéd verbal offerings. In spite of his physical qualities and meticulous grooming, I couldn't imagine that Ben would be a particularly passionate or tender lover. But also, I had to acknowledge, even if only to myself, that I couldn't bear to visualise him with Rebecca in that context.

For a moment, I couldn't help thinking about how it might have been if Ben had stayed behind in Edinburgh and instead of going to work, Rebecca and I had walked out alone together, along the path by the River Dee towards the Meadows, the way we had that evening all those years ago. I imagined how we might have begun to speak to each other candidly, in the unguarded ways we had done when we were younger, but with the confidence and advantages of maturity. My mind began to build up a picture of us, this time hand in hand, side by side, exchanging the missed details of our histories, lost in continual conversation – light, as well as serious, not caring that we were collecting the river's mud on our hems and shoes.

Whereas at one time I might have deliberately stopped myself, I let my imagination be free to carry us on. To the moment where I would have felt compelled to take hold of Rebecca, to physically confirm the depth of my feelings for her. Beyond the hesitancy of my adolescence, secure in my own certainty that, whatever anyone else thought, I had regarded her as my best friend, but never as my sister. Given the least encouragement from Rebecca, I would have allowed passion to overwhelm me. I would have surrendered to the truth of it, the way I unquestioningly let myself be absorbed into the life force of one of

Beethoven's sonatas. I realised that the time we had spent apart, in silence, had taken nothing away from the undeniable chemistry that I felt was between us.

I felt distracted that night as I worked at The Narrow Boat, mentally replaying what had happened that afternoon in the sitting-room, analysing my own and Rebecca's behaviour, reflecting on my appraisal of Ben. I had been eager to find fault with him. He was undoubtedly doing his best to adapt to an unfamiliar situation, but I was still puzzled by Rebecca's attraction and commitment to him. The thought that she would continue to offer herself to him, when he seemed incapable of returning the same measure of feeling, seemed almost unbearably poignant.

'Something on your mind tonight, Jacques?' Laura asked me behind the bar. The pub was busy. Terry kept coming down, making his scrutinising presence felt, then returning upstairs to his flat. Usually quick to serve and settle with customers, I was dropping glasses and making mistakes on the till. 'Sorry, Laura. Yes, I'm a bit preoccupied, I suppose.'

'Your love life, is it? Usually is.' I had come to like and trust Laura. She was humorous and flexible, interested without needing to pry. Not at all intellectual, but intelligent when it came to understanding people.

'Maybe. Something like that. I'll try and focus more on the job, Laura.'

'You're doing alright, love. You've learned pretty quickly. Actually, while we're ...' Laura stopped and glanced swiftly around the pub, then motioned that I join her as she prepared some whiskies at the rear shelf of the bar. 'It's OK. I thought he was still about, but he's gone back upstairs. I shouldn't be telling you this, probably, but ... I've heard from a couple of friends working in other pubs that there's a new place opening, closer to the centre, near Eastgate, by the walls. They're looking for staff, apparently. It might suit you better, love. The owner's not from here, he's from somewhere up north, so I've heard. More than just an ordinary pub by the sounds of it. Kind of a bistro bar, I think. They'll be serving food and putting on some live music. If you want, I'll try and get you more details.'

I was touched by the fact that Laura had been thinking about me and was genuinely concerned for my happiness. 'Thanks, Laura. I'd appreciate that. Though I don't mind it here. The work's fine.'

'I know, love. I mean, it's alright for the likes of me, but you're a bright young man, Jacques. You could do with a place with a bit more life and younger people about it. I'll get some more information, soon as I can.'

The following morning, it was after ten by the time I got downstairs. There was no sign of Ben or Rebecca. Anna was making coffee in the kitchen. 'How was dinner last night?' I asked, trying to sound as casual as possible.

'Oh, it was fine. But we missed you, Jacques. You would have livened up the party. Ben's a very polite young man, but he doesn't quite ... have your sense of humour and particular spark. Slightly limited range of conversation – though not a word of that to Rebecca.'

'I wouldn't dream of it!'

'How was work?'

'Alright. The usual.'

'You look dreadful, by the way. You should get some fresh air.'

'So ... have Rebecca and Ben gone out?'

'Ben's still in bed. Rebecca's out in the garden. Why don't you go and talk to her? She was hoping you'd be up soon. I think she was wanting to have some time to see you when she's on her own. Take some coffee out.'

I couldn't immediately see Rebecca. Then I noticed that the door of the garden shed was ajar and discovered her inside. She was standing staring into the semi-darkness, holding one of the old badminton rackets we had once played with. My unannounced arrival startled her. 'Oh! Jacques?'

'I've brought you some coffee.'

'Put it down on the grass outside for me, would you? I'm so glad you're up. Ben's still asleep. Look what I've found! Remember all those evenings the two of us used to play in the garden?'

'Of course I do. You don't really think I'd forget that, do you?' I stood beside her in the doorway of the shed.

'No ... I don't ... of course I don't,' she said quietly. She held my gaze for a moment, then we both stared ahead again. 'I think the net's in that bag in the corner. And the other racket's bound to be here somewhere. I thought we could put the net up between the trees like we used to and have a game of badminton. Ben plays too, you know. He goes to this club in Edinburgh. I haven't seen him in action yet, but I'm sure he's good.'

'Of course. I mean, he's bound to be.'

'Don't be sarcastic, Jacques! I always know when you're being sarcastic.'

'Yes, you do. I'm sorry, Rebecca. That was out of order. And after all the time we've wasted not speaking to each other ... the last thing I want is for us to have another argument.'

'Yes, I know. I feel the same, Jacques. I hated what happened. I couldn't stop going over and over what we'd said on the phone. I knew from Mum what you were doing and I knew you'd know about me, but it wasn't the same as hearing it all in detail, in your own words. I feel we've wasted so much time. There are so many things to go back over ... everything that happened when you were at Manchester ... the job you have now ...'

'And everything that's happened for you, in Edinburgh,' I responded. 'I know but do we have to go on being critical of ourselves, Rebecca? We can't change what happened now and we're both sorry for what we've missed. I'm sorry ... you're sorry. Can't we let ourselves enjoy being together again now and in the future?'

'Yes, we can. You're right of course. You know, I've often thought ...'

'You've thought ... ?'

'You're a year younger than I am, but in so many ways, when you talk ... it feels that you're older ... and somehow, between us, things always balance out.' She put her hand on my arm as she said it and looked up at me. In that moment her face seemed particularly open and receptive. 'Do you remember the time, after we'd played badminton, when we walked together by the river? I remember feeling so free and grown up. It was such a special moment, wasn't it?'

'Yes, it was … it was so still and secret and …' As I looked at her, I felt the warm buzz in my body I'd felt with her when we were younger, the urge I'd had to touch her mouth when she first left to go to Edinburgh. Now, the urge was much stronger. I longed to kiss her. I wanted to, I was so ready, but I knew I couldn't. I had to remind myself that she was with someone else. Rebecca was with Ben now.

'Let's get the badminton stuff out then, shall we?' I said, needing to distract myself from thoughts of kissing Rebecca before I acted on them. She gave me a slightly puzzled look, questioning, I guessed, my sudden change of mood, although afterwards she nodded thoughtfully and didn't comment.

Between us we took the net and the rackets out of the shed and set them down on the grass. The racket strings were much less taut and the net was full of dust, but Rebecca still seemed determined to set up for a game in the garden.

'The rope should still be there too, Jacques, if you don't mind having a look?'

Rebecca was shaking the net out when I emerged from the shed with the lengths of old rope we'd used to roughly mark out the court.

I was reluctant to spoil the new beginning we were making with each other. But also I couldn't stop thinking about how Rebecca had chosen not to challenge Ben's suggestion – that anyone might feel the need to have an abortion. I felt driven to confirm that the Rebecca I thought I knew still existed.

'When Ben was talking about abortion … Why didn't you say something more to him about what you felt, Rebecca?' I asked, as gently as I could.

'Well, sometimes it's just better to leave things unsaid, isn't it? And anyway, I think that Ben and I can have our own ideas about things and still get on, can't we?'

'Even if he hadn't told you before yesterday that he wouldn't have minded doing abortions if he hadn't chosen to pursue his dream to be a cosmetic surgeon?'

The pained look on Rebecca's face told me that I had hit a proverbial nail on the head. I immediately felt sorry for her, regretted what I had said. 'Well, no, but … that's alright. I mean, he did acknowledge, didn't he, that he knows I would object to being involved in abortion on the grounds of conscience? I'm sure he would have told me, in his own time, if the opportunity had presented itself. Sometimes you have to forgive small things in a relationship, don't you, Jacques? Swings and roundabouts …'

'Yes, of course, I know what you mean. Sorry, Rebecca, I didn't mean to … '

'It doesn't matter, Jacques, really. It's fine. But let's just change the subject now?'

'I think I might get another job,' I told her, as I helped her unroll the net, trying to compensate for my earlier lack of tact.

'Oh? What kind of job, Jacques?' Ostensibly at least, Rebecca had always been able to shift her mood, especially when there was the prospect of a good conversation.

'Still bar work, probably, but apparently there's this new place opening that's looking for staff and doing live music, food as well as drinks. Laura at The Narrow Boat is going to get me more details about it.'

'Certainly sounds better than what you're doing at the moment, Jacques. But are you still convinced that it's what you want to do? I'm sure you could get something where you get better pay and a bit more … recognition … and please don't jump down my throat for that! Honesty has to work both ways. Looks like the mice have been at this net, doesn't it?'

I knew that I had to allow Rebecca her turn, after what I had said to her. I responded to her observations as openly as I could. 'Recognition isn't so important to me at the moment, Rebecca. Maybe it should be … maybe it will be, but I don't have a problem with working in a bar. I can learn different things. Life doesn't have to be an academic, competitive sort of exercise, does it? We can be satisfied with other things. Yes, probably I will have to get something that's better paid in the future, but …'

'I do admire you for that, you know, Jacques. Sometimes I wish I could be more like you. Not so swayed by other people … less obsessed with a single goal … feeling more comfortable when things aren't under control. I'm sure you're more rounded than I am.'

'Oh, I doubt that!'

My joke helped to break the tension still between us. When the old net was suspended in its usual place between the trees, we stopped our discussion and turned our energy towards cleaning up the rackets. 'Let's have a quick game now!' Rebecca shouted at me from the other side of the net. 'Can't believe Ben's still in bed, can you?'

'No, but … do you want to serve?'

'Yes. I haven't played for ages.'

Rebecca delivered the shuttlecock with such power that I hardly had time to react. I had been a good enough player, but she had always been better. On this occasion, I felt more than happy to let her win.

'Oh, Jacques. This really takes me back. We never wanted those badminton games to end, did we?' Rebecca said, her voice softening. 'Remember, you said it made you feel as if you were a shuttlecock yourself, flying through the air?'

'I did! Fortunately you knew me well enough to give me the benefit of the doubt. People have probably been locked away for a lot less … an eccentric boy, wasn't I?'

'You were only going on thirteen! Anyway, all the best people are a bit quirky, aren't they?'

'I think so,' I replied, enjoying the implication that I was being included in the 'best people'. 'Speaking of which, remember all those strange voices you used to put on when we talked about teachers? The way you would snort and snuffle like a pig?'

When Ben eventually emerged, holding a cup of coffee, Rebecca and I had finished our match and were sitting on the chairs on the patio, at the back of the house. We had sunk into enjoying ourselves, talking non-stop, making each other laugh. The period of silence between us seemed only to have made us appreciate our history more. With Ben's appearance, suddenly the relaxed atmosphere between us was broken. I noticed Rebecca stiffening, her face growing immediately more controlled and serious. Ben seemed like an intruder.

'Sorry I slept in, darling,' he said drowsily, pecking Rebecca's cheek. 'Morning, Jacques! Good night at the pub?'

'Yes, fine, thanks. Nice dinner?'

'Wonderful! Your stepmo—, I mean Anna is the perfect hostess. So, what have you been up to this morning, darling?' Ben asked Rebecca. He stood next to her chair, looking down at her.

'Jacques and I have just had a game of badminton, actually. And I won!' Her voice grew more animated as she mentioned our game.

'Where did you play? Surely you've not had time to get to a club?'

'Oh, no! We didn't have to. We've just been playing in the garden. We found our rackets and the old net in the shed.'

Ben turned sharply and looked towards the lawn, then down at the rackets on the patio.

'You mean you've actually been playing with those, over that old thing? With bits of rope on the ground for a court? For Christ's sake people!'

'Why not?' Rebecca answered abruptly, her happy mood instantly punctured.

'Well, you're not exactly ... you're hardly playing a proper match then, are you?'

'No ... but that doesn't matter. It was fun! Jacques and I enjoyed ourselves, didn't we, Jacques? It took us back, didn't it?' Rebecca's words were quickening. She was attempting to sound breezy, but I sensed that she was hurt, annoyed and embarrassed.

'Yes, it was great. A good game,' I said simply, avoiding looking in Ben's direction, aware that, for Rebecca's sake, I needed to restrain my impulse to punch his arrogant face.

As Anna and I said goodbye to Rebecca and Ben later, I couldn't resist holding Rebecca for longer than I should have. Now that we'd made up, I didn't want to be without her. I was aware of Ben in the background, saying his polished farewell to Anna, studying us for a moment, then striding stiffly over to his Land Rover.

'Take care of yourself, won't you?' I whispered fiercely at the side of Rebecca's head. 'Whatever else you do, be yourself. And make sure you have some fun. You always liked to have fun, Rebecca, didn't you?'

Momentarily, she turned her face against my chin. I could feel that her eyes were moist.

'Yes I will, Jacques. I promise.' She pulled away suddenly, sniffed and took a deep breath, before saying goodbye once more to her mother.

'Goodbye, Rebecca. Safe journey. Best of luck on the wards!' Anna said, as Rebecca made her way round to the other side of the Land Rover.

Rebecca's childlike words, 'I promise', had been barely audible, but they resounded loudly in my mind, filling me with acute tenderness and sadness for her.

As Ben drove off, there was something about his expression that proclaimed his assumed ownership. I had an urge to shout after him that a man like him had no right to take Rebecca away. That I loved her and appreciated her more than he did, that I knew who she was. And a small part of me felt that she might feel the same way about me.

I needed so much to break free from the mental constraints that had prevented me from relating to Rebecca in the way that I had really wanted to since I was a teenager. I knew that I wanted her to be free, but also, I realised, more exclusively mine.

12

Although I had never been to Keys before in my life, I immediately felt that it was familiar. I knew that I had come to the right place by the freshly painted sign against the red brickwork: black, simple lettering on a white background. It was late morning, the beginning of November 1994.

The entrance to the bistro opened onto an enclosed cobbled courtyard, off one of the back streets close to Chester's Eastgate.

Straggling remains of plants persevered in a clutch of rusting buckets and flowerpots gathered into one place for watering. The collection of rattan chairs and round, marble-topped, metal-edged tables with bowls of sugar sachets, reminded me of the cafes in Neuilly I had occasionally visited with Maman and Papa. I had always loved sitting out on the street, the feeling of importance as one of the waiters took your order and almost instantly, it seemed, set it in front of you with a magician's flamboyant turn of the wrist. I had often envied other people talking over cups of chocolate and *café au lait*, and had imagined that when it came to my turn, I would be appropriately envied too.

The wooden frames of the glass doors and large windows of Keys, like the rest of the woodwork, were weathered and in need of renovating, although there was something about their worn quality that made me feel comfortable, a feeling that persisted when I went inside.

The interior was arranged on two levels, floored with scuffed, bare boards. It reminded me slightly of some of the student bars I had frequented during my time at Manchester. The upper level, closest to the entrance, was cluttered with small wooden tables and chairs. It was dominated by a metal-edged, curving bar, in a similar style to the tabletops outside. On the back shelf behind it, there was a large coffee machine, surrounded by an untidy arrangement of white cups, saucers and cafetières, a small refrigerator stocked with bottled beer and soft drinks, and the usual lines of optics, wines and spirits that I had become so accustomed to seeing at The Narrow Boat. The darker lower level, down a few shallow steps, was also scattered with tables and chairs. Its red painted walls were covered with posters and framed black-and-white photographs of performing musicians. The floor had a cleared area at the front. In one corner there was an upright piano.

I didn't immediately see that there was a young woman behind the bar, crouched down at the shelves below the coffee machine. 'Sorry! Just stocking up. How can I help?'

'I've been told that I should speak to Peter Bateman.' I was feeling apprehensive, although eager to give an impression of confidence.

'About the work, is it? Jacques Lafitte? Sorry if I've not pronounced it properly. Yes, Peter's expecting you. He's downstairs, painting.'

I went down the steps and found Peter round the corner with a black-tipped brush and a line of open paint pots at his feet. He was obviously dissatisfied with his artistic efforts. He was a big man, well over six feet, probably in his late fifties, I thought, with a broad face and large nose. The precise, dark glint of his eyes contrasted with the rugged, spacious terrain of his features, like sparks of mica within a rock face. He had square shoulders, huge hands and feet, thick grey hair, neither long nor short. His accent was different from the accents I had got used to hearing around Chester.

'Oh, hello, lad. Jacques, isn't it? Excuse the paint on the hands!' He set his brush down on top of one of the pots and shook my hand firmly. 'I'm Peter. Peter Bateman.'

'Pleased to meet you, Mr Bateman. Jacques Lafitte.'

'Peter's fine by me, Jacques. You've come about the job?'

'Yes.'

'And I gather you've had experience at The Narrow Boat?'

'Yes. Since the summer.'

'You come highly recommended by Laura. I'd say you must be tough enough to have survived that one! I've not been in Chester long, but bad news travels fast! Our Terry's not the jolliest of souls by the sounds of it.'

'No, that's true.' I wasn't quite sure whether to say anything else. I had got used to Laura's forthrightness at The Narrow Boat, but I wasn't quite prepared for Peter's bluntness. His ability to read me was even more unexpected.

'Aye, lad. You'll have to get used to me! I'm from the spade's a spade school. Have to say what I think most of the time. Bit different from Cheshire people, us Yorkshire men. But we don't usually mean much harm! So, how soon could you start? I'm looking for someone to work evenings on the bar. Coffees and drinks mostly. Someone else'd be doing the food. I'm after someone reliable, with a bit of personality. I'm hoping we'll get plenty of students in. It'll be pretty lively, so you'd need to keep your wits about you. Interested?'

'Yes. Laura needs me to work two more weeks. But after that I can start when it suits you.'

'Right, then. Two weeks it is! If only other things were as straight forward ...'

Peter turned back to scrutinise his project, a life-size silhouette of a man playing a saxophone, painted directly onto the wall. 'Not good, is it? I'm not bad at the ideas but cack-handed when it comes to the execution. Do you paint yourself, Jacques?'

'Yes, I do. Though what you've done ... it isn't bad.' The painting was perhaps a bit clumsily done but I hadn't quite meant to be as direct. It seemed as if Peter had already influenced me.

'But not good either, eh? Clarity appreciated here, Jacques.' Peter seemed both amused and impressed by my honesty.

'I'll try and do something with it for you, if you like,' I offered impulsively. 'If it doesn't offend you? I haven't got any plans until this evening.'

'I'd be very grateful! And of course I'll pay you something for your time. Drinks on the house while you're at it. Don't be too long, mind. I'm a Yorkshire lad after all!'

I felt more confident when Peter put a paintbrush in my hand and gave me permission to do what I liked. 'You might be better to start again, Jacques! There's plenty of red emulsion there. Paint over my mistake and do something of your own. I'll make you a coffee, will I? Or do you want a beer?'

'I'd like a coffee with milk, please, Peter.'

I did as Peter had suggested and started by painting over his attempt, letting it dry while I drank my coffee. I had my own image of a sinuous saxophonist in mind. It was larger and more impressionistic than Peter's, but I was hopeful that, judging by the style of some of the other artwork he had displayed on the walls, he would like my idea.

Peter didn't come back until I had finished painting. He seemed to understand that I needed to work alone and was obviously busy, moving between the bar and a nearby doorway, carrying boxes and crates full of bottles, serving coffee to the occasional customer. When I finally put down my brush and stood back to evaluate my work, he came downstairs to join me.

'I like that, Jacques! Bloody good, in fact!' he said approvingly. 'Exactly what I had in mind but lacked the talent to do myself. You've captured the spirit of the instrument in the painting. Full of energy.'

'Thanks, Peter,' I said.

'Made your mark already, lad! I'd say you've definitely got your own Unique Selling Point! So ... what brought you to Chester from *la belle* France? If you don't mind me asking?'

'I've been in Chester since I was eleven,' I said, feeling at once acknowledged and more potentially vulnerable. 'Both my parents died within a short time of each other. I had to come here to live with my legal guardian.'

'That must've been bloody difficult ... to say the least.'

'It was, but I didn't have any choice.'

'No.'

'And what brought you here from ...?'

'Bradford! A few different things, I suppose. Needed a change, was the gist of it. I'd had an old pub there on my own since my wife died – she was only thirty-six – had a sudden heart attack. We'd had this country pub out in the Dales together. But I wanted to move into the city again. I felt too lonely out there without her. And then ... I started to get fed up with Bradford. I'd always had a dream to have a different kind of bar. A good place to meet, more than a basic watering hole. Not that I've ever had anything against people getting drunk. Wouldn't be in this business if I had. But I liked the idea of somewhere that would be really good for young people ... never had any children myself. Somewhere with food, and especially music.'

'You played an instrument yourself?'

'Always liked jazz. Dabbled a bit with the tenor sax. Occasionally take it up when I'm on my own. Though let's just say we've both seen better days.'

'Perhaps you play better than you think.'

'Probably not, Jacques! But I'm past worrying about it, if I'm honest. I enjoy myself, that's enough for me these days. Lost that go-getting intensity of my youth. What about you? Play something yourself?'

'The piano. Classical music.'

'Good for you! Don't mind classical myself. I'll definitely keep you in mind, if you like, when I finally get my venue fully operational. In the meantime, please feel free to avail of our facilities. Probably desperately in need of tuning, but ...'

Peter was pointing towards the piano in the corner, on a low platform. After years of seeing Anna's Bechstein covered when not in use, the upright looked strangely exposed. Although its surface was dull and scratched, I was still curious to know how it sounded.

'Have a go now, if you like.'

I approached the piano, sat down on the plain wooden chair behind it and carefully lifted its lid.

'You'll need more light.' Peter was already running up the steps and quickly switched on the lights above the piano. The keys were old, yellow and greasy. I held my hands above them for a moment, the way that I always did before I started to play. It was my own equivalent to saying grace before a meal: a brief acknowledgement, a prayer to my own kind of god.

I began to play lightly, building the arpeggios of Bach's Prelude No.1 in C Major, from *The Well-Tempered Clavier*. In spite of its down-at-heel outer appearance, the piano was surprisingly in tune. The acoustics of the room were good. I felt my neck loosen, my head lower slightly towards the keyboard. I paused briefly at the end of the Prelude, before moving into the more melancholic, less easily harmonious mood of Satie's 'Gymnopédie No.1'. Every time I played it, I had an image of myself, swimming alone, in the deep, cool water of an edgeless lake, into the reflected rays of a slowly sinking sun.

'Bloody 'ell, you're good!'

I had come to the end of the piece. Peter was applauding me from the top of the steps near the end of the bar and the young woman was joining in. I stood up and bowed, mock seriously.

'Encore! Go on! Play something else, Jacques!' Peter shouted in encouragement. He was clearly touched by the music.

'Some other time, maybe,' I shrugged.

In spite of Peter's insistence that he wanted me to continue to play, I suddenly felt self-conscious and reluctant to impose on him further. 'I've got a few things I've remembered I need to do before this evening,' I lied.

'Fair enough, Jacques. Look forward to seeing you again, in a couple of weeks. Best of luck with Terry Bostock in the meantime!'

I left Keys that afternoon, wishing that I didn't have to return to The Narrow Boat that night, genuinely excited, for once, at the prospect of my future employment.

The day before I began my new job at Keys, I was getting ready to go to work at The Narrow Boat for the last time when Anna told me that there was something she needed to discuss with me in the kitchen. 'I don't really want to have to tell you this, Jacques, but I've not long come off the phone with Rebecca and ...' Anna closed her eyes. She opened them again, covered her mouth briefly with her hand and leant on the back of one of the kitchen chairs as if to steady herself.

'What's wrong, Anna?' I knew it had to be something serious, judging by Anna's strained expression. 'Rebecca's not ill, is she?'

'Well, no ... Rebecca's ... she's pregnant, Jacques.'

'Pregnant?'

'Yes. Still in the very early stages. It's Ben's.'

I could hardly connect with Anna's words. It was as if I had a cold, fast river running through me.

'But why didn't she mention it when she was here? She must have known then.'

'I gather she suspected that it was a possibility, although she was trying to make herself believe that she wasn't.'

'So ... what's going to happen?'

'Ben wants her to have an abortion, Jacques. He says he isn't ready to be a father, is arguing that Rebecca ought to think about the importance of her career. Rebecca is adamant, of course. She says she has to go ahead and have the baby, with or without his involvement.'

'But ... isn't he going to marry her?' Even as I said them, the words seemed nonsensical. 'I mean ... yes, OK, maybe the idea about them having to get married is out-of-date and old-fashioned but what I really mean is isn't he going to look after her?'

'Doesn't sound like marriage or long-term commitment is on the cards, Jacques. Ben has told Rebecca that if she won't have the abortion, she'll have to go ahead on her own.'

'Evil bastard!'

'Yes.'

'So ... what about Rebecca? How will she manage?'

'She says she's going to carry on with her course, speak to someone in the faculty when things are more advanced. Do her best to have the child and her career, work around things. You know what she's like. Always very determined. She knows she'll have our support but ... this is going to be very difficult for her, Jacques. I can hardly believe it's happening, although I'm the last person who should be surprised.'

'I need to speak to her, find out how she is.'

'She was going out when she went off the phone. She asked if you could call her back tomorrow.'

I could think of nothing else for the rest of that evening. In spite of Laura's attempts to make my last shift as relaxed and easy as possible, I was tormented by thoughts of Rebecca and what I could only think of as Ben's inhumanity. I felt a surge of anger every time I thought about him, his selfish, neat little ultimatum, the way he was prepared to walk away and leave Rebecca alone to deal with the consequences of their actions. Although Rebecca was a strong person and would be convinced that she was doing the right thing, I also knew that she was unnerved by chaos. She would struggle with the feeling that she was no longer entirely in control of her life. There would be nothing that I could do to fundamentally change her situation, but I needed to speak to her as soon as I could.

'Cheers, Jacques! Hope you really enjoy your new job, love,' Laura toasted me warmly, after the pub had closed later that night. Terry had disappeared upstairs and I had no expectation that he would re-emerge to wish me well.

'Thank you, Laura. You've looked after me.'

'It's been my pleasure. You haven't needed much looking after. And I do hope you can sort things out. Something's obviously still eating away at you, isn't it?'

'You're right, Laura. I do have something on my mind, but ... here's to you! The best barmaid in Chester!'

Suddenly, quietly, without warning, Terry appeared at the bar counter. He was wearing a fraying Paisley-patterned nylon dressing-gown and old leather slippers with splaying sides and heels.

'Something I forgot. Might not be seeing you again. Special leaving bonus for our posh French boy. Best put it away ... before I change my mind.' Terry had placed a roll of notes, fastened with a rubber band, on the bar in front of me. Before I could say anything, he turned the corner again and disappeared.

'Well! How about that?' Laura said immediately, lifting the notes and passing them to me. 'I did say he's not as bad as he seems, didn't I? Must be fifty quid there, at least! Get that in your pocket, love, in case he comes back!'

I found Terry's gift strangely moving, all the more so because it was so unexpected. He was hardly the most pleasant or sociable of people, but in his gruff generosity, I thought there was something more dependably real than in any of Ben's smooth, carefully considered gestures.

The following morning, I tried to phone Rebecca as soon as I could. It wasn't until late afternoon that I found her in. 'Jacques!

I was hoping that you'd call.' Rebecca's faint voice sounded drained of its usual vitality. Its nasal quality suggested that she had been crying.

'Anna told me your news and I ... I'm sorry, Rebecca. This is awful for you. Ben's a selfish bastard.'

'He won't change his mind, Jacques. As far as he's concerned there's no future for our relationship unless I have an abortion. And you know I can't, Jacques. I really couldn't.' Rebecca began to sob. I could hardly bear the raw, broken sounds. I closed my eyes, not knowing what to say next, still wanting to offer her something.

'It'll be alright, Rebecca. You're better off without him if this is the way he is. You're a strong person, you'll manage. We'll manage everything, together. I'll help you as much as I can. You know I'll do anything to help you.'

'Yes, I know that, Jacques ... and ... I'll be fine. Lots of people are, aren't they? Lots of other women go through the same thing. They have babies on their own and they juggle careers, and they're absolutely fine, aren't they?'

'Of course they are.' I tried to sound as convincing as I could, although it was impossible for me to accept objectively that Rebecca was simply like 'lots of other women'. 'Why don't I come up and see you? We could talk things through. It would be better than trying to talk on the phone.'

'No, Jacques. I'd really love to see you but you're starting your new job ...'

'It isn't that important. Not compared to this. I can always get another job. I want to be there for you, Rebecca. I could come tomorrow.'

'No, Jacques. I'll be fine on my own. I'll manage. It's my fault, my responsibility. Mum offered too, but there isn't anything really to be done at this stage. I should try and just concentrate on work ... and I need some time to think, on my own. Look, I'll phone you again in a couple of days. And I'll come down soon to Chester. I'm coping, honestly, Jacques. But thank you. It has helped, just talking.'

'I can still come, whenever you want. You will tell me if you need me, won't you?'

I didn't want to take away from Rebecca any sense of control that she had. At the same time, I found it difficult to believe that she really was 'coping'. I couldn't imagine how it was to have a new life suddenly taking root and growing inside and have any feeling of normality. It was clearly something I would never properly understand, but which I had always found awe-inspiring. At school, I had poured over a picture of a foetus enclosed in a womb in one of my science text books: the miniature limbs, the praying hands, the disproportionately large head, which seemed to heighten the small being's appeal and vulnerability. The thought that I had once been in such a form myself and could remember nothing at all about that phase of my life belonged to the order of thoughts that I believed were bound to overwhelm my own and any other human mind if considered too much.

Before I went to Keys later that evening, I felt driven to paint: a series of muscular wombs, holding tiny, curling forms. As

I worked on the curved, crimson lines of the wombs, my hand moved confidently. I felt the same boldness that I had felt when I had outlined the silhouette of the saxophonist on the wall of Keys. When it came to the tiny, detailed bodies inside, however, as I began to carefully trace the delicate digits and sealed eyes of the innocent heads, I could feel myself curling forward, my breath becoming more shallow. The paintings seemed to come from somewhere wordless, profound within myself. I thought they were disarmingly beautiful, more beautiful than anything I had ever painted before.

13

Although I continued to be preoccupied with thoughts of Rebecca, my new job at Keys gave me many reasons to be otherwise content. The main reason was Peter Bateman. While Peter was obviously my employer, age, personality and experience had brought him the capacity to eschew any tendency to assume a false superiority over his employees. While the running of a good pub was important to him, and he would never hesitate to correct someone if necessary, Peter's *raison d'être* went far beyond an attachment to power or professionalism as ends in themselves. First and foremost, Peter was genuinely interested in people and in the mutual benefits of storytelling and honest relationships. As soon as Peter had got the measure of a person and felt that they had earned his confidence, he was more than willing to deal with them on a level free from artificial role restrictions. From the beginning, he treated me as a person worthy of trust.

Mostly, I worked evenings as arranged, although occasionally I would help out during the day. As Peter had anticipated, the majority of the bistro's clientele were students, which gave it a robust, lively atmosphere, a welcome contrast to the busy but dull environment of The Narrow Boat. I enjoyed being surrounded by conversations turning on the concerns of student life, quite happy that I was no longer a student myself.

Two weeks after I started, Peter organised the first of the musical events that he had had in mind since he bought the place. By word of mouth, he had discovered Suzie, an aspiring young jazz singer from North Wales, who came accompanied by her anaemic, painfully shy pianist, Mike. Like many musicians, Mike fortunately found courage behind the keyboard, a confidence not unlike my own, which was more to do with being totally absorbed, than with the thrill of exhibitionism. Suzie was a petite, finch-like creature, with a halo of soft hair, thin arms and legs and a small rounded body. Her neck was surrounded in soft, shimmering fringed scarves. The power of her disarming and expansive alto voice seemed almost miraculous, given the daintiness of her frame.

At the end of the night, as Suzie sang the moving 'Summertime' from Gershwin's *Porgy and Bess*, I knew that I had to stand still and do nothing else except listen to her. Conveniently, most of my customers were equally mesmerised and seemed to forgive me for temporarily forgetting their orders. Suzie's Blues voice took me back to a small, bustling bar, in which I had once sat while on holiday in Provence with Maman and Papa.

The door of the bar had been open, there were people constantly coming and going. It was warm, but still pleasantly cool, compared to the unrelenting heat of the summer day outside. I was drinking a tall glass of grenadine, Maman and Papa were drinking beer.

Suddenly, a lithe young black man had appeared, wearing a long white shirt and pale trousers. Unaccompanied, he had started to sing 'Summertime' in English, just where he stood, right in the middle of the bar. In that moment, it had felt as if there was nothing more important than his beautiful, mellow voice, the poignant, wending, completely consuming melody that connected in my mind with the fields of Provence, the meandering streams, the luxurious feeling of being effortlessly harmonious on holiday. Even though I couldn't understand everything at the time, I had felt a lump gathering in my throat. When I looked at Maman, I saw that her eyes were filled with tears. I wanted the music to go on and on. I knew that I would remember that ecstatic moment forever.

In *Porgy and Bess*, 'Summertime' is the lullaby first sung by Clara to her baby. Later, when Clara and her husband die in a storm, Bess sings the song again to the orphaned child. As I continued to listen to Suzie, the quality of her voice and the tenderness of the song's lyrics made me feel increasingly emotional. I leant forward on the bar on my elbows and, without thinking, covered my eyes with my hands.

For a moment everything seemed to draw together, the intensity of my past happiness with Maman and Papa, those idyllic days in the south of France, the strength of my feelings for Rebecca, the sadness of her situation, the thought of the beginnings of a child forming in her womb, her courageous vow that she was prepared to have it, whatever the cost to herself.

'Oh, Rebecca,' I said, uncontrollably, under my breath.

'You alright there, lad?' It was Peter. He sounded concerned.

'Sometimes ... sometimes everything seems to come together, doesn't it?'

'It does, Jacques. And a voice like that, that kind of music, can set light to the fuse. Anything you need to talk about?'

'Not really. I was just thinking about my parents ... a long time ago when we were on holiday in the south of France and ... and a woman who I ... who ... but, no, Peter, thank you.'

'Look, why don't you get yourself a drink, Jacques? Have a seat for a bit. Lucy and I can finish up here on the bar. Get yourself a cognac or a whiskey or something.'

I accepted Peter's offer, poured myself a large glass of cognac and took it to one of the empty tables close to the bar. Suzie was singing her last song, a piece that I didn't recognise, which probably soothed me more accordingly. I let the cognac warm my throat, the sound of Suzie's voice and the constant babble of the students at the surrounding tables wash over me.

When I returned home after midnight that night, Anna was still downstairs. I had intended to go straight to my room, but she intercepted me at the bottom of the stairs. She looked cold and pallid with tiredness, and had a tartan travelling rug draped around her shoulders. I had the immediate feeling that she was steeling herself to tell me something. 'We need to talk, Jacques. I'll get us a pot of tea.'

I waited for her in the dining-room, still dazed from the effects of 'Summertime' and the large glass of brandy I had had at Keys.

'We'll go and sit in the lounge and put the fire on, will we? It's too cold in here,' Anna suggested, when she returned with the tray. We had never sat in the lounge before together, but I wasn't in the mood to question her.

Anna's hand was trembling as she passed me my cup. She turned on the electric fire and sat down on the sofa, with her legs curled up. It was strange to see her like that. Undoubtedly her body knew such postures from sleep, but I was used to seeing her straight-backed and upright. I sat down in the armchair opposite her. 'I have two less than pleasant pieces of information to impart, I'm afraid, Jacques. The first ... Rebecca has miscarried. It happened a few days ago, in fact, but she wanted to handle things herself. One of her flat-mates went with her to hospital. These things happen. We don't always know why. Nature has a way of dealing with situations ... often for the best.'

'She lost her baby? She's been in hospital?' I could scarcely keep pace with Anna's words, her neutral, factual tone so apparently separate from the information that she was delivering. 'So where is she now?'

'She's out of hospital, Jacques. Things were still at a very early stage and there wasn't need for much intervention. She'll have to rest for a while, although she's keen to get back to work and study as soon as she can. I've offered to go up and see her, but she says she doesn't want any fuss. Said she'll come back here soon instead.'

We both sat in silence for some time, staring at different angles into the space between us. I lifted my cup mechanically without really tasting the tea, hearing the clock ticking, the heat from the electric fire stinging the side of my leg. 'How did Rebecca sound?' I asked, finally forcing myself to speak.

'She was upset. By the whole exhausting physical process of it, but more by her own thoughts, I think. She admitted that she felt sad and guilty. She hadn't planned it ... even though she had decided to go ahead with having the baby, she couldn't help wondering if her reluctance, and her uncertainty about Ben, had somehow played a part in her losing it. Not a rational thought, although I do feel for her, Jacques.'

'Yes. I do too. I'd like to go and see her, but I don't think she'll want that, will she?'

'Probably not yet. Rebecca does need space sometimes, to gather herself. Best to allow her to come here, I think, when she's ready.'

I vaguely recalled that Anna had said that she had two things to discuss with me at the beginning of the conversation. As there was nothing more I could do at once for Rebecca, I made myself ask her what the other matter was. 'Oh, yes, that.' Anna drank slowly from her tea before continuing. 'I've discovered, Jacques, that I'm ... ill. Before you start thinking or fretting about me, don't. I'm not worried myself. These things don't frighten me. They're more inconvenient, if anything. It's cancer. Cancer of the breast. I'll need to have some surgery and radiotherapy. The prognosis is reasonable. I'll have to take some time off work for the initial treatment and face the tedious prospect of regular follow-ups, but I'm hoping it won't interfere too much with my usual routine.'

'I am so sorry, Anna,' I began. 'I don't know what to say. I did think that you looked less well.'

'There's no need for us to talk about it any more, Jacques. You had to know at some stage, but the main reason why I mentioned it was because I've decided at this point to revise my will. I want you to share my estate when I die. I'm still in the process of getting advice, but roughly my idea is that this house or its value will be shared between you and Rebecca, and that Matthew will receive the equivalent in funds. I know that you're not my son, Jacques, but I've grown fond of you and I'd want to help you to succeed in whatever way I can.'

'Thank you, Anna. I'm very grateful that you would think about me. But you're ill – you should be thinking more of yourself.'

'You're tired, Jacques. You've been working all evening and it's a lot to take in. You must go to bed.'

I kissed Anna quickly on the cheek and went towards the door. My response felt too abrupt. I turned towards her again, but she waved me back.

As soon as I was inside my room with the door closed, I took the chair from the side of the bed and positioned it directly below the skylight. I loosened my shirt and tie, climbed onto the chair and undid the latch, pushing the window open above my head. The keen, damp air of the winter night rushed in. I stood there with my head tilted back, inhaling, exhaling, losing track of time. I cried for a while, silently, felt the tears running down my face. My mind reeled with all the information I had been given.

Such a short time ago, it seemed, my thoughts had centred on Rebecca's unborn child, her courage and determination to look after it. I had already begun to integrate it into my vision of the future. Everything I knew about Rebecca told me that she would have been a wonderful mother. That was the sort of person she was, had always been. The rescuer, the protector of the 'baby bud'. I found it almost unbearable to imagine how alone she must have felt, how the loss of the child had affected her. Although her sense of guilt and responsibility was, as Anna had said, not rational, it was completely in keeping with who Rebecca was. While in many ways she wasn't as analytical as I was, she had a capacity for acute anger, which she could turn back, in punishment, against herself. I wanted desperately to be with her, to convince her, in whatever way I could, that the miscarriage wasn't her fault.

In spite of how cold Anna had once been towards me, in spite of her declarations that she could cope single-handedly with everything to do with her cancer and its treatment, I couldn't stand the thought of her being seriously ill. Over the years, I had come to appreciate the abiding honest and solid relationship that had developed between us. She was someone I had come genuinely to respect and depend upon. I hated the idea of her suffering, having to confront such uncertainty.

As the night went on, I looked out at the distant pinpricks of the stars above my head. It felt almost selfish to think about it, but for a moment I imagined how much less complicated it would have been if I had had the choice to exist as a ball of gas and rock, among a non-human population, in a spacious, mindless universe.

My brief phone call to Rebecca the following evening confirmed that Anna was right. Rebecca was grateful to me for making contact, but said that she wanted time to reflect and recover physically from her ordeal as well as she could by herself. She repeated to me how she felt guilty, how she feared that in some way she had brought the tragedy upon herself and her unborn child by subconsciously willing the pregnancy to end. However much I tried to reassure her, I guessed that she would continue to have such thoughts and that it would be misguided and even arrogant to believe that I could immediately persuade her to adopt another, more positive view. I wanted to see her, to make her feel better, but I knew that it would be more respectful of her needs to give her time alone.

Anna, as she had indicated, had said everything for the time being that she needed to say on the subject of her illness. She would be keeping me informed, she said, with respect to her will. She expected that her treatment would start in a few weeks and that it would inevitably be 'less than pleasant'. She stated that she would cope with it as best she could, repeated that she had no fear of serious illness or her own death. It was difficult to know exactly what she was really thinking. She told me that she felt as if she had already been so many times to those territories bordering the edges of life.

I tried deliberately to immerse myself in my work at Keys and accepted any offers of extra shifts. Increasingly, Peter came to depend upon me to share the managerial as well as the daily practical tasks of running the bistro. I enjoyed pushing myself to achieve tasks quickly and as well as possible. It became a running joke among staff and customers how rapidly I could calculate bills, how many separate orders I could keep in mind at once. To further challenge myself and to add to my own and the customers' entertainment, I began to cultivate a new 'Jacques the Bartender' persona. It was also an attempt to force myself to set aside the more introspective, anxious side of myself, the self that seemed to have become so entangled with complex situations of love and loss. With Peter's encouragement, I added paintings to the walls of big, wide-rimmed glasses, brimming over with colourful fruit and cocktail parasols.

My larger-than-life 'Jacques the Bartender' was so much more self-assured and suave than my less socially confident self, made espressos at lightning speed, juggled handfuls of glasses jangling with ice, always remembered regular customers' particular drinks. He effortlessly charmed men and women, could offer a view on almost any topic, serious or humorous.

Peter was amused by my performances, encouraged them. 'Think you're something out of *Cocktail*, do you? Tom Cruise, is it?'

'Maybe. Although, no. I'm much more talented. Much more handsome,' I joked back.

'Can't see a smooth operator like you staying for long in a place like this!' Peter also often joked.

'You'll just have to pay me more!' I teased him back. 'Forget about the music. I could be your main attraction here, if you gave me enough incentive.'

I wasn't a light-hearted person by nature, but I appreciated Peter's humour and sense of perspective. Occasionally he would speak about how he still missed his wife Celia and the happiness they had had together. He was always alert to other people's difficulties and ready to take them seriously, but he also seemed to have resolved to try to enjoy himself as much as possible and deliberately to live in the moment. He didn't attempt to ignore or detach from the past in the way that Uncle Oliver did. Peter's strength was both a more and less solid kind, a mature, open-hearted acceptance of both the pain and pleasure of living.

I particularly admired Peter's ability to 'think on his feet'. While many people I had observed, including myself at times, felt the need to respond from a pre-prepared mental script, Peter seemed to be comfortable without one. He was like a man who trusted his parachute to take him safely to the ground. However buffeted he had felt on the descent, however bumpy or imperfect his landing, he would climb back into the plane and keep going back up to jump.

Peter could talk to anyone. He taught me a lot about the art of creating the beginnings of a conversation out of very little. In the steady base rock of his personality there was a slightly manic streak that glittered like his eyes. Whether he chose to begin with a crack in a wine-glass, a cardboard beer mat or the possible meaning of someone's surname, Peter could take a topic and elaborate upon it endlessly, then select another and repeat the process. Peter's own surname, 'Bateman', became an ongoing source of humour and mock debate between us. The name, of Saxon origin, had various possible meanings, which Peter argued were different facets of his 'true self'. I was surprised and delighted to learn that it was related to 'Baitman', a 'keeper of a house of entertainment'. It might also have meant 'boatman' or, if connected to the Saxon 'bate', meaning 'to beat', Bateman could have signified 'a contentious man'.

'The keeper of this particular house is feeling right contentious today, Jacques,' Peter would say. 'Not sure what I should do about it.'

'Get your boat,' I would suggest. 'Take yourself somewhere far away. Before you get into a fight. I'll manage on my own until you return.'

'Anything to be the king of the castle, eh? Here. Take the keys. Go and bring some more crates up. Cheeky scullion!'

As time went on, I started to play the piano in the evenings as well as working on the bar. Peter was keen to pay me for performing for a whole evening like the other musicians, but I told him that I preferred to play a few pieces occasionally when I had the energy and the inspiration. I was always anxious when I walked down the steps and cut through the tables on my way to the piano, but relaxed as soon as I began to play. I was surprised by how warmly

I was received by the students and how some customers started to request particular favourites from my repertoire of Beethoven, Chopin, Schubert and other classical composers.

One December evening approaching Christmas time, I completed a set of pieces with Chopin's Nocturne No.1 in B Flat Minor. The nocturne invariably filled me with images of a romantic sort of solitude. I often felt as if I was on a quiet, moon-lit walk, on a shadowy path through a park, walled either side with dense, clipped conifers and yews. When I came to the end of it and stood up to gather together my music, I heard a familiar voice, loudly shouting approval from the bar end of the bistro. 'Well done, Jacques! Well played!'

It was Wheelie. Larger than I remembered him and undeniably older, but unmistakably Wheelie. He was sitting in the corner with his back to the wall where I had painted the saxophonist. Inevitably he had company – this time, a striking, curvaceous woman, with milky skin, long, ebony-dyed hair and dark red lipstick. I guessed she was possibly in her thirties. I closed the piano lid and made my way over to speak to them. Wheelie and I had phoned each other now and then when I was at Manchester. He knew that I was considering leaving with the intention of getting a job in Chester, but we hadn't been in touch since.

'Hey, Jacques! How's it going? Your performance has come on leaps and bounds. Bloody impressive! Great to see you. Sorry not to have been in touch for so long. My fault completely. Oh, forgive me, Rosalind. This is Jacques Lafitte, a good friend from my Chester past. A sickeningly intelligent, suave and good-looking Frenchman. We went to school together. Jacques, meet Rosalind. Rosalind's a journalist. We met in Bristol. She's streets ahead of me, of course. I'm still plodding away on my English course. I'll get there in the end, but ... anyway, the most important news is that Rosalind has eventually agreed to take me on!'

I was momentarily puzzled by the meaning of Wheelie's last statement, but Rosalind was quick to clarify. She lifted her left hand and waved it flamboyantly in front of me, showing off what I assumed was a diamond ring, with a large stone. 'How good to meet you, Jacques! I loved you on the piano. You could be my personal pianist any time.' She spoke slowly and almost lazily, in what I thought sounded like a southern English accent.

'I'm not sure that your fiancé would approve,' I responded lightly, as well as truthfully.

'Oh, don't worry about me,' Wheelie supplied smoothly, pretending, as always, to take everything in his stride. 'Rosalind's unstoppable! Totally her own woman.'

I noticed that he still chose to steer the next part of the conversation in a different direction.

So, you're working here now, Jacques? Sorry the old history thing didn't work out, but anyway, good for you, getting a job! Heard from Mitchie recently? I should make an effort to get in contact with him.'

'I was thinking the same thing myself. I haven't heard from him for a while.'

'This must be a pretty lively place to work, Jacques? The big guy behind the bar seems good fun. Is that your boss?'

'Yes. Peter Bateman. He's a good man. Great to work for. Speaking of which, I probably need to be getting back on the bar, Wheelie. Perhaps we could meet another time? I don't know how long you're in Chester?'

'Probably will have to be another time, Jacques. We're going to see Rosalind's parents. Big announcements and all that. Fingers crossed I meet with everyone's approval. But I'll be in touch again soon anyway. I need to make sure you'll be available to help me out on the Big Day!'

'Help you out?'

'As my Best Man? Only if you feel you'd like to, of course ...?'

'Oh, right! Well I ... appreciate the invitation, of course, but ...'

'The appropriate answer is "I will, Wheelie". Speak to you soon, Jacques.'

'Wonderful to meet you, Jacques! Keep those fingers nice and supple, won't you? Can't wait to see you again,' Rosalind told me flirtatiously.

I was pleased to have seen Wheelie again. He was as keen to impress as ever and as driven by his own passions, but he was never consciously condescending or negative about what I chose to do.

'Friends of yours, are they?' Peter commented as I stood back beside him again behind the bar. 'Beautiful-looking woman.'

'Yes. I knew Wheelie from school. He's studying at Bristol now. They're getting married! Wheelie was always interested in the older woman.'

'Can't say I blame him either, especially a woman like that! Tended to go for girls my own age myself, although that's a long time ago now. So what's your type, Jacques? That night when Suzie was here you mentioned something, didn't you? About a woman?'

Peter rarely missed a trick. He had a way of sounding casual, as if he was distracted by preparing drinks and wasn't properly listening, although I knew that he was. 'Yes, I did. She's ... although ... I probably shouldn't say anything.'

'Entirely up to you, lad! I'm not the prying sort. Don't see that there's any harm in openly talking about a woman or three if you want to, but only if you want to.'

'There is ... someone. I can't tell her how I feel. It's complicated and there are other people to think of who ... and I doubt if my feelings would be reciprocated anyway.' As I spoke, I wanted to say more. I had been repressing so much on the subject for such a long time.

'Sounds like an old, old story, if you ask me. Though, why complicated, Jacques?'

'Well, actually, I'm talking about Rebecca. She's the daughter of my guardians. We grew up together – at least since I was eleven and she was twelve. A lot of people still might describe her as my sister or my stepsister, but we're not at all related by blood, and ... we've never thought of each other as siblings. We've been good friends, even if we haven't always agreed on everything.'

'Who does? Celia and I ... well, opposites, so they say. I mean, perhaps I can see some of your dilemma, Jacques, psychologically, and if you're concerned about the reactions of other people. Personally, I don't think there's a problem. She isn't your sister or your stepsister. You were almost teenagers when you were first introduced. Given some time and if both of you felt the same way, well there wouldn't be anything wrong in trying to make a go of it.'

'You're right. But I don't know if Rebecca ... I don't know for sure that she would ...'

'And there's only one way to find out.'

'You won't mention it to anyone else, will you?'

'Jacques! Am I not a man who can hold his drink? You'll not catch me spewing over the bar! Take your time, lad. Not too long, but think about it. The world's your oyster.'

'Thank you for listening, Peter.'

I felt some relief after my conversation with Peter. I was certain that I could trust him to keep the information to himself. I still didn't know what exactly I was going to do, but I felt better having such strong, long-hidden feelings finally out in the open.

After meeting Wheelie that evening, I decided to try to contact Mitch when I got home. It was after midnight and Anna was in bed. I wasn't sure if Mitch would have already returned to Chester for the Christmas holidays, but I thought that I would try calling him in Manchester. I knew that he and his Welsh flatmate, Owen, generally didn't go to bed until at least two in the morning.

'Mitch, it's Jacques. Wasn't sure if you'd still be in Manchester. I hope I'm not calling too late?'

'Never too late, Jacques. You know what I'm like. Owen and I have decided to stay on here for a few more days. We've got some boozy parties lined up. To what do I owe the pleasure of the call?'

'Wheelie.'

'Wheelie?'

'I was going to phone you anyway, but I saw Wheelie in Keys tonight and we both said we should get in touch with you. He's just got engaged.'

'Engaged?'

'To a woman called Rosalind. Older, very glamorous.'

'The old wheeler-dealer! The last time I spoke to him he was with someone called Penny. Wasn't that long ago. How was the fat dog then?'

'In his element, of course! Obviously in love, the height of sartorial elegance, as usual! How are things with you, Mitchie?'

'Pretty good. No current romance to boast of myself, but ... drawing the crowds ... enjoying life. Yourself, Jacques? How's the job going? Any wild women in tow?'

'The job is going well, Mitchie. No wild women attached at present. Sorry to disappoint.'

'I expect better next time, Jacques. Look, we should meet up sometime soon. I've just joined this foreign film club. They show a lot of French stuff, usually with subtitles, but you'd like it. You could come and stay overnight here when you've got a night off. Last week it was a late night Marcel Pagnol double bill. *Jean de Florette* and *Manon des Sources*. The film club girls would love you. And you could get your fix of French actresses.'

'Sounds good. I'd like that, Mitchie. So how's your course going? Any ideas about what you're going to do at the end of it yet? I'm beginning to sound like my guardian, aren't I?'

'Not sure yet, Jacques. I'm thinking I might go into teaching, but time will tell. Speaking of guardians, how's Angel Oliver? Has he recovered yet from your decision to leave Manchester?'

'I doubt it. My decision to work in a bar was a personal insult to him after all. Fortunately we don't see each other much these days. Uncle Oliver's commitment to guardianship has always been intermittent. Occasionally it suits him to be seen to care, but generally he has much more important matters on his agenda. He needs to be on the receiving end when it comes to attention.'

'Selfish toad! You always deserved better, Jacques. Especially after what happened to your own parents.'

'Thanks, Mitchie. Fortunately I don't need to rely on Uncle Oliver for my happiness. I've been lucky enough to find other good people along the way, such as yourself.'

'You're welcome, Jacques. Any time.'

It was after two in the morning when Mitch and I finally finished our conversation. The fact that we had talked was more important than what we had talked about. Although I chose not to disclose any of my thoughts about Rebecca or Anna to him, I felt encouraged by our continuing connection and the affirming power of real friendship.

14

I was pleased when Rebecca called to say that she would be spending some time with Anna and me over Christmas. She was behind with studying, she said, and would probably only stay for two days, but she was keen to get away from Edinburgh and was looking forward to seeing us.

'We need to catch up, Jacques. I want to come and see where you work. Keys, isn't it? And I need to see Mum as well. She always says she isn't worried, although it must be awful for her, facing the surgery and radiotherapy. Not knowing exactly how things are going to go. I know she won't really want to talk about it, but at least we can be together.'

Anna's treatment was planned for the beginning of the New Year. She would continue working until Christmas, but she intended to indulge herself before having to submit to inevitable restrictions. 'I'm going to make a point of it, Jacques! I've asked Mrs Chad to make sure that we are overstocked with good food and alcohol before she goes on holiday. If this has to be my last supper, so be it. May as well be as epicurean as I can.'

I felt uncomfortable when Anna made jokes about her mortality. It was difficult for me to envisage being able to be equally humorous in her position. Any time that I had tried to contemplate the thought of my own death, I had felt my mind start to struggle. It was a slightly similar feeling to the one that I had when confronting the fact that I had once been an embryo in my mother's womb – but much less pleasant. The idea that at one time I had not existed, and that at some point I would cease to exist again, would occasionally hit me in an acute, visceral way. It happened particularly when I was doing something apparently relaxing, but less mentally absorbing, like having a bath or taking a walk. I would begin to feel a cold panic flashing through me, would feel trapped in my body, surrounded by an absurd, meaningless universe, unable to definitively make sense of things or simply escape. The persistent thought, that I had no way of advancing my knowledge about how death would be until I came to experience it, made it seem even more impossible. If I allowed myself to continue dwelling on it, I would break out in a sweat and go round and round, in constricting, anxious inner circles.

When such moments came along, I learned to distract myself by thinking about something entirely different, by recalling a particular tune, or by observing an object, anything from a stone to a bar of soap, in the same kind of detailed way in which I would study it for a painting. Alternatively, I would try to console myself by remembering that Maman, Papa and Stephen had gone ahead of me already. Impossible though the

thought seemed, death was our natural and common inheritance and destination. Surely there could be little to truly fear
about becoming more fully integrated with Nature, persisting
somewhere, perhaps in the atoms of a rock, a pine tree or a
blackbird?

Rebecca arrived on the morning of Christmas Eve in a small
Renault. She loved to drive and was proud of her new car.
Although I had taken lessons and had passed my test when
I was at Prince's, I had no particular ambition to have a car
myself, a fact that she had always found puzzling and amusing, as well as 'typical' of me. She looked slighter and more
fragile than when she had visited with Ben. Her sharp eyes
were circled with shadows, her hair cut even shorter. She
looked much more like her mother than she had done before.
She was wearing an ink blue coat over a long black wool dress.
Instead of throwing herself at me boisterously, this time she
approached me more slowly, quietly put her arms around me
for a moment.

'Jacques! You look so well! Your hair suits you when you wear
it a bit longer like that. I'm sure I must look awful. I wanted
to have an early start and I was so worried I wouldn't wake up,
I hardly slept at all.'

'You look lovely,' I said quickly. While Rebecca looked less
radiantly healthy, I could feel my heart racing with the excitement of being with her again. 'Can I give you a hand with your
bags? Anna's in the kitchen, making mulled wine.'

'Oh, good for her! If anyone needs to relax, it's Mum. I'll come straight in. Don't worry about the bags. I haven't brought much with me. I'll come out later.'

I followed Rebecca inside. Although Anna didn't usually go in much for Christmas trimmings, this year she had insisted that I help her put up a tree in the hall and decorate the downstairs rooms with red candles, evergreen cuttings and wreaths she had asked Mrs Chadwick to get from Chester Market. Usually faintly scented with furniture polish, the house smelled strongly of a mixture of pine, bay leaves and spices. 'The house looks great, Jacques!' Rebecca exclaimed as she made her way in. 'I love the tree, especially with just the white lights. It doesn't need anything else, does it? Mum! I'm here!'

I could tell that Anna was pleased to see Rebecca, even if she continued to busy herself with preparing the wine. 'I'm so glad you've come earlier, dear! How was your journey? You look seriously in need of something to warm you up. Let's all sit at the table, shall we? Get me down the glasses, would you, Jacques?'

'Why don't we sit in the lounge, Mum? You'd be more comfortable on the sofa, with the fire on, wouldn't you?' Rebecca suggested.

'Fine by me! Though you know I don't need to be fussed over, Rebecca! I can't abide bossy physicians, you know.'

'Takes one to … Yes, I know, Mum. I promise I'll keep fuss to the minimum,' Rebecca agreed, good-humouredly. 'Can I help carry something through for you?'

'We'll bring the whole pan and the ladle in on a tray, I think. I refuse to keep my mulled wine at a distance. And everyone can help themselves, without to-ing and fro-ing unnecessarily to the kitchen. If you take the small tray with the glasses and nuts, Rebecca, I'll ask Jacques to carry the pan.'

We made our way in procession to the lounge, Anna following with a large box of Swiss chocolates. She clicked on the fire. 'We can put everything on the table,' she suggested, pulling a low coffee table into the middle of the room. Rebecca and I sat down on the armchairs opposite the sofa. Anna ladled the wine generously into the glasses and passed them over to us.

'Thanks, Mum. This is really nice. All very festive! Very unusual for me to be able to drink at this time of the day but ...'

'It'll do you good, Rebecca. You need some colour in your face. You look terribly drained, and you've lost weight.' While Rebecca and Anna were in many respects very different, they shared a tendency to clinically observe, as if everyone was a patient.

'Now who's fussing, Mum? I'm just a bit tired. I'm still trying to work as hard as I can to catch up after ...' Rebecca stared down dolefully.

'Yes, I know. I'm not surprised you're exhausted. There's no point in pretending, Rebecca. You've had a pretty trying time, haven't you?'

'Well ... yes.' Rebecca held her glass in both hands, swirled her wine, apparently absent-mindedly. 'But I'm better now.'

'And no further contact from Ben, I suppose?' Anna enquired acidly, with unmasked bitterness.

'No. There won't be. Ben's ... got someone else now,' Rebecca said quietly. 'One of the first year students. Sweet, gullible little thing, I'm afraid.'

'Psychopath!' I had nothing but contempt for Ben. His behaviour continued to validate my initial gut feeling about him, which I now wished that I had trusted completely from the beginning.

'Well put, Jacques!' Anna agreed. 'Never judge a book by its smooth little cover. I know it's been a trial, Rebecca, but you really are best rid of someone like that. Anyway, let's not give Ben a moment more of our lives, shall we? How's everything going otherwise, Rebecca? How are you finding things at the hospital? What about the post-mortem? I can still remember my first one! I was as green as a Martian – crouching and heaving over the toilet bowl all night afterwards!'

'I didn't mind too much. Though I have to say I prefer contact with the living rather than the dead. I'm looking forward to things being more hands-on,' Rebecca replied, laughing. Although at times Anna's instinct to move on rapidly prevented Rebecca from expressing herself as fully sometimes as she needed to, I could tell that at other moments it suited her well.

'Always a promising sign when you're wanting to be a doctor!' Anna quipped. 'Pass me your glass, Rebecca. Can't have you drinking the dregs. Jacques? Another one for you?'

'Half a glass, please, Anna. I'm working tonight. Don't let me forget.'

'Oh, you'll handle it, Jacques. It's not until after six, is it? You can have a little nap before then.'

'So ... can we come and see you later on then, Jacques?' Rebecca asked me directly. I noticed that she was suddenly looking better. Her eyes were brighter, her cheeks flushed. 'Mum and I could call into Keys for a drink, couldn't we, Mum? I'm desperate to see Jacques at work.'

'Of course! Why not? Unless it would make you feel uncomfortable, Jacques?'

'No, not at all. I might be a bit busy, but you could have a drink together, meet Peter.'

'Peter?' Rebecca asked quickly.

'It's Jacques' boss, Rebecca,' Anna answered, yawning. The wine was making her more drowsy, her speech slower. 'Actually I'm quite curious to meet him myself. Sounds like an interesting character.'

'Keys it is tonight then!' Rebecca affirmed briskly. 'So what are we doing for the rest of today? Want me to help you make some lunch soon, Mum, or would you like to go out somewhere?'

'Actually, I'm starting to feel quite sleepy, if I'm honest, Rebecca. If you two don't mind, I might take the nap now that I recommended to Jacques. Why don't you go into Chester? Have a bite of lunch, a wander round the shops? Come back later and we'll have a cup of tea?'

Chester city centre was bustling with shoppers making last-minute purchases for Christmas. The usual street buskers had adapted their performances to include more Christmas songs and a small Salvation Army brass band played ebulliently. Our appetites sharpened by the cold and the mulled wine, Rebecca and I bought pancakes spread with butter and chocolate from a kiosk close to Northgate and ate them out of the paper as we wandered around the Rows.

I had never been particularly fond of shopping for its own sake, although even as a child I had appreciated the leisurely conversations and time spent in cafes that I came to associate with it. I had enjoyed watching Maman trying on a new scarf or a coat, listening to her speaking to shopkeepers, telling me all kinds of small things and stories triggered by our shared experiences. 'You're such good company, Jacques!' she had often told me when we were out, which made me feel grown-up and proud of myself.

I could hardly believe that I was strolling with Rebecca through the centre of Chester – just the two of us, alone after all this time. I was relaxed by the wine and I could tell that she was too. At the same time I couldn't ignore a sense of urgency I felt about having to make the most of our time together, and the constant questions in my mind about our relationship. Was there any possibility that Rebecca could feel the same way for me that I did for her? There had been moments in the past that had made me think that she did. The time when we'd walked arm-in-arm by the river. When we'd said goodbye as she left for university. When she'd touched my face and started to say something that had had to be left unsaid. When we'd stood side by side at the shed and she'd seemed so happy playing and talking with me and disappointed when Ben appeared. We were both unattached now and we were going to have an unpressured opportunity to talk. Why couldn't I tell her how I felt?

'So ... do you feel that you have ... do you feel better now? Don't talk about it if you don't want to, but I don't want you to think that I'm ignoring the subject ...' I explained tentatively.

'I do appreciate you asking, Jacques. It was really awful. Physically and emotionally draining. I still feel guilty at times, that I let it happen in the first place. Especially that I didn't make a good judgement about Ben, why I didn't see through him earlier – let myself be humiliated ...'

'You shouldn't blame yourself. He was attractive and charming.' I didn't want to say it, but I forced myself to attempt to see things from Rebecca's past perspective.

'Well, yes. But I have to move on now, Jacques. However much I need to punish myself, I can't keep looking back, can I?'

'No. You don't have to. Not if it damages you.'

'That's what I mean. You always know how to put it better than I do, Jacques. So, tell me about how things are with you. You're enjoying your job?'

'Yes. Peter's a good man. It makes a difference. It's a lively place, always something happening. And I get to play the piano to an audience, when I want to.'

'That's good! You'll play something tonight when we come, won't you? Promise me you will!'

'I might. If I'm in the mood.'

'Please, Jacques!'

'Yes. I was only joking. Of course I'll play something, if you want me to.'

We walked in silence for some time. I felt much more vibrant than usual, constantly on the edge of a slightly nervous excitement, mentally and physically. I knew that it was the effect of Rebecca's presence. It made me feel sharper, although less able to concentrate on anything else but being with her. 'Let's go into Browns!' Rebecca said suddenly, energetically. 'I could do with a new dress! I haven't bought a dress for ages. You know about colours, Jacques. You can help me look.'

Before I had time to reply, Rebecca was already halfway up one of the steep stone stairways leading from the street to the Rows. I followed her into the department store, pushed through the heavy glass doors, felt a sudden wave of dense heat and heady perfume as I stepped inside.

'Come on, Jacques! It's on the first floor. Let's take the stairs instead of the lift, shall we?'

We climbed the thickly carpeted, rather grand staircase, with winking Christmas lights, and joined the jostling shoppers perusing the bays of clothes on the floor above.

'What do you think of this, Jacques? A little Chanel, isn't it?' Rebecca asked, after she had been browsing the rails for a while. She was holding up a red dress with short sleeves.

'It's quite nice, I think,' I replied, pretending to be non-committal, already knowing how she would react.

'Nice? It's gorgeous! You know it is!'

'Yes, so why don't you go and try it on, then?'

'Yes. I will. You'll wait outside the changing rooms, won't you? I want you to see it. Tell me what you think.'

I waited beside an elderly man who had sat himself comfortably on a chair with a newspaper while his wife was in the changing room. 'Serious sort of business, this. Been here hours, so it seems. I was only fifteen when I arrived!' he remarked wryly to me, before turning back to his paper.

Rebecca soon appeared, making a show of posing and twirling round playfully in front of me. She looked as beautiful in the dress as I had anticipated that she would. Its simple style suited her perfectly.

'So what do you think?'

'You look like a tulip!' I said, meaning it.

'Is that a good thing or a bad thing?' Rebecca enquired, looking me straight in the eyes.

I made myself return the directness of her gaze. It felt like a risk. Surely she couldn't fail to sense the strength of my attraction to her? Wasn't the chemistry between us palpable? It felt so good just being with her. No other woman had come close to making me feel the way I felt with Rebecca. I couldn't imagine that anyone else ever would.

'Oh, it's a good thing. Definitely a good thing,' I replied quietly, smiling, aware that my facial muscles were tense, slightly twitching. As she kept looking back at me, Rebecca's quizzical look gradually began to shift into something different. Her face started to look more exposed somehow, her still, open mouth lost its smile. Her eyes became more serious and narrowed in the way that they did when she was becoming more deeply thoughtful. 'Jacques? What are you ...?'

Her half-finished question hung in the air. There was no hostility in her tone, but I couldn't be certain about what exactly she felt. Was it a moment of recognition, a candid, however small, disclosure of reciprocated desire? I couldn't assume it was. And I didn't want to guess any more. I wanted to know.

'You look really beautiful. That's all I was thinking,' I simply said, finally breaking eye contact with her, looking in the direction of the elderly man reading the paper.

'And that's an understatement!' the man interjected, looking up towards Rebecca and then at me. 'I hope you'll be taking her somewhere good enough for a dress like that?'

'You'd like to think so, wouldn't you?' Rebecca answered him, light-hearted again.

'I'm sure he'll wait while you look round a little longer,' the man said, indicating by a movement of his head that he was referring to me. 'He'd better, eh?'

I was grateful to the old man for diffusing some of the tension. I could tell that Rebecca was affected by what had just happened between us. 'I think I will get it, Jacques. I won't be long getting changed. I'll be back in a minute.' Rebecca appeared slightly flustered. She looked down at the dress this time as she spoke, smoothing its already smooth fabric. She didn't look at me directly, turned quickly and went back into the changing room. When she emerged, I asked her if she wanted to look for anything else.

'No. I've got some shoes and a black jacket that would do well enough. I'm sure you don't want to spend any more time here, Jacques. You probably can't wait to do something else.'

'I don't mind staying, if you want to look.'

'No. I'll just take this to the counter and then we'll go, shall we?' She continued not to make eye contact with me, held the dress on its hanger out in front of her and began to walk ahead, in the direction of the cashier.

'Look, why don't I pay for the dress for you?' I called after her, impulsively. 'I've only got you something small for Christmas. Let me get you another treat.'

Rebecca stopped and looked at me awkwardly. She seemed moved by my offer. 'Oh, no, Jacques! I mean it's really generous of you, but I can't let you do that!'

'Why not? I've just been paid. You should take advantage of me, before I spend the money on something else. I insist.' I was determined to make her accept my gift.

'Well, alright, then. Only if you're sure. Thank you, Jacques.'

I paid for the dress, waited for the shop assistant to wrap it carefully in tissue and handed the smart, heavy paper bag to Rebecca. 'Thank you,' she repeated, less stiffly this time. 'I didn't expect you to ...'

'It's my pleasure. I really want you to have it,' I told her. 'You deserve it. I want you to be happy ... more than anything.'

'Oh, Jacques! Thank you, it's so lovely of you. I'm very touched. You'll have me crying if you say any more now.' She laid her hand for a moment on my shoulder, then rubbed her eyes.

I was feeling deeply moved myself by how delighted she was. Making her happy, even in a small way, really was a pleasure.

'Can't I get you something too, Jacques?' Rebecca asked.

'No. I appreciate you offering. But there's nothing I need, Rebecca, honestly. I'd rather we spent the time talking, just enjoying ourselves. So, what do you want to do now? We could go for a bit of a walk?'

'Yes. Let's make our way back slowly. We could walk through Grosvenor Park, couldn't we?'

I had always liked Grosvenor Park. It was much bigger than the little park near our apartment I had been so attached to in Neuilly, but there was something similar about its well-maintained curving paths and tended flower beds. Rebecca and I had often walked through it when we were younger, chased after the pigeons, fed the grey squirrels on red-skinned peanuts, sat reading or picnicking on the short grass in the summer.

It hadn't yet started to turn dark. We made our way along one of the central paths, our breath visible against the cold air. Ahead of us, on the other side of the park, there were several paths down through tiered shrubbery to the perimeter gates, leading towards the banks of the River Dee. In contrast to the bustling city centre, the park was virtually empty. The beds were studded with modest winter pansies, the grass frozen hard, many of the trees stripped back to the stark beauty of red, grey and black skeletons.

As we walked, Rebecca looped her arm through mine. She held the bag with her dress, swinging slightly, in her other hand. I wanted her close to me, but could hardly bear it at the same time.

'Odd how you live your life in different worlds, isn't it?' she began, thoughtfully. 'I feel as if I'm in another world here, apart from the one in Edinburgh. You must feel it yourself, Jacques, especially having lived completely in France and then here?'

I understood her and in many ways agreed, but simultaneously didn't like the idea that the worlds Rebecca and I moved in were separated. 'Yes, though I try not to let it make me feel divided. We might feel like we change slightly as people in other places but we're still always ourselves, aren't we? The notion of the separate worlds is just a way of managing things, isn't it? It's all really just one world. We're in the same world, together. Especially... when we choose to be. That's what I think, anyway.' Having Rebecca so close to me was making it more difficult for me to think. I suspected that my argument, while it suited me, was full of contradictions.

'Well, yes, I know what you mean, Jacques – you always go into these things far more deeply than I do. I was only saying that sometimes it feels strange … when you start to think about it … a lot of things do, I suppose. They feel quite ordinary and natural when you're just doing them, but when you start to think about them …'

'Yes. That's true.'

We continued walking in silence, took one of the more secluded paths down through the shrubbery, left the park and headed towards the bridge over the Dee.

'So, do you think you'll ever go back to France? To live there, I mean?' Rebecca asked.

'I don't know. For a holiday, yes. But to live … I don't think so. There's no one I know there any more so probably not.'

'I think I could. All that light, the heat – the beautiful countryside …'

'But if you didn't have someone there you knew, what would be the point? Having people you know and you like … that's what matters most, doesn't it? The countryside is important enough, but not compared to …'

'Yes, I know. I'd … have to ask you to go out there with me, Jacques, wouldn't I?' Rebecca tightened the loop of her arm around mine. Her tone was light, but I felt my pulse quickening as she spoke.

'You would,' I stated, as factually as I could, walking faster across the bridge, feeling Rebecca match my pace.

'And you'd have to agree, of course, wouldn't you? Hypothetically speaking, that is?' she continued, in a way that I couldn't help feeling was patently provocative.

'Of course. Hypothetically speaking. If you wanted me to ...
if I wanted to ... then ...'

'Jacques! You're so ...'

Rebecca stopped where she was on the bridge, bringing me to a
halt. She set the bag containing her dress down, disengaged her
arm from mine. She placed her hands for a moment on her hips,
screwed up her eyes then opened them, turned and looked up
at me. My whole body ached with wanting to hold her, I felt my
hands lifting, twitching as I tried to keep them still at my sides.

'I'm so what?' I asked, without properly thinking.

'You know.'

Rebecca stared at me thoughtfully. Then all of a sudden she
lifted her arms and placed her hands lightly on top of my shoulders. She stopped smiling, bit her lower lip when I looked back
at her seriously, without pretence. Her hands moved and slipped
around the back of my neck. I felt her body against mine and put
my arms slowly round her waist.

'Is this what you want, Jacques?' Rebecca asked quietly.

'Yes,' I said, scarcely able to speak. It was the most exquisite
and the most frustratingly painful moment. I lowered my head,
rested the side of my face against hers. 'And what about you,
Rebecca? Is it what you want too?'

'Yes. Yes, Jacques. Can't you tell? I've often thought ... especially
more recently ... I've not been able to help myself imagining
how good it would feel to be so close to you like this. But should
we be ... don't we risk losing ...' Rebecca whispered, 'even if it feels
like it might be what we most want? Is it right?'

'Yes. If we feel it's right. Then ... yes.' I moved my head so that we were face to face again.

The longing behind Rebecca's tender expression was unmistakable. I could feel my head sinking towards her, turned my neck, stopping just short of her mouth. Her confession that she shared my feelings made me feel so relieved and euphoric. All I wanted to do was to surrender to the moment. I felt sure she wanted to kiss me as much as I wanted to kiss her. Instead, she lifted her hand and gently put a finger against my mouth

'Jacques ... shouldn't we...? Shouldn't we think more about this ... about what it means? I don't know if ...' she whispered, so that I could feel the small exhalations that came with her words on my lips.

'You don't know ...?'

'I just don't want us to do something we'll both regret. We can't spoil everything we already have, Jacques.'

'No, although ...'

From my perspective, the word 'spoil' seemed to have nothing to do with my relationship with Rebecca. The whole thing felt so perfectly right to me, but I didn't want to pressurise her into doing something she wasn't completely sure about.

'I'm sorry,' Rebecca continued sincerely. 'I'm not trying to mess you around, Jacques. It's just that I ...' Her mouth started to tremble, she was on the edge of crying. I lifted my head quickly, desire shifting into concern and a need to comfort her.

'Don't worry, Rebecca. Everything's fine. It's just me here, isn't it? You know I'd never try to persuade you to do anything you didn't want to do.'

'Yes, I know. I'll always love you, Jacques,' she said fiercely, squeezing me hard.

'Yes. I'll always love you too,' I replied immediately, automatically, as I hugged her back.

'Come on,' I suggested. 'Let's go back. I've got a few things I need to sort out before I go to work tonight. Your mother will want time with you, without me about. Let me carry your bag.'

I broke away from Rebecca and lifted the bag with the dress. She slipped her arm back through mine. We carried on across the bridge and made our way home, in silence.

15

For Rebecca's sake and my own, I went straight upstairs when we returned from Chester. 'I've still got to wrap a few parcels for tomorrow,' I told Anna. 'You know what I'm like. Always doing things at the last minute!'

'Yes, I know, Jacques! I'm always intrigued, of course, to see what you've got me!' she said, easily accepting my excuse. 'What was it last year? Oh, yes. That light little read called *Being and Nothingness*!'

It wasn't a complete lie. I had to wrap the presents that I had bought for Anna and Rebecca. Mrs Chadwick had been delighted with my gift to her: a silver cake slice, engraved with a pattern of grapes and vine leaves, from a cluttered antique shop in Watergate Street. In the same shop, I had discovered a set of glasses and an ornate wine-bottle stopper for Anna. In Browns, I had also bought silk scarves, a green one for her and a red one for Rebecca, with the eager guidance of an effusive assistant. I still had the series of womb paintings I had done when Rebecca was pregnant. I couldn't bear to destroy them, but I didn't feel that it was the right time for me to give them to her. Instead, I had had three small paintings of crimson peonies, which I had done during that summer, mounted and framed. I wrapped the presents in gold paper and attached plain paper labels. On the label for Rebecca's paintings I wrote, 'Hope you like these. Don't feel you've got to hang them. Reminded me of you – for some reason.'

I set off slightly earlier than usual for Keys that evening. I knew that Peter would be happy to have the extra help. 'Off already, Jacques?' Anna asked, when she found me putting on my coat in the hall. She was carrying a wooden bowl of tangerines. 'Thought I'd better have something healthy for a change! Want one for your pocket?'

It was a small thing, but I found it touching. It reminded me of Maman, the way she used to offer me polished apples and peaches to take out to the park.

'Thank you, Anna, I will. Yes, I'm going in early. Peter will be glad of the extra help. Then you and Rebecca can have more time on your own. Are you still planning to come to Keys later?'

'We certainly are! Probably around half-past eight?'

As I had anticipated, Peter was grateful that I was early. The bistro was already crowded, most of the tables were full, groups of young people were standing everywhere, some sitting, others leaning along the edge of the bar. 'Glad you're here, Jacques.

Lucy has cried off, I'm afraid. A headache apparently. Too much Christmas cider, no doubt! So, it's only you, me and Emma tonight.'

'We'll manage. I don't mind being busy.'

I got to work quickly, tried to focus my thoughts completely on the tasks in front of me. I was still holding the unrelieved tension of my desire for Rebecca, and kept replaying our conversation as we had walked through the park, remembering particularly the aching suspense of the moment when we had almost kissed each other.

'Anna and Rebecca are coming down later tonight, Peter,' I said, as I stopped halfway through pulling a pint, waiting for the foaming head to settle.

'Oh, are they?' Peter answered in a knowing tone. 'I look forward to that. Anna sounds like quite some woman and Rebecca, of course I'm keen to meet Rebecca. How's that going, Jacques? Made any ... progress?'

'Yes and no, Peter. Actually, I really don't know.'

'Fair enough, lad. A possibility's always better than none.'

'Yes.'

'Oh, look. Here comes Emma. Reliably late at least, our Emma.'

Emma had only recently started work at Keys. She was only nineteen, studying law at Chester. She was a slim, well-groomed girl, who reminded me of a long-maned, energetic pony. She had perfect, large, straight teeth, a long face with prominent cheekbones and wore her hair pulled back into a high pony-tail.

'Sorry, Peter! Sorry, Jacques! Running late again, I'm afraid. Had to drop something off with a friend. Got talking, you know what I'm like.' Emma was good-humoured and likeable. I found her easy company, forgave her for not always working as hard as she should. I was clear that as far as I was concerned, my feelings for her went no further than liking. I had begun to notice some signs, however, that Emma was attracted to me. It wasn't just my imagination. Peter had obviously noticed it as well and occasionally teased me on the subject.

'That was some fluttering smile you've just had from Emma, Jacques, wasn't it?' Peter told me later that night, when Emma had gone into the kitchen. 'She was virtually on top of you when she was waiting for you to finish that pint earlier on, wasn't she? Wouldn't take much encouragement, I'd say … if you showed any interest in her.'

'You know I'm not interested. Emma's nice, but she's not …'

'I know, lad. I was only joking.'

Anna and Rebecca arrived as planned at half-past eight. Fortunately, a small table had just cleared close to the bar. 'That's Anna and Rebecca,' I told Peter. 'Do you mind if I sort out a table for them?'

'Of course not! Once they're settled, give me a wave. I'd like to come and introduce myself.'

'Jacques! It's great to see where you work, at last!' Rebecca told me. She seemed less tense than earlier and looked at me apparently easily. I noticed at once that she was wearing the dress that I had bought her that afternoon.

'Jacques! How wonderful!' Anna was obviously relaxed with her continued consumption of alcohol. She had a rare touch of glamour about her. She wore a white wool jacket with light-reflective threads instead of her usual choice of olive-green and beige. 'This table's perfect for us. We have a good view of you at the bar. And can I say, Jacques, in case I forget, the dress you bought Rebecca is absolutely exquisite. You can take me shopping!'

'Yes, it suits her, doesn't it? Though Rebecca chose it herself, of course. What can I get you both to drink? A glass of wine? Something different?'

'Wine, of course, Jacques. Same for you, Rebecca?'

'No. Actually I'd prefer a small drink of something to warm me up. A whiskey or a liqueur, or ...'

'Suggest something, Jacques,' Anna said brightly. She seemed louder, larger than life, determined to be exuberant.

'A glass of Cointreau. I think you'd enjoy that, Rebecca.'

'Yes. A Cointreau. Perfect, Jacques.'

Rebecca slipped off her black jacket and arranged it over the back of her chair. The sight of her revealed shape, the faintly freckled skin of her arms and décolletage, was incredibly arousing. To distract myself, I waved over to Peter at the bar. 'Peter wants to meet you both. You don't mind if he comes over, do you?'

'Absolutely not, Jacques!' Anna said, clapping her hands repeatedly in a childlike way I had never seen her do before.

Peter strode over straightaway, introduced himself to Anna and Rebecca and warmly shook hands with them. 'So pleased to meet you, Peter. I'm Anna Clark. Jacques has told me all about you,' Anna responded with the self-assurance of an older woman. I had never observed her in such an effusive, flirtatious mood. While not drunk, she was undoubtedly slightly tipsy. I might have felt shocked by the shift in her behaviour when I was younger, but I now found it amusing and endearing. The fact that she was ill and facing an uncertain future made me more aware of her poignant frailty. I had briefly confided in Peter that she had been unwell, without going into much detail.

'Equally pleased, Anna! Welcome to my humble house. And delighted to meet you too, Rebecca.' I was glad that Peter avoided looking at me after acknowledging Rebecca, which further assured me of his intention to be discreet. 'A bit on the busy side tonight, I'm afraid. But I hope we'll get the chance to talk later. All drinks are on the house, by the way.'

'How good of you, Peter!' Anna replied. 'We'll do our best to drink you completely dry!'

'You drink as much as you like, Anna. Don't want anyone to have reason to say that I didn't show you a good time on Christmas Eve,' Peter ended generously, digging his hands almost boyishly into his trouser pockets, returning Anna's flirtation, smiling broadly before returning to the bar.

'I'll get the drinks then,' I said. 'Sorry, I probably won't be able to talk to you much tonight.'

'Don't worry, Jacques. Mum and I will be fine. Looks like someone else wants to speak to you,' Rebecca finished, pointing behind me. It was Emma. She was struggling to open a bottle of wine, had broken the cork and wanted me to rescue her.

'Sorry for interrupting, Jacques. I'm so stupid. I've broken another cork. Can you have a go at getting it out? You're always so good at things like that.' Emma looked up at me coyly through her long fringe, put her hand on my arm as she passed me the bottle. I was aware, out of the corner of my eye, that Rebecca was watching us closely. I removed the cork quite easily with my knife.

'I don't know if we can serve this, Emma. It might be corked. We'd better keep it behind the bar until we can test it.'

'Anything you say, Jacques,' Emma gushed. 'Haven't had a chance to tell you yet … that black shirt really does something for you. You've got the right body for trousers and suits. Can't wait to hear you play the piano tonight, Jacques. You will be playing, won't you?'

'Yes, probably,' I said, briefly, irritated by the way she was so unashamedly flirting with me, so close to Rebecca and Anna. 'I'll be back to the bar in a minute, Emma.'

I turned to Anna and Rebecca.

'The drinks won't be long!'

'Pretty little thing isn't she, Jacques?' Anna remarked freely, with reference to Emma. 'Fresh, clear skin, lovely long hair.'

'She's nice enough, I suppose. I hadn't particularly noticed.'

'Though she has obviously noticed you,' Rebecca said, trying to smile as she said it.

'Maybe,' I shrugged and held Rebecca's gaze. In spite of her apparently light-hearted remark, I could read her pain and frustration. I wanted her to understand that I knew what she was trying to do – to appear to be going along light-heartedly with her mother's joke, for the sake of normality, however difficult it was for her.

'Interesting woman, your Anna,' Peter told me, when I got back to the bar. 'Striking, lively, honest character. And Rebecca's beautiful, Jacques.'

It was around nine-thirty when Peter suggested that I play the piano. We had been working constantly. I was aware of Rebecca's presence, how she was watching me when I was at the bar, the way her eyes followed me around the bistro. I had only been able to talk briefly to her and Anna between serving drinks.

I felt so tense, I wasn't really in the mood to play, even though I had told Rebecca that I would. Finally, however, Peter managed to persuade me. Without saying anything to Anna or Rebecca, I cut through the tables on the lower level, went directly to the piano, opened it and sat down. Peter was in the process of adjusting the lights. I blinked against the contrasting brightness, held my hands above the keys.

I began to play one of Maman's favourite pieces: Beethoven's hauntingly moving Bagatelle in A Minor. For me, 'Für Elise' has always seemed an exquisite statement of longing in the face of all obstacles. Hope and love irrepressibly bursting out, running free for a while, bound to be thwarted but never giving up.

A heart beating, contracting, but also involuntarily relaxing, helplessly opening.

My tension gradually dissolved as I became absorbed and my emotions moved with the patterns of sound. Waves of sadness and happiness alternating. Moments of lull, gentle lyricism. High-spirited peaks of joy. At the back of my mind, my time in the park and on the bridge with Rebecca was running like a succession of scenes in a film.

When I came to the end of the piece I paused, only for a moment and kept my head down over the keyboard. I was only vaguely aware of people clapping and cheering, Anna's distinctive, strident voice in the background shouting, 'Bravo, Jacques! Encore! Play more, Jacques!' My fingers returned to the keys, easily remembering the bars of Beethoven's Piano Sonata No. 8 in C Minor, the Rondo Allegro. I had always found it exciting, compelling, expansive, energising. It felt like a walk, in Spring, into a lively, invigorating breeze that you couldn't possibly ignore. In moments of sheer ecstasy, you would be swept up into a chaos of light and exhilarating movement. The piece seemed to deny nothing, gathered together so many varied feelings. At the same time, the refrain felt reassuring, restored balance. Perhaps because it gave me a sense of completion that I lacked otherwise. That, I had often thought, was Beethoven's profound gift, his capacity to acknowledge everything and keep moving along with it, to carry his listener, his player, with him.

As I continued to play, the restlessness that I had felt building all day, was slowly seeping away. In those moments of surrender, I felt more quietly powerful and peaceful than I had done for as long as I could remember. From the Rondo, I moved to Liszt's 'Liebesträume No. 3'. It was like strolling into an enchanted avenue, a vivid, yet fragile dream, fluttering with gently falling snowflakes, arriving at the foot of a curving staircase, an invitation to a fairy tale of everlasting love and beauty. And still, a compassionate acknowledgement of every real, tentative, vulnerable feeling.

At the end of the 'Liebesträume', I finally stopped. I felt tired, but not unpleasantly so. I sat still with my head down for a few minutes, without moving. 'Yes, Jacques! Wonderful! Superbly played!'

I could hear Anna's voice again. This time I looked up, saw her standing, clapping excitedly. I searched for Rebecca. She was on her feet too. Even from where I was sitting, I could see that her eyes were full of tears. She was clapping intermittently, then putting her hand to her mouth.

I stood up and bowed slightly, like I always did after a performance, acknowledging the appreciation of my audience, which rapidly died back again into a low babble of conversation.

I walked back through the bistro, straight to Anna and Rebecca's table, the whole time looking straight at Rebecca. Anna touched my arm in a congratulatory gesture as I passed.

'Rebecca ... don't.' I put my arms around her and held her tightly, could feel the slight spasms of her sobs.

'You're really great, Jacques,' she whispered, in a broken voice, against me.

'It's OK, Rebecca. We'll talk later,' I whispered into her hair. I held her for a moment longer, then released her quickly.

'Jacques? Rebecca?' Anna was staring at us quizzically. There was nothing judgemental in her expression, but I could tell that she was reaching towards comprehension.

'It's OK, Anna. It's really fine. I'll ... I'll get you and Rebecca another drink. Cointreau again for you, Rebecca?'

'Yes. Thank you, Jacques.'

I went back to the bar. Peter was waiting for me.

'Take it from me, Jacques. That was bloody marvellous! You could have played all night with no objections.'

'Thanks, Peter. Though, that was enough for me. I'm just getting Anna and Rebecca another drink.'

'Want me to take them over for you? It'll give me another opportunity to chat them up! You could have a quick breather if you wanted?'

'Yes, thanks, Peter. Wine for Anna, a Cointreau for Rebecca.'

I watched Peter as he went over to Anna and Rebecca's table and delivered their drinks. Rebecca glanced briefly at me, then smiled as her mother said something to Peter that made him laugh. I envied him for a moment, the confidence that came with his experience.

At the end of the evening, after last orders, Peter urged the final lingering groups of students to leave his bistro. 'Give me a few minutes at least to get the chimney cleaned up for Santa Claus,' he joked. 'Come on! Haven't you got gnomes to go to?' When the place was finally empty, he went to the bar and started making coffee. 'Does everyone want coffee? Keys special blend?'

'Perfect, Peter! I'm ready and waiting. Just hope I'm not too sozzled to appreciate it!' Anna shouted back.

'Oh, no. The palate is definitely more experienced towards the end of an evening. Some might disagree but that's what I say anyhow,' Peter returned. 'Stop what you're doing and come and sit down for a bit, Jacques. I'm not opening till late tomorrow and only for a few hours. I don't mind leaving some of the clearing up.'

We gathered round the table, each with a cup of coffee. Rebecca and I sat quietly listening, while Peter and Anna happily carried the conversation between them effortlessly.

'So, you're a surgeon, Anna? What kind of surgeon, if you don't mind me asking?'

'I work in women's clinics. I mainly do terminations of pregnancy, some sterilisations ... hardly the jolliest of topics to discuss over a coffee, Peter, but that is what I do.'

'Rather you than me, Anna. Don't get me wrong. Has to be somebody's job, but I wouldn't have the bottle for that, if you'll pardon the expression.'

'Expression pardoned. Unfortunately I do have the bottle. I have had years of the stuff, Peter. Though I'd prefer another kind of bottle any time, given the choice. How about you? You're not long in Chester are you?'

Anna and Peter seemed to go on talking and joking endlessly. I was pleased that they were so obviously enjoying themselves, but after a while I began to feel impatient to leave. I was tired after the events of the day. And I wanted to be alone again with Rebecca. 'I'm sorry, Anna. I wouldn't mind getting back soon.'

'Of course, Jacques! I'm sure you're exhausted. I'm sure you are too, Rebecca. Don't like to have to put an end to the party, Peter ...'

I could tell that Anna was genuinely disappointed at the thought of having to go home.

'Tell you what, Anna,' Peter intervened. 'Why don't you stay here with me? I could give you a bartending lesson. We could operate on a few lemons ... you could help me develop my knife skills ... finish off with some more coffee at my place, just across the courtyard. All perfectly respectable and above board! When you've had enough of me we can order you a taxi, make sure you're back for your Christmas Day breakfast.'

'Why not, Peter?' Anna replied, clearly delighted by the unexpected offer. 'As long as that's alright with you two?'

'Of course, Mum. You should stay on. Jacques and I can get a taxi back.'

'Mum was enjoying herself, wasn't she?' Rebecca said, as we climbed into the taxi. 'Peter's good for her. He's considerate, as well as funny.'

'Yes. He's an intelligent man.'

'Do you think she'll stay all night?' Rebecca asked, as if she felt she shouldn't really be asking the question, lowering her voice.

'Maybe not, although I don't think it's something for us to worry about, do you? Whatever happens, Peter will take care

of her. She can take care of herself. Two consenting adults ...'
I couldn't help leaning on the words.

'You're right, Jacques.'

We sat close together in the back of the taxi, feeling the
warmth of the heater, hearing sounds erupting occasionally
from the driver's radio behind the glass partition, staying silent
ourselves for the rest of the short journey.

When we arrived home, Rebecca unlocked the door and
I followed her into the darkness of the hall. I expected her to
switch the lights on straightaway, but she didn't. She turned
back towards me. There was enough light reflected from outside through the glass of the front door for me to see her face
quite clearly. We both kept our coats on, held our hands in our
pockets.

'Want a drink or something?' I asked, unsure how else to begin.

'So ... what are we going to do, Jacques?' Rebecca started,
ignoring my question. 'I feel so frustrated and confused, don't
you?'

'Not any more. Everything feels clear to me now, Rebecca.
But we don't have to do anything, do we? If you don't want to,
then ...'

'Oh, come on, Jacques! Once something changes like this ...
You can't live forever suspended, can you? We're not like that,
you and I, are we?'

'No, we're not. I just want to ... I need ... you to know
that I love you, Rebecca. I want you and ... it's up to you to

choose what makes you happy. Love shouldn't always be a source of sadness or pain, and if it is, then there's no point, is there?'

'But don't you feel the complexity of this, Jacques? I mean … I love you so much. I want to be with you too. But I can't risk losing your friendship and, whatever we feel, there would be my parents and other people, with their judgements.'

'People will always judge you for something. At the end of the day, this is just about you and me. There isn't anything wrong about this, Rebecca. We don't share any blood. We've never considered ourselves brother and sister, have we?'

'No, that's true. Absolutely not.'

'It's up to us. If we both feel the same way, then …'

'If we allowed ourselves to … there wouldn't be any going back, Jacques.'

'No. I'm sure that I wouldn't want to go back. I know what I think, Rebecca. You need to decide what's best for you.' I felt there was nothing more that I could say. To be fair to us both, I couldn't go on trying to persuade her indefinitely. 'I'm going to go to bed. Sleep well. See you in the morning.' I didn't want to, but I made myself turn away from Rebecca and start to climb the stairs.

'Wait, Jacques. Please don't go like that. Come here.'

I went back, stood facing her again. We were much closer than before.

'What I'm saying is …' Rebecca lifted her face and looked up at me, 'I need more time. I want you too, Jacques. You must know that? If only things were simpler. But … I need to feel for certain that what we're doing is completely right, Jacques. This can't be just some passing fling between us, can it? We have to be sure. There's so much at stake. Hold me, will you ... before I make myself go upstairs?'

I immediately put my arms around her and held her hard, so tightly that we could hardly breathe.

'I don't need any more time, Rebecca. I've loved you for so long. I don't have any doubts about this. But just take all the time that you need.'

It took hours for me to go to sleep that night. I was divided between frustration and a new feeling of happiness. Rebecca's words gave me reason to hope. At the same time, given the chance, I wouldn't have hesitated in making love to her all night. Everything in my body and mind had been telling me that it was the right thing to do.

16

When I woke after eleven later that Christmas Day morning, I could hear the distant clatter of dishes in the kitchen. I got dressed and went downstairs. I was tempted to knock on the door of Rebecca's room, but I didn't want her to feel that I was putting further pressure on her.

Anna was at the kitchen sink, preparing a large pile of Brussels sprouts, peeling off the outer leaves, methodically cutting crosses into their stems. She had an energetic air about her, and looked smart and efficient with her rolled up sleeves and apron over a white shirt, pearls at her neck.

'Morning, Jacques. Merry Christmas! I've made coffee.'

'*Joyeux Noël*, Anna!' I kissed her lightly on the cheek. 'Have a good evening?'

'Yes. We had a wonderful time. We ended up going to Peter's house across the courtyard, having coffee, listening to jazz, looking at some of his photographs of Yorkshire. Peter is a perfect gentleman. Oh, good morning, Rebecca. Merry Christmas, dear!'

'Happy Christmas, Mum! Happy Christmas, Jacques!' Rebecca was still in her dressing-gown. She kissed her mother, hugged me briefly. I was relieved that she didn't avoid contact with me. I was very conscious of Anna watching us.

'Happy Christmas, Rebecca,' I said, hugging her back.

'So … was it good last night, Mum? I didn't hear you coming back. Did you stay the night at Peter's?' Rebecca asked her mother directly.

'I'm not sure that a mother should have to answer her daughter a question like that, Rebecca!'

'No … but what I meant was … is it romantic, Mum? You did seem to be getting on very well.'

'We do! I had a great time. And we're going to do it again. You won't persuade me to say any more on the subject. Except that I've asked him to come and have Christmas dinner with us. He won't stay very long. I hope you both don't mind?'

'Of course not, Anna. Hence, the mountain of sprouts?' I observed jokingly.

'Yes. I'm turning over a new leaf, Jacques. I'm having more vegetables, which means I can feel less guilty about having more wine! I can't believe you two – you're not usually so restrained about opening your presents, are you? Let's all open them now, shall we? Your Dad – your Uncle Oliver, Jacques – phoned to say that he would be dropping in briefly with something for you. He should be here any time.'

We brought our presents to the lounge and opened them. Rebecca was particularly moved by the paintings. 'How beautiful, Jacques,' she said, as she arranged them in a row on the carpet. 'Of course I want to hang them. I'll put them above my desk in my room in the flat. You're very talented. You should be exhibiting your work. I'm so lucky,' she ended, meaningfully, smiling up at me.

'Stunning, Jacques,' Anna commented. 'And I do love these wine-glasses and the stopper. People could be forgiven for thinking that wine was my only hobby!'

'Open my present to you now, Jacques,' Rebecca said quickly.

It was a book of Beethoven sonatas, carefully wrapped in red paper, tied with ribbon. 'To Jacques, love from Rebecca' was written on the inside cover. My hands began to tremble as I held it. The thought that the woman I loved had given me a copy of the music that most deeply inspired me heightened the value of the gift. 'Thank you, Rebecca. I can't tell you how ... all my own copies are held together with tape, so ...'

I was aware that Anna was studying us. She didn't say anything, but I wondered if she was reflecting on how I had comforted Rebecca at Keys the night before and the reason why her daughter had been so emotional. If my relationship with Rebecca did develop in the way that I wanted it to, I knew that we would naturally have to discuss the situation with Anna. There was no doubt that, although I couldn't be certain exactly how she would react, I dreaded her response much less than Uncle Oliver's.

'That's the door-bell, isn't it? Must be your father, Rebecca,' Anna remarked, without enthusiasm.

'I'd better go and get dressed,' Rebecca said, leaving the room immediately.

'No. It's Peter,' I corrected Anna. I could see him from the lounge window, standing outside the front door, smartly dressed in a shirt and jacket, holding a bottle behind his back.

Anna ushered Peter into the lounge. She was being flirtatious again, touching his arm frequently. He had a freshly scrubbed, sleeker appearance than usual, which suggested that he had made a particular effort. 'Happy Christmas to you, Jacques! Bet you hadn't planned on having me for Christmas dinner!'

'Well, no ... you're right. But it's good you could come, Peter. I think it's a great idea!'

Before I had time to ask Peter to sit down, the door-bell sounded again. When Anna went to answer it, I heard Uncle Oliver's voice.

'We're in the lounge, Oliver,' Anna was explaining. 'Why don't you come in?'

'Amanda's waiting in the car,' Uncle Oliver replied briskly. 'We're going to the Christmas Service and then on to visit Julie as well. I think it's best that we don't stop. Although perhaps I could just give these to Rebecca and Jacques?'

'By all means! Go through. Rebecca's just gone to get dressed, but she won't be long.'

When Uncle Oliver strode into the lounge, he was clearly surprised to see that I wasn't alone. He passed me a carrier bag full of Christmas parcels. 'There you are, Jacques. Few things for you and Rebecca in the bag. From myself and Amanda. Mainly her choice, I have to say!'

'I've got something for you as well. It's in the kitchen. I'll get it before you go.' I had bought Amanda some chocolates and Uncle Oliver a bottle of cognac. 'Sorry, I haven't introduced you. This is Peter. Peter Bateman. Peter, this is Oliver Clark … my guardian.'

'Pleased to meet you, Oliver,' Peter said courteously.

'Ditto, Peter. Not a local accent?'

'No, I'm Yorkshire born and bred!'

'So, what brought you here?'

'Anna's generous offer of Christmas dinner! Otherwise, nothing more glamorous than a pub, I'm afraid, Oliver.'

'Peter's my boss at Keys,' I explained. 'Actually he's being very modest. He runs a really good place.'

'Glad to hear it, Peter. Good to hear that someone else has a head for business. Pity Jacques here couldn't take a leaf out of your book. Wouldn't mind him working in a pub so much if he was involved in the managerial side.'

'Have to say, Oliver, Jacques is pretty good at everything,' Peter said in my defence. 'Don't think he'd have any trouble taking charge if he wanted to. Though I'm sure you'd agree he's blessed with much more important talents. Bloody great pianist, isn't he?'

Uncle Oliver's smug, condescending attitude irritated me even more than usual. I resented the way that he assumed that he had the right to talk to Peter about me in such an arrogant fashion, even if I also knew that Peter wouldn't find it impressive. For everyone else's sake I didn't want to lose my temper. I was relieved when Rebecca appeared at the door of the lounge.

'Happy Christmas, Dad!'

'Your dad has just given us these, Rebecca,' I stated flatly, handing the carrier bag to Rebecca.

'Just a little gesture,' Uncle Oliver explained. 'From Amanda and me. You don't need to open it now. Must dash in a minute. Amanda's waiting in the car. We're off to one of the Christmas services. True meaning of Christmas and all that! Haven't always made time for things spiritual, but better late than never, eh? Amanda has persuaded me to put in an appearance.' Uncle Oliver beamed, I guessed at the thought of his own righteousness. He seemed unaware of the irony inherent in his reference to 'appearance' and adjusted his tie self-importantly. 'How's medicine going, Rebecca? Won't be long until you're fully fledged. I assume that little Renault on the drive belongs to you? Maybe you can get yourself a real car some day!'

'There's nothing wrong with my Renault! Everything's going fine in Edinburgh, thanks, Dad. Always exams, but ...'

'You've never had any problems with those!' I always had the impression that despite having had little to do with Rebecca's successes, Uncle Oliver automatically assumed some personal credit for them. 'Still sharing that Morningside flat with the same girls? And how's Ben these days? Surprised you've not brought him down with you!'

Rebecca hadn't told her father about her pregnancy or subsequent miscarriage.

'I'm not with Ben any more, Dad.'

'Sorry to hear it. Sounded like a promising sort of chap. Set your sights high, Rebecca. A man of the right calibre.'

'I'm afraid Ben wasn't the man we thought he was. Enough said, I think!' It was Anna. She was carrying a tray of glasses.

'I see.' Uncle Oliver acknowledged curtly. 'Hard to know these things when you're not told.' It was a criticism of Rebecca and Anna, Anna especially.

'Water under the bridge, Oliver. Anyway, this is where we are now, isn't it?' Anna answered brusquely, before moving towards Peter with her tray. 'Aperitif, Peter? You still can't be persuaded to join us for a drink, Oliver?'

'No, Anna. Amanda and I need to go. Peter, pleased to have met you. Keep Jacques on his toes, won't you? Who knows? Maybe one day he might surprise us!'

'Oliver.' Peter simply raised his glass and smiled, apparently amiably.

We all felt more relaxed when Uncle Oliver left. Anna and Peter sat down together on the sofa, Rebecca and I took the armchairs opposite them.

'Dad's so ...' Rebecca began, in exasperation, 'so predictable. So full of his own ... and the way he is with you, Jacques. I'm surprised that you don't say more than you do.'

'My sentiments precisely, Rebecca,' Anna affirmed. 'Still, let's not go there now.'

'No,' I agreed. I didn't want to think any more about Oliver. It seemed increasingly meaningless from then on to call him Uncle Oliver.

'Another good choice, Peter!' Anna said, changing tack, making a performance out of tasting her wine, smelling it slowly, closing her eyes as she savoured the first mouthful.

'I aim to please!' Peter replied, delighted with her compliment.

'And you do succeed, Peter,' Anna returned, unashamedly. She sat back, extended her arm almost languorously, I thought, along the top of the sofa cushions. Peter seemed quite unembarrassed, eased himself back, smiled at her directly.

Rebecca and I exchanged a glance. Although at one time the situation would have embarrassed me, I was now simply interested by it. Rebecca widened her eyes meaningfully, comically.

'So, are you still opening up later, Peter?' I asked.

'Yes. A lot of places are closed, but just for a few hours, I thought.'

'You work much too hard, Peter,' Anna remarked. 'But perhaps I'm not one to talk! I have to say, it really has been very agreeable stopping work earlier this Christmas, having more time to wind down.'

'Why shouldn't you? Life's too short not to allow yourself time to just enjoy it.'

'Absolutely. And ... with what's on the horizon I ...' Anna faltered momentarily. '*Carpe diem*! I'm determined to have the best time I can!'

'Oh, Mum,' Rebecca said sympathetically, sitting forward on the edge of her chair. 'Don't worry. Everything will be fine, you'll see.'

'Oh, I'm not worried, dear! I just … I'm not a person for anticipation, am I? I like to go ahead, quickly. Make a clean breast of things as they say. Terribly bad taste by way of a pun.'

'Dreadful, Anna,' Peter said, laughing lightly. 'But I think we could let you off the hook this time. As long as you don't make a habit of it.'

Peter put a hand on Anna's knee. There was nothing salacious or flirtatious about it. He had the confidence to trust that it was totally appropriate. Anna had obviously discussed her illness further with him when they had been alone. She lifted her arm from the back of the sofa and set her hand on top of his. 'Thank you, Peter. I'll try not to. Now, enough of that! I must have a look at the turkey. Make sure that he hasn't escaped. Might not like the thought of surrendering to a fate with all those sprouts. Not sure that I'd abandon myself to them so happily. Jacques, check that everyone's topped up, will you?'

The imaginative details of Anna's Christmas dinner – the glittering candle centrepiece, the foiled chocolates at each place setting, the green and red napkins within embossed silver rings – brought back memories of Maman's magical feasts which, like my birthday parties had always reinforced my fantasy of being a prince. One of the unforgettable elements of the Christmases of my childhood had been the decoration my mother had made for the centre of the table, which had varied slightly from year to year, but had remained fundamentally unchanged. From a brightly polished oval mirror, a collection of moss, ivy, berries and miniature figurines of animals and fairies, Maman had elaborated her own fantasy of a frozen winter lake. It was an image that stayed with me through many of my own dreams. Every year I had anticipated the moment when Papa would light the circle of small candles around the lake, when we would each make our silent wishes for the year ahead. As Maman and Papa talked afterwards, I would be mesmerised by the wavering flames, the reflections flickering against the glass, willing myself to shrink temporarily to the size of the Christmas cake Father Christmas, imagining how it would be to skate across the surface of that enchanted lake.

We ate in the dining-room. Anna's food was magnificent. While Uncle Oliver had lived with us, meals, however supposedly celebratory, had always been rather dull, perfunctory occasions. It seemed that since she and Uncle Oliver had divorced, Anna had increasingly been able to revisit life's simple pleasures.

'You seem to enjoy cooking much more now, Mum,' Rebecca remarked. 'You didn't, did you, when we were younger?'

'No. I didn't. I wasn't able to relax. And your father ... well, he liked to be looked after, of course, but he was never really interested in the taste or the finer qualities of food. He liked the idea of it – that he was doing the traditional celebratory family thing – but it didn't seem to be in him to linger. He needed to be moving on again. *Quelle surprise*, what, Jacques?'

'*Eh bien ...*'

'Anyway, let's not linger there!' Anna suggested briskly. 'Sorry, Peter. Can't imagine that this is of any interest to you!'

'I don't mind. Feel free,' Peter answered. 'Very good meal, Anna. Haven't had something as good as this for a long time.'

'I'm delighted, Peter. Though I can't take full credit, of course. Mrs Chad, as usual, has dependably played her part. I think that calls for another toast, actually. To Mrs Chad!'

We all clinked our glasses.

'So, what was Matthew's reason for not coming for Christmas this year, Mum?' Rebecca asked suddenly. She very rarely mentioned her brother. None of us referred much to Matthew. It seemed that he referred even less to us, especially since he had succeeded in getting a research job at Cambridge.

'The usual things, I gather. Too much work. Not wanting to be distracted. You know what he's like ... nothing personal.'

'Exactly!' Rebecca said emphatically. 'At least I imagine that's how things are. I don't feel I really know Matthew any more. Perhaps I never did.'

'Yes, I know, dear. Matthew was always very self-contained. Even as his mother, I ... though I wouldn't judge him for it. It does seem to be how he is. It might not be for everyone, but his way of life appears to suit him well enough. Can't blame him for cutting loose. Had enough turkey, Jacques?'

'More than enough, Anna! How about you, Peter? I imagine it might take more than a single portion of turkey to defeat The Boatman?'

'You're right there, Jacques. Don't mind if I do, Anna. And a few extra roast potatoes wouldn't go amiss either.'

'Of course, Peter. We will stuff you like a goose! You may have problems taking off afterwards, but ...'

'Oh, don't worry about that. I'm quite content here, feeding on the ground.'

Anna delighted in piling Peter's plate while Rebecca and I looked on. He resumed eating unselfconsciously, clearly relishing the experience.

'So what would you usually do on Christmas Day, Peter?' I asked.

'Oh, not much. I've never been a religious man. When Celia was alive we'd have a nice dinner. Since then I've not bothered much. Always kept pretty busy round the pub anyway. Seemed to spend a lot of time listening to other people talking about their festive family feuds!'

'The way we've made you listen to the details of some of ours?' Anna enquired, laughing.

'Oh, no! I'd say you sound fairly civilised compared to some. Much less kicking and screaming!'

'Peter, don't underestimate me. I assure you I can do my share of kicking. Perhaps it might have been better if we'd simply allowed ourselves more of that. It might have been more honest.'

'We do what we can,' Peter shrugged. 'Hindsight can be a punishing bugger.'

'Couldn't have said it better myself!' Anna agreed.

'You're right, Peter,' Rebecca said thoughtfully. I was fairly sure she was thinking about what had happened with Ben.

We sat for some time talking at the table after dessert. When Anna went to make coffee in the kitchen, Rebecca insisted on showing Peter the paintings I had given her for Christmas.

'Very good, Jacques. Even better than my saxophonist at Keys! You have a distinctive style, haven't you? Intense, vigorous. Makes you want to reach out and ...'

'Yes,' Rebecca said, abruptly. I noticed that she was blushing slightly. 'He's very talented, Peter. I keep telling him that he should be exhibiting his paintings. I'm sure a lot of people would pay good money for his work.'

Although it had been completely Rebecca's choice to show Peter the paintings, I sensed that as he had begun to describe them, the meanings of my present in the context of our private, changing relationship had become more clear to her. I guessed by the way that she cut Peter short and started to speak more rapidly, that she was feeling more exposed and wanted to avoid the development of a situation in which we might both be made more intensely conscious of our feelings for each other in front of Peter, and especially her mother. She was obviously unaware that I had spoken to Peter about her, a fact that was making me feel uncomfortable, however much I trusted him.

'You're right, Rebecca. I'm sure people would pay. So, why don't you exhibit, Jacques?'

I had always disliked being cajoled, especially when it involved deliberately putting myself forward for public judgement.

'Perhaps I might in the future. I don't know if I'm an exhibiting kind of person.'

'Wouldn't be any harm in trying!' Peter suggested affably. 'Why hide your light under the proverbial bushel?'

'That's what I think, Peter,' Rebecca added. 'You shouldn't hang back. You can step up, push yourself forward. You're a man now.'

'Yes, I am, Rebecca. I hadn't forgotten. Point taken,' I replied quickly. I never doubted that Rebecca's intentions were good, but she sometimes could speak without pausing to reflect on the implications of what she was saying.

As we fell into silence, Peter gave us both a glance and looked back down at the paintings in front of him.

'Coffee and chocolate!' Anna announced, as she carried in the tray and set it on the sideboard. 'We can have it here, or in the lounge?'

'How about the lounge?' Peter suggested, obviously trying to divert attention from the discomfort between Rebecca and me. Anna poured coffee for herself and Peter, and suggested that we pour our own and follow them.

'I am sorry, Jacques. I'm not finding this very easy,' Rebecca said, as soon as they had left the room. 'What I said, it wasn't very insightful, and I didn't mean to be bullying or condescending. You're much more decisive about a lot of things than I am, aren't you?'

'Not really,' I said, quickly forgiving her, pouring her coffee. 'Don't worry, Rebecca. I'm pleased actually. Reassured that I have more explicit permission to push myself forward. You'd better take your coffee and go to the lounge straightaway before I step up ...'

I set Rebecca's coffee down and pretended to move towards her. She began to laugh softly, lifted the cup and left the room.

After Peter left later that afternoon, Anna and Rebecca became immersed in a long conversation about studying medicine. I took the opportunity to go for a walk along the River Dee. I knew that there was nothing more I could do about my relationship with Rebecca by thinking. I had no choice but to wait. As I was on my way back, I found myself following a familiar figure. It was Wheelie. He was walking slowly, without, I couldn't help thinking, his usual verve. As I arrived alongside him, I had to say his name twice before he answered.

'Jacques!'

'Wheelie! Didn't expect to see you here! I thought that you'd be ...'

'Afraid not, Jacques. Well and truly home and alone – apart from mother and siblings – for Christmas.'

'But what about Rosalind? I thought you were engaged?'

'We were … but not any more.'

'Why?'

'Because she cheated, Jacques. It came out just before we were about to go and see her parents. She'd kept getting these phone calls … and lied. I had to confront her with what I'd felt for a long time and wanted to pretend I hadn't. End of story, basically.'

'I'm sorry, Wheelie.'

'So am I!'

'There'll be someone else.'

'I have no doubt of that, Jacques. Although perhaps there comes a time when you get tired of just another someone else. You just want one good person … a bit of … continuity?'

'I know what you mean, Wheelie. Look, why don't we have a walk? Unless you're meeting someone? We could have a longer chat?'

'Very thoughtful of you, Jacques, but no thanks. I told my mother I'd be back soon. She'll only worry about me. Another time, definitely. I want to hear all about you and your bartending adventures.'

I felt sorry for Wheelie for a moment. He had been so buoyant when I had met him at Keys. His brightness seemed to fade so quickly in the absence of romantic love. My next thought was about how similar we were in that respect. I was no less dependent on being affirmed by the love of a woman than he was.

When I arrived home, Rebecca confirmed her intention to return to Edinburgh early the next morning. That evening seemed to stretch endlessly ahead. We helped ourselves to cold food in the kitchen, filled and refilled our glasses. I kept going back to the piano, played for short bursts then stopped, unable to fully harness my restlessness and transform it. When talking with Anna and Rebecca, my mind was divided, agitated. I kept losing track of the conversation. Although I didn't want to begrudge Anna the time with her daughter, I could only think about being alone with Rebecca. We all went to bed at around midnight. Rebecca was planning to leave at five o'clock and I had agreed with Anna that I would get up, while she slept on, to see her off.

I lay on top of my bed, fully dressed, tormented by the thought that Rebecca was such a short distance away. In spite of the fact that Anna was nearby, I could so easily have gone to Rebecca's door. I willed her to knock on mine but eventually slipped into a fitful sleep.

I woke with a start. It was almost five o'clock.

'Jacques?' It was Rebecca, knocking lightly.

'Come in,' I answered. I felt exhausted, cold, jittery.

'I'm sorry, Jacques,' Rebecca whispered, closing the door quietly behind her. 'I meant to wake earlier – have more time. I wanted to come and knock on your door last night, but I thought you might not want me to ...'

'Really?'

'Well, no. It was more that I didn't know if ... if it was fair.'

'Fair to whom?'

'To you. And I was aware of Mum, just downstairs.'

'I know, so was I.'

'I wish I wasn't going now,' Rebecca said faintly, coming closer to me.

'Don't, then! Why do you have to?'

'Because I have to try and get back to work. Because I think that some time has to pass before I'm clear about this and I can't stand being here any longer. You, me and Mum – the strain of holding myself together, as if nothing has changed when it so obviously has!'

'Rebecca, please! Don't talk any more.'

I couldn't bear the tension any longer. I pulled Rebecca towards me and kissed her passionately. I had no doubt that she wanted it. Her jaw relaxed, her mouth opened, responding to mine. As I moved my hand firmly down her spine, I felt her hands falling down against the length of my back, then reaching up to stroke my face. The only thought in my head was that I wanted to keep kissing her, tasting her warm, soft mouth forever. Until she broke away.

'Jacques, we have to stop now ... or I won't be able to stop.'

'You don't have to, Rebecca. All you have to do is ...'

I moved my mouth onto her neck, took in the intoxicating smell of her, felt the smoothness of her skin under my lips. My hands lifted instinctively towards her breasts. 'Don't go now, Rebecca.'

Rebecca held my hands against her body.

'Jacques, you know I don't want to, but I have to. We'll be together again soon. Do you want me to go down to the car by myself, or are you coming with me?'

I felt like crying with frustration, but forced myself not to and held Rebecca tightly.

'Yes. I'll come down with you. You won't be able to manage your case.'

After she had left, I went round to the back garden. I was shivering but I didn't care. I paced the length of the grass between the two willows where Rebecca and I had always hung our badminton net.

17

Anna went for surgery in Manchester as planned, three weeks into the beginning of 1995. She was in hospital for only two days and was told that it had been possible to remove completely the lump in her breast, with a surrounding margin of healthy tissue. While she still faced the prospect of travelling back to receive three weeks of radiotherapy treatment as an outpatient, she was clearly relieved that there was no evidence to suggest that the cancer had spread elsewhere in her body.

'I have to admit, Jacques. The idea that I'm apparently clean does bring some consolation to my obsessive little surgical brain. Of course I know that there's no real guarantee that the problem won't reoccur. I suppose at the back of my mind there is always the thought that cancer might well be a fitting nemesis for someone like me. All those untidy, burgeoning cells … chaos made flesh.'

In contrast to her previous workaholic approach, Anna decided that on this occasion she would take at least a month away from her job. 'Occasionally an old bitch should learn a new trick. I've decided that it's time I loosened my grip a little. I'm not totally indispensable after all. There are plenty of young pups who are willing and able to take over. If this whole thing has taught me nothing else, I hope at least that I've gained some perspective.'

For the three weeks of her radiotherapy, after Mrs Chadwick had brought her home, Anna grew increasingly fatigued. She would eat lightly and then sleep for hours, curled up on the sofa in the lounge. Each evening, she woke before I went out to work and asked me to play the piano to her. Going upstairs made her feel too much of an 'invalid', she said. Peter called occasionally to see how she was, sent her cards, flowers and crates of bottled ginger beer and sparkling elderflower, a gesture that she found very touching. Rebecca also phoned regularly, for what Anna described as 'a progress report'. If I was there, we would exchange brief words about our work and about Anna. Rebecca would end the call with, 'You know I love you, Jacques.' I would have to resist the urge to force her to make up her mind.

Towards the end of that February, Amanda called one afternoon to speak to me. At first I assumed that Mrs Chadwick had made a mistake.

'Are you sure it isn't Anna she wants to speak to?'

'Oh, no, Jacques. Says she wants to talk to you. Sounds quite tearful actually.'

I took the call in the hall.

'Amanda? It's Jacques. Is everything alright?'

'Jacques. Oh, I am glad you're there. I wanted to ...' Amanda began to cry, 'I wanted to talk to someone. I couldn't get hold of Julie.'

'What's happening, Amanda?'

'It's Oliver, Jacques. He's ... he's left me.'

'When?' I couldn't immediately think of another response.

'Last night. We haven't been getting on for quite a while, but ... he's involved with another woman, Jacques. Someone younger who he met when travelling on business. He says he has to be with her.'

'Really?' I said irritably.

'He says he's passionately in love. That he's found his soul mate. And I thought that was me, Jacques.'

'Yes, of course you did, Amanda!' I replied sharply.

'He always said that I was the love of his life – that there would never be anyone else. And now it's like I don't matter any more. I'm just something he wants rid of. I don't know what I'm going to do without him.'

'*Connard*!' I snapped, no longer able to restrain myself. 'He doesn't know anything about really loving someone, Amanda! He will always have his own self-centred agenda. Selfish, immature bastard! You'll be better off without him.'

'It isn't so easy, Jacques. When you ...'

'I know you're upset, Amanda, but the best thing you can do is to try and forget about him. None of this is your fault. It's just the way he is. Is there something I can do to help you?'

'No, thank you, Jacques. I'm sure that Julie will call me back soon. I'm sorry to have imposed. Tell Anna I hope that she's better soon.'

I didn't want to disturb Anna, but found that she was already awake when I went into the lounge.

'Who was that on the phone, Jacques?' she asked drowsily, rubbing her eyes.

'It was Amanda. She told me to say that she hopes you feel better soon.'

'That's thoughtful. Though, it's unusual for her to phone, isn't it?'

'She wanted to talk about something else as well. I may as well tell you. Oliver left her last night. He's found someone else, younger. Another love of his life!'

'Huh! And why am I not surprised, Jacques?' Anna replied, contemptuously. 'The technical term I believe is "love rat", Jacques! Although the average rat, I think, would be much more intelligent and considerate.'

'Amanda sounds devastated. Really upset.'

'She would be. He really had her, didn't he? I suppose our circumstances didn't lend themselves to us being friends, but I do feel sorry for the girl. She will find it difficult to see what I had to recognise a long time ago.'

'What's that?'

'That Oliver's behaviour is never actually personal, as such. He doesn't really feel the existence of the other person, even if he tells himself that he does. He isn't capable of love or a real relationship. He's attracted to pretty things, but they are just things to him. After a while the novelty of a particular thing wears off and he feels driven to find himself a different one. His life revolves entirely around his own needs, Jacques. His needs for recognition, for strokes.'

'Yes. You're right, Anna. Must have been hard for you to discover that.'

'At first, yes, perhaps. But then self-preservation kicks in. You know that you have to cut off the creeping tendrils, so that you can remain intact. Rebecca will be furious, I've no doubt. She has little enough patience for him at the best of times. And he'll be angling for us all to be happy for him again, of course.'

Anna's prediction was quickly proved correct. Two days later, I answered the front door to Oliver. He was standing behind an impressive bouquet of rosebuds and ferns, wrapped in an ostentatious flourish of cellophane. The flowers were for Anna, he immediately explained.

'Just popping by to wish her a speedy recovery, Jacques. Apologies for not arranging the visit in advance. Meant to call long before now, but life's been rather hectic! She is in, I presume?'

'Come in. She's been sleeping. I'm not sure if she'll be awake … if she'll want to see you.'

I deliberately omitted 'Uncle Oliver', the words that I had used for so long, which seemed to imply a degree of relationship that I no longer felt, a role that he had never properly been able to fulfil.

When I went to see if Anna was awake, she was sitting up and had already folded up the rug that she had covered herself with. 'It's Oliver, isn't it?' she said, wearily. 'He can come in for a while, Jacques. I don't imagine he'll stay for longer than he needs to anyway.'

Oliver followed me into the lounge, presented Anna grandly with the bouquet, then perched on the side of one of the armchairs, without taking off his coat.

'Sorry not to have come before now, Anna. Surgery went well and so on?'

'Yes. I'm fine, Oliver. Thank you for the roses. You didn't choose these yourself, did you?'

'Well no, but actually there's something I've been meaning to tell you – some news.'

The smugness of Oliver's smile alone was enough to rile me.

'I think we know the news already. I've spoken to Amanda,' I said bitterly. 'You've left her for someone else, haven't you?'

'How could she? I told her that I wanted to tell you myself!' Oliver replied, petulantly. 'Without her putting her own spin on things.'

'So, what's your spin, Oliver?' Anna asked sarcastically.

'I have to hold up my hands, Anna. I know what you're thinking and I know that you'll say you've heard it all before. I really am in love this time. I know what I said about Amanda, but

Emily really is the one. She's young, exciting, talented. She's fresh, pure and adores me, just as much as I adore her.'

'Naturally!' Anna smiled, falsely. 'How could she not? And how young is she, Oliver?'

'OK, OK. You've got me. She is only twenty-five – she could be my daughter – but so what? She makes me incredibly happy.'

'How sweet,' Anna said, coldly.

'Oh, come on, both of you!' Oliver said impatiently. 'I just want you to be happy for us. I haven't told Rebecca yet. Though I'm sure she'll understand. I mean, you and she aren't children any more, are you, Jacques? You're old enough to accept these things. You can do what you want, can't you? You have your lives, I have mine. That's how it works, isn't it?'

'Yes, you're absolutely right. We are old enough to make our own decisions about things …' I answered, deliberately ambiguously. I could hardly bear to look at Oliver's complacent face.

'Although, of course, I'd always like to think I could offer you the benefits of my age and experience. A guardian and a father always likes to have his say,' Oliver continued.

'I'm not your child, though, am I?' I was past caring any more about pleasing or making things easy for him. 'And while, in principle, you were my guardian, you've never really been particularly interested in me as a person, have you? And as far as I'm concerned, I think you've forfeited any right you might have had to try and teach me about what really matters in life, especially about relationships. It's despicable how you behaved towards Amanda … and Anna … and Rebecca.'

'Jacques! Steady on. Let's not get too personal. I don't expect you to understand all of this. A young man of twenty, I was pretty green myself when I was your age. Still in the process of finding, becoming myself. There was so much I didn't understand about commitment and people and life.'

'And you understand it all now?'

'Well, no, not everything, obviously. I've always thought that a person should have a degree of humility. Although I do believe I'm more in a position to know myself, Jacques.'

It had never been clearer to me how much Oliver's words worked at the level of a fluent performance, their meaning unconnected with the reality of his life. 'Even if that puts you in even less of a position to really know anyone else?'

'Jacques, Jacques. Let's not fall out. I do appreciate change can be difficult for us all, but we can learn to rise above our fear. That must be one of the most important things I've learned from business, I'd say. Look, I'd better be going. Don't want to tire you out, Anna. You will let me know when Rebecca next proposes coming down from Edinburgh, won't you? I'll bring Emily over with me. Whatever you say, you'll love her, Jacques. I have been truly blessed. I really mean that. Most sincerely. A total angel, I can assure you. If I can't win you over, trust me, Emily will. She really is adorable, Jacques.'

'For a month, for a year, two years?' I was determined for things to end awkwardly between us, not to allow Oliver to leave with the impression that he had in any way won us over.

'Goodbye for now, Anna. I'll phone next time before I come. Maybe by that stage you'll have time to see some reason, Jacques?'

I continued to feel angry that evening when I went to work at Keys. I found it impossible to relax, was short with my customers, a fact that Peter didn't fail to notice. 'Something on your mind, Jacques? I mean, I know that Anna's still not back to her usual self yet ...'

'It isn't about Anna. It's about Oliver. He's an arrogant ... I just want to feel indifferent towards him.'

'But you can't?'

'No. I want to hit him.'

'Sounds healthy enough to me! Where I was brought up ... But you're thinking of Rebecca too, I imagine?'

'Well, yes. Although, I don't know how that's going to work out, Peter.'

'No, but there comes a time, I think, when you've got to make things happen, Jacques. When, setting aside any macho crap, you've got to state what you want and it's quite reasonable to ask someone to make a decision. A man can't wait forever, can he? Or perhaps he can, but he won't be happy while he's always waiting.'

'Yes, I know. I'm not.'

The next day when Rebecca phoned, I told her about Oliver's visit and also about how I had first learned of his affair from Amanda. She was furious, as I had anticipated.

'How he expects us to have any respect!'

'I know. I think he honestly can't see it from any perspective apart from his own.'

'That's always the way he was. Egocentric. Only wanting people to confirm his rosy view of himself. And she's only twenty-five? I suppose at least he knows that someone of his own age would probably see through him. It's pathetic! Anyway, how are you and Mum?'

'Your mother's fine. She intends to go back to work soon. The radiotherapy's finished. She'll need regular check-ups but she seems very positive. She's been spending some evenings again with Peter.'

'Oh, has she? That bodes well, doesn't it?'

'It does.'

'And you, Jacques?'

'As Wheelie once said to me, I'm "chugging along".'

'Which means?'

'I need you ... to make up your mind, Rebecca.'

'I have, Jacques.'

'And?'

'I'm coming back, this weekend.'

Anna was delighted when Rebecca announced her plans to return. 'Much sooner than I had expected. Did you persuade her, Jacques?' She looked at me directly as she asked the question.

'A little, perhaps, although you know Rebecca. She can't be persuaded to do something if she hasn't already thought about it herself.'

'That's very true, Jacques.' Anna smiled thoughtfully. 'It is a woman's prerogative, isn't it? To be open to persuasion?'

'Yes,' I said, not quite sure what she was thinking. 'I know that she's really keen to see you. On the other side of your ordeal.'

'The only thing is ... I did say that I'd let Oliver know if Rebecca was visiting,' Anna said flatly. 'I could choose to ignore the request, but these things can't always be avoided, however much we might want to.'

Rebecca arrived late that Friday afternoon. She looked much more robust than she had done on her previous visit. In spite of her height, Anna looked frail and bird-like in comparison.

'Mum! You've lost a lot of weight, haven't you? Look at your little wrists. You need feeding!'

'Don't fuss, dear! I'm perfectly fine. The worst is behind us, I hope. You look wonderful. A picture of health. Not slacking, I hope?'

'No, Mum! I've started running again. Jacques.' I hugged her briefly on the front steps, conscious of Anna standing close beside us.

'Why don't you two have some time on your own to catch up?' I suggested. 'Peter has let me have this evening and the rest of the weekend off. So we can talk more later, can't we?'

'Yes, Jacques,' Rebecca replied. 'And ... I can't wait to see some of your new paintings.'

'Yes. Come up and see my etchings,' Anna said brightly, as a parting joke, before she went back into the house.

'Why don't you go and see Jacques' paintings now?' Anna suggested later, when we had had dinner. 'I'm going to sit and vegetate in the lounge. I'll probably go to bed soon. I want to be in good form for your weekend, Rebecca!'

'What do you think, Jacques?'

'Why not? I haven't got a lot of new work to show you, but ...'

I followed Rebecca upstairs to my room. I couldn't help feeling there was something unreal about the moment, the way we had even been invited by Anna to spend time alone. Anna was one of the most perceptive people I'd ever known. It did seem unlikely that she was oblivious to the atmosphere between me and Rebecca. Rebecca bounced down on my bed and clasped her hands around her knees, the way she had always done when we were younger.

'Show me then, Jacques! It doesn't matter if you haven't got much new work. I'm interested in seeing anything!'

I gathered up an armful of sketch-books and set them in her lap.

'Forget about anything,' I said. 'How about everything?'

I sat down on the bed beside her, flipped back the top cover of the first sketch-book. They were old watercolours, ones that I had chosen not to destroy. I was probably about twelve when I had done them. I turned over page after page: paintings of the Dee, impressions of the Meadows, the city centre, abstracts of people.

'This is you. I always painted you in yellow, with stars.'

'Oh, Jacques!'

'And these are of the back garden. I did a lot more but ... I destroyed them.'

'These are amazing, Jacques! I haven't seen these before, have I?'

The next sketch-book contained a collection of my earlier charcoal drawings, including some sketches of Rebecca and the more abstract drawing of how I had imagined she might look naked. I couldn't help feeling nervous still about her seeing it, although I had to trust that she wouldn't think any less of me for it. 'I hadn't realised you had done so many drawings of me, Jacques. I thought that I'd only sat for you a couple of times?'

'Yes, you did, but I ...'

'This nude is great, Jacques. You didn't draw this from life ... or did you?'

'Yes and no. From my imagination ... of life ...'

'So ... who ...?'

'OK, actually it was you as well. At least, how I imagined you might look – even then I ...' Rebecca started to laugh. 'Oh, I am sorry, Jacques. I didn't mean to laugh.'

'Actually, I'm relieved that you did! You could have reacted much less positively. Here, these are better. Look at them instead.'

We went through book after book. Finally we came to the womb paintings that I had done when Rebecca was pregnant. 'You don't have to look at these, if you don't want to. I did them more recently. Before ... before you had the miscarriage.'

'Oh, Jacques. The details are so delicate. These are really beautiful. I can't believe that you ... that a man could ... I'd like to have them, if I could?'

'I was thinking of giving them to you, but I didn't think that you would want to be reminded.'

'I feel better about that now. More clear that it wasn't all my fault. It's in the past, Jacques, although I'd still like to have the paintings. And what about these? The saxophonists? These abstract paintings of landscapes or waves?'

'I did those after I'd painted the saxophonist on the wall at Keys for Peter. And these were inspired after I'd been listening to music – they're a bit rough.'

'They're really good, Jacques. You should have more confidence in yourself.'

I closed the books, took them off her knee and set the pile down on the floor.

'Give me reason to, Rebecca. You know that I'd be better if ...'

I laid a hand lightly on her leg. She put her hand over mine, looked down as she spoke.

'So, how about this, Jacques? Why don't you come up to Edinburgh? We could ... get our own place and ...'

'Yes.'

My response was barely audible. I hardly dared to believe what I had heard. 'We could start a new life. Have the space to be our own people. I could help you find a job. There are places you could play the piano. I could finish my course. We could arrange to exhibit your paintings. It would mean that you'd have to give up your job at Keys, which I know would be hard for you ...'

'Rebecca! I said yes! The idea of living with you was enough.'

'I haven't stopped thinking since Christmas. I can't imagine being without you, Jacques. The thought that you might spend your life with someone else because I didn't have the sense to make the choice that I knew was right all along. I would regret that forever.'

'But now you won't have to.'

I lifted her hand and pressed my lips hard against it.

'No, I won't.'

Rebecca turned, leant towards me, kissed me slowly on the mouth.

'Rebecca? Jacques?' It was Anna, calling from the stairs below Rebecca's room. 'I'm off to bed. See you tomorrow.' She didn't wait for a reply. We listened as she went downstairs again.

'You won't go, will you?' I asked Rebecca.

'No, not this time,' she replied.

We lay down together on my narrow bed. Lost track of everything but each other.

Later, after we had made love for the first time, Rebecca and I lay talking, looking up at the skylight. It was a view that I had had so many times alone, but then it seemed that I had passed into another world, where what was still objectively the same felt very different.

'So when do you think you knew ... that you felt something for me that wasn't just friendship?' I asked her.

'I'd always thought you were handsome. I told you that, didn't I? But then I think it was ... when I was leaving to go to university, but particularly the time when I came back with Ben. When you played the *Moonlight Sonata*. I suddenly saw you very differently. You were no longer a boy. You had a man's capacity for passion. You really wanted to know what I thought. You wanted me to be myself in a way that Ben didn't and never would. So what about you? When did you see me differently?'

'For a long time. I think from the time that we walked by the river. Especially when you started to go out with Sam. I was very jealous.'

'Oh, yes, Sam! Sam was very sweet for a while. Oh, look, Jacques! Did you see the bat?'

'Yes. You see a lot of them up here.'

'I used to hate them. The thought of their skinny little wings touching my face really frightened me.'

'But they're beautiful. Delicate, fragile creatures.'

'Well, yes. I do think that now. One flew into the hospital one night by accident. They had to catch him in a sheet. There was something about him that suddenly reminded me of a child. His tiny ears, his head on its little wobbly neck, the velveteen softness of his wings. I felt sorry for him and guilty for having hated his species. I wanted to wrap him up, keep him warm against me.'

'And now you only have me!' I teased her, laying my head on her chest.

'Jacques!'

The contradictions in Rebecca's nature had never ceased to surprise me. She could be calculating, clinical, worldly. At the same time, she had a flexible imagination and an abiding sympathy for small, vulnerable beings, a quality that I had always found particularly endearing.

'I always envied you, Jacques. I wished that I had a skylight in my room. I wanted to see all that space in front of me as I went to sleep. Like a future, I suppose, full of endless possibilities.'

'I know what you mean. Although sometimes in a confined space, within the limitations of the present, we can have everything.'

18

It was eight in the morning when I woke. Anna was already downstairs in the kitchen. Rebecca was still asleep. There was something distinctly cat-like about her sensuality. She purred softly with each exhalation, settled her relaxed, animal warmth against me. I watched her silently for some time, wanting to savour the experience of waking beside her. She soon opened her eyes, seeming to be conscious that she was being observed.

'Jacques.' Rebecca stretched quickly, then pulled me down to kiss her. I couldn't help feeling relieved, that she hadn't changed her mind.

'I can hear Mum, downstairs. Do you think she suspects anything?'

'I don't think so, although your mother isn't always predictable.'

'We'll have to tell her soon. And Dad, unfortunately.'

'Yes. He's coming to see you this weekend so, perhaps ...'

'I'm not worrying about it the way I was, Jacques. Dad certainly won't like it, but I gave up looking for his approval a long time ago.'

'What was it that he told me when he last came here? You have your lives – I have mine. That's how it works, isn't it?'

Anna was having toast and tea at the kitchen table when we got downstairs. 'Before I forget, Rebecca, your father has just phoned. He wants to call in and see you later this morning, with Emily. I've said that if it doesn't suit you, you'll call him back. Don't feel under any pressure, dear. He shouldn't always expect to see you just when it suits him.'

'It's fine, Mum. I don't mind. I shouldn't think he'll stay long.'

'And now, I'll start again. Good morning!'

We were standing shoulder to shoulder in front of Anna. She stared back at us openly. I couldn't quite fathom what was behind her half-smile.

'Have to say. You two are looking quite ... conspiratorial.'

'Well, actually, Anna ...' I began, simultaneously placing an arm around Rebecca's shoulders, before I could think about what I was doing.

'Yes, Jacques?' Anna set down her knife, indicating that she was giving us her undivided attention. Her eyes darted in the direction of my arm.

'There's something we have to tell you. Rebecca and I have fallen in love, Anna ... actually, we ...'

I had no idea what Anna was thinking. She continued to stare at us, with an opaque, wry expression. Finally she spoke. 'Actually,

Jacques, believe it or not, I know. I've known for some time. Call me a merciless old bird, but I have a tendency to pick up on these things.'

'So are you shocked, Mum?' Rebecca asked.

'What? No, dear! A weather-beaten old thing like me? Why would I be shocked?'

'But what do you think, Mum?' Rebecca enquired, impatiently.

'I think that this isn't about me, Rebecca. It's what you and Jacques feel that counts. Although, for what it's worth, I think that when it comes to compatibility you couldn't have picked a better man. Probably clichéd and totally sentimental, but ...'

'Thank you, Mum!'

Rebecca was clearly delighted with Anna's response. She hugged her mother for as long as she would allow.

'Thank you, Anna,' I said, gratefully. 'I was afraid that you might have reacted very differently.'

'Oh, no, Jacques. Why would I want to pass judgement on my favourite pianist? I can't guarantee, unfortunately, that your father will respond in quite the same way, Rebecca, but ... let's not stand on ceremony. Let's have breakfast, shall we? You can tell me about your plans.'

Oliver arrived with Emily just before midday. My immediate thought was that she looked younger than Rebecca. She was petite, slim and pretty, her smooth corn-coloured hair cut into a neat bob. She wore an immaculate matching pink jacket and skirt, had small, even teeth that reminded me of polished rice grains. She exuded a quiet confidence, smiling pleasantly when she was introduced.

'This is Emily, everyone,' Oliver said proudly, pushing out his chest, as we all stood gathered in the hall. He was dressed in a bright green shirt and a fat, speckled silk tie under his suit jacket. As he introduced Emily it struck me that Oliver was like a prize rooster. 'She's been feeling very excited about this morning, haven't you, Emily? We even chose a new shirt and tie for me, in honour of the occasion, didn't we, darling?'

'Yes, we did!' Emily acknowledged, with a grace and patience, I thought, that Oliver didn't deserve. 'I've been looking forward to meeting you. I appreciate you allowing us to come – I know you're only back for a weekend, Rebecca.'

In spite of her connection to Oliver, I couldn't help liking Emily. She seemed quite straightforward and was trying her best to adjust to a situation in which she probably didn't feel entirely comfortable. And knowing that, in time, Oliver was likely to treat her in the way that he had treated her predecessors sickened me. I couldn't put the thought out of my mind.

'Why don't we all go into the lounge?' Anna suggested. 'I'll make us some coffee. I wasn't sure whether you'd be here for lunch, but there's plenty of bread, cheese and salad, so you're welcome to stay if you want.'

'Thank you, Anna. That's very kind of you. I'd like that – if it wouldn't be too much trouble for you?' Emily replied.

'No, Emily!' Oliver insisted abruptly, stamping his foot slightly as he said it. 'Remember, darling? I said I'd take you out to eat somewhere really nice later?' He was attempting to modulate his tone, but there was an undeniable undercurrent of impatience beneath his words. Oliver had his own fixed agenda and was determined not to change his mind, even if Emily was prepared to be more flexible.

'But are you sure, Oliver?' Emily asked, amenably, slipping her arm through his. 'We could eat out another time, couldn't we? I don't mind. I would understand if you wanted to spend more time with your family. Especially with you seeing so little of Rebecca.'

'Oh, no. That won't be necessary, darling. Let's just have coffee.' He didn't turn towards her as he spoke, but kept his chest out, his hands in his pockets, and made a show of shaking his head vigorously. He felt himself to be in command. I could almost see his cockscomb quivering.

Emily obviously felt awkward, briefly glanced at us, then looked down at the floor. I could tell by her puzzled expression that she was struggling to understand Oliver's attitude.

'Don't worry, Emily!' Anna said brightly, by way of reassurance. 'We don't mind. I can tell that Oliver is keen to have you to himself as much as possible. I have no doubt that you have a proper treat in store for you, dear. Just coffee it is then!'

While I appreciated Anna's wit, I couldn't help feeling sorry for Emily. She was almost certainly completely oblivious to the irony in Anna's words.

'And I think we should sit in the sitting-room instead of the lounge,' Oliver suggested, as Anna was on the point of going to the kitchen. 'The lounge used to be more for the children, didn't it? The sitting-room is much more suitable for entertaining adults. Especially on occasions like this.'

'Excuse our little altercation, Emily, but I beg to differ, Oliver,' Anna pronounced sharply. 'I have a strange little attachment to organising things in my own house. Actually, I think that Emily might feel more comfortable in the lounge. I'll make the coffee and meet the four of you there, shall I?'

Oliver looked momentarily embarrassed, but made a show of strutting on quickly. 'Yes, yes, Anna. Whatever you say. You know me. Always willing to take orders from a woman. I know my place, eh, Emily? Lead us through to the lounge then, Jacques!'

Rebecca and Emily sat on the armchairs in the lounge while Oliver and I stayed standing at opposite ends of the room. 'This is lovely,' Emily said immediately. 'You're lucky having such beautiful high ceilings and all this space! My entire flat would probably fit inside two of your rooms!'

'Although these chairs and the carpet are starting to look quite worn. Whatever Anna says, the sitting-room is better for visitors – much more smart,' Oliver declared. He had quickly recovered from his confrontation with Anna, was almost visibly puffing up again in her absence. He was still fixated on his earlier theme. I hated his snobbery, his undis-guised materialism.

'Oh, I think this is very grand, Oliver,' Emily persisted. 'And it's warm and comfortable as well.'

'So, where are you living at the moment, Dad?' Rebecca asked, pointedly.

'Actually I'm staying at Emily's flat, near Manchester, Rebecca,' Oliver answered, forcing a smile, avoiding eye contact. He put his hands behind his back and rocked back and forward slightly. I sensed that he was feeling uncomfortably exposed. 'Only a temporary arrangement, of course. I have my sights set on a much bigger place for us, not as close to the city centre. Something uncluttered, stylish. Emily likes modern properties, don't you, darling?'

'I do. Although I have said, Oliver, I don't really mind so much where we live. We both travel a lot anyway. When we're at home it's just about enjoying being together, isn't it? Having such a special relationship is the main thing. I just feel so lucky we found each other.'

'Oh, yes, of course. Absolutely, darling!'

Oliver seemed to swell with Emily's words and their implica-tions for his self-image and sense of esteem. He then made eye contact with her, but only momentarily. She had given him what he needed. He looked down at the floor again, this time with a self-satisfied look on his face, clearly giving himself time to gather strength from the thought that he was appre-ciated. I always had the impression that he quickly hoarded compliments, somewhere deep down inside himself. I imagined that afterwards he would self-indulgently revisit his accumulated stores. He liked to keep them put away jealously, rather than share their benefits. Finally, he released his hands from behind his back and lifted them in the air, theatrically. It was his moment of glory, his time to crow. 'Have to say. Wonderful to be loved! Even at my age!'

'So, do you work somewhere in Manchester, Emily?' I asked, determined not to allow Oliver the undivided attention that he craved.

'I'm based there, yes. Although I do travel quite a lot. I'm in public relations. That's how Oliver and I met. We ended up sitting beside each other on a flight. He offered to buy me a gin and tonic … we got talking.'

'And it wasn't long before I charmed the pants off you!' Oliver declared brashly, angling his shoulders, tilting his torso arrogantly. 'If you'll pardon the expression.'

Emily giggled awkwardly, fiddled with one of her tiny pearl earrings. I imagined that she was cringing inwardly at Oliver's off-beam joke, the way his stagey gesture to excuse himself simply heightened his own and her potential humiliation. If Oliver's final words to Rebecca and me were designed to appeal in any way to our sympathy or humour, they had the opposite effect. I pitied Emily even more for being involved with him.

'Dad! Too much information!' Rebecca said, vehemently. It was obvious that she was disgusted. 'I'm sorry, Emily. My father is very clumsy sometimes. I don't know what gets into him.'

'Oh, no, it's OK. It was only a silly joke!' Emily replied, blushing slightly, trying to make light of it. 'Anyway, what about you, Jacques? You work in Chester, I hear?'

'If that's what you call it!' Oliver snapped irritably. He was annoyed, offended, I knew, that his joke had been so badly received. 'Actually, I'd rather that you didn't go there, Emily. For my sake, darling. Jacques has a dependable habit of getting angry with me when I attempt to broach the subject of his career!'

'You don't need to broach it!' I answered him, impatiently. 'Yes, Emily. To reply to your question, I work in a bar in Chester. I enjoy it, in fact. I get the chance to play the piano there as well.'

'The piano? I always envy people who can play an instrument,' Emily confessed. 'I never managed to myself. You must be very good if you have the confidence to play to an audience, Jacques.'

'I enjoy it, so ...'

'Oh, yes. Life is a cabaret, isn't it, Jacques?' Oliver said to me bitterly, spitting as he spoke. 'Some of us have to live in the real world!'

I had a sudden urge to grab Oliver by the throat and hurl him across the room, in spite of Emily's presence. She was looking down at her knees, fidgeting with the edge of her skirt. Fortunately Anna appeared with the coffee.

'So, you're studying medicine, Rebecca?' Emily enquired, putting her hands together in her lap, changing the subject.

'Yes, Emily. Another year after this and I'll be finished with the basics. That's only the beginning of my training, of course.'

'Any particular specialism you'd be interested in?'

'Medicine rather than surgery, I'm sure of that.'

Oliver had become taciturn and had withdrawn all his energy inwards. While she was a relative stranger, Emily seemed more interested in the details of our lives than he was.

'So have you had a chance yet to …?' Anna asked, looking in turn at Rebecca and me meaningfully, after she had poured everyone's coffee.

'No, not yet,' I said.

'What's this?' Oliver suddenly became more upright and alert. He set down his cup and saucer, returned briskly to stand with his back to the fireplace.

'Jacques and I have something important to tell you, Dad,' Rebecca said, edging forward in her chair.

'Oh?' What Oliver hated most of all was to face the unknown. He began to blink rapidly, twitching with the surge of adrenaline. 'And are you sure, being as Emily is here at the moment, that this is the appropriate time to discuss this particular matter with me, whatever it is?'

'Oh, don't worry about me, Oliver. I don't mind, if Rebecca and Jacques feel comfortable,' Emily offered helpfully.

'It can't wait,' I stated. 'And it might be a long time before you see Rebecca again in person, so … this may not be easy for you to understand, but …'

'For Christ's sake, Jacques! What is this? Spit it out, will you?'

'Rebecca and I are in love.' I'd imagined for such a long time how that moment would be, the words I might use, how anxious I would feel. In the midst of the reality, though, I felt remarkably calm.

'We're going to live together in Edinburgh. I'll get a job, she'll finish her course and we'll—'

'Rebecca and you are what?' Oliver stared back at me, made strange little jerking movements with his neck.

'In love.'

'Yes, Dad. It's true,' Rebecca added quietly, looking up at her father directly.

Oliver lifted both his hands to the sides of his head. His fingers pressed hard against the top of his scalp. 'No! No!' he said, incredulously, repeatedly shaking his head. 'This isn't happening! This really isn't on! You aren't telling me what I think you're telling me?'

'I think you'll find that they are, Oliver,' Anna suggested, nodding.

'So, you knew about this? And you never told me?' Oliver hissed back, his jowls flushing with rage. His hurt, wounded rage at not being included.

'Only since this morning, Oliver,' Anna responded quietly. 'Before you came, though I'd suspected for some time.'

'You'd suspected and you didn't do anything to stop it, Anna?'

'No. There was no need to. They're both over eighteen – consenting adults. I can appreciate that you might feel a tad surprised, although, as you've always said, it's important that individuals do what they need to do for their own well-being.'

'Surprised? I feel as if I'm in a bloody nightmare, Anna! This is our daughter we're talking about here. And he's been living as a ward in our home, which to all intents and purposes, in most people's eyes, makes them siblings! Hasn't it occurred to you? I mean, what the hell are people going to make of this outrageous ... ? I dread to think ...'

I was seething with anger. Any sense of amusement that I had been feeling at Oliver's expense suddenly left me. His insensitive, stupid words set me churning inside. I noticed that Rebecca's eyes were filling with tears.

I was also aware that Emily was listening silently and I still felt terribly sorry for her, but I had reached a point of overwhelming anger. All I could think about was defending Rebecca and what we had.

'Don't be so bloody stupid, Oliver! Rebecca and Jacques are right for each other. They were almost teenagers when they met. They're certainly not siblings and they've never seen each other in that way at all,' Anna intervened. 'You're prepared to put the irrelevant opinions of a handful of petty-minded people above the happiness of your daughter?'

'You can't just whitewash over these things, Anna. Don't expect me to give my blessing to something that is bound to make public fools of us all!'

'We don't! We don't expect your blessing. We don't need it,' I said. 'We don't, do we, Rebecca?'

'No. I don't care what you think any more, Dad! You don't really care about me. I love Jacques. We're going to be happy together. I'm not going to give him up, for you or anybody else.

You can keep the rest of your negative thoughts about us to yourself. And don't worry, we'll stay far away from you. No one will be able to associate you with our foolishness!'

'Rebecca …' Oliver's tone softened slightly. It was soon evident that his sympathy was more for himself than for Rebecca. 'Don't do this to me. I'm your father. Don't ask me to give up my daughter.'

'But you did that a long time ago, Dad, didn't you? And you did it again, in the way that you described the most precious part of my personal life. So why don't you just go and get back to your own world? It's the only one that you believe is real, isn't it? Like you used to say, let's keep facing ahead.'

'I think you should go,' I said coldly to Oliver. 'I'm sorry, Emily. That you've had to listen to this.'

'It's OK, Jacques,' Emily replied quietly, getting up from her chair. 'I can't pretend I understand everything. I hope we'll meet again and that things can be worked out, for the best. Goodbye for now. Thank you for the coffee, Anna. I'll go and wait in the car, Oliver. You might want some time to …'

'No!' Oliver was irritable, hostile again. The thought of spending a single moment with the rest of us, without the presence of a soft, sympathetic female devotee in the background, clearly didn't appeal to him. 'There's no need, Emily. I'm coming with you. I have nothing more to say. I'll get the coats myself, Anna. Don't see us out. And don't expect to hear from me soon!'

'I won't, Oliver,' Anna called back, deliberately nonchalantly. As soon as the front door slammed behind Oliver, she got up.

'Right! I'm having a glass of wine. Cognac, Jacques? Rebecca?'

'Yes, Mum. I'll have the same as Jacques. A large one.'

'Won't be long,' Anna said, leaving us alone.

Rebecca got up from her chair and put her arms around me.

'That was horrible, wasn't it? I don't know if we'll ever speak to my dad again.'

'We might, we might not. I think that's up to him. We've said what we had to say.'

'Yes. There isn't anything else that we can do. I'm not changing for him. I'm going to be with you, Jacques. Forever.'

'Forever?'

'Yes. Let's take it from there, shall we?'

Later that afternoon, I suggested to Rebecca and Anna that we go to see Peter at Keys.

'I'd like to talk to him. Tell him about our plans, Rebecca. He'll have to start looking for someone to replace me. It's only fair to give him some notice.'

'Why don't you go by yourself, Jacques?' Rebecca offered. 'You can speak to him on your own for a while, have some space? We can stay here. Unless you want to go and see Peter too, Mum?'

'No, dear. I'm seeing him on Monday anyway. You go, Jacques. Have a man-to-man talk. The perfect antidote to a meeting with Oliver.'

On my way to Keys, I passed the Reids' house. Although I had spoken to Stephen's parents several times when we had happened to meet in Chester, I hadn't visited them at home since the summer before I had gone to Manchester, when Jane and I had parted. I had a sudden impulse to see them again, to let them know, however briefly, that I would soon be leaving to live in Edinburgh. It might feel awkward if Jane answered the door, but I decided to take a chance.

From what I could observe, the house seemed to have changed very little over the years. As I pressed the front doorbell I could see through the open blinds into the sitting-room. Stephen's hi-fi tower was in the same place, pictures of him were still arranged in the same patterns on the walls.

It was Mr Reid who came to the door. He was wearing a half-apron over his shirt and tie, had his sleeves rolled back, and was drying his hands on a towel. 'Jacques! This is a surprise!' He shook my hand warmly and seemed genuinely pleased to see me.

'Yes. I'm sorry I didn't call you in advance. I just wanted to ... but you're in the middle of cooking ...'

'Not at all! Mary isn't home yet, so I'm just preparing the vegetables. You'll come in, won't you?'

I followed him inside. He took me into the sitting-room, in exactly the same way that he had done when I had visited him after Stephen died, removed his apron and gestured for me to sit on the sofa. 'Have to say, you don't often catch me wearing my apron! You won't tell anyone, will you? My reputation could depend on it, Jacques!' he joked. In spite of everything that had happened to him, Mr Reid always seemed so resilient.

'Your secret's safe! Don't forget, I'm used to working along-side chefs.'

'That's a relief! Would you like a drink or something? You don't mind if I do, do you?' Mr Reid went to the sideboard and helped himself to a small glass of whiskey.

'Not for me, thanks. But you go ahead. I'm on my way to Keys. I won't stay long. Are you on your own, or are Jane and Michael ...?'

'Both away, Jacques. Michael lives in Coventry now and Jane's at music college in London. Just the old worker bees at home these days. So, how are you doing?'

'I'm fine. Much better very recently. Actually, that's partly why I'm here. I wanted to let you know that I'll be moving up to Edinburgh ... to live with Rebecca, in fact.'

'That sounds good, Jacques. Edinburgh's a pretty lively place. I'm sure you'll be very happy there. It'll give you the chance to stretch your wings. Still painting and playing the piano?' Mr Reid had always been respectful of my privacy. He clearly didn't feel the need to quiz me about the details of my relationship with Rebecca.

'Yes, both. I hope to carry on, get a job in a piano bar, perhaps. So, how are you and Mrs Reid? Busy as usual?'

'Always, Jacques. Quite why we have to be so busy I don't know. Although, on reflection, to be honest ... the hustle and bustle often saves us, doesn't it, Jacques? From our own thoughts, you know ... When we keep doing, we manage to live with some things that otherwise we ...' Mr Reid shrugged slightly, looked at me meaningfully for a moment, then swallowed the remainder of his whiskey. He studied his empty glass, turning it loosely in his hand. I had no doubt that he was thinking about Stephen, that my very presence was triggering many memories.

'I'll never forget Stephen, you know,' I said quietly. 'People say you move on, that there are stages of grief that you move through, but I ...'

'I know what you mean, Jacques. Real life is always much less tidy than theories about it. Actually, before you go, I wonder if you might like to have something to take with you.'

Mr Reid got up and returned to the sideboard. Instead of pouring himself another drink, he set down his glass, crouched down and opened the cupboard doors. 'Might have to go upstairs, but I think it's in here,' he said, half to himself, half to me. He began to search through the bundles of papers inside the cupboard. 'Yes. Here it is. There you are, Jacques. One of the best ones of him, I think. With his special canine friend! We've got some more copies, so you can keep it.'

I stood up and took the photograph from Mr Reid. It was a smaller copy of the picture of Stephen and his dog Mack that was hanging on the sitting-room wall. 'Thank you,' I said, hardly able to reply for a moment. 'It's very kind of you. I'm really glad to have this.'

'Kind, selfish, I don't know, Jacques – just wanting your child to be remembered, carried forward. Some slight con-solation, perhaps in feeling that a loss ... that memories are shared ...' Mr Reid was standing with his back to the sideboard with his hands in his pockets. He closed his eyes, momentarily screwed up his face, as if feeling, quite literally, the pain of a nerve being touched. He then opened his eyes and carried on briskly. 'Anyway, must let you get to Keys. Really do appreciate you calling in. Mrs Reid and I wish you all good things for your new life in Edinburgh.'

I put the photograph carefully into the inner pocket of my jacket. As I walked through Chester towards Keys, I took comfort from the idea that I had an old friend resting close to my heart.

As usual on a Saturday night, Keys was thronging with students. Even Emma was working hard, lifting handfuls of empty glasses, running to and fro between the tables and the kitchen with plates of food. Peter was assembling lines of pints along the bar, still finding time to talk to customers.

'Jacques? Didn't expect to see you tonight! What are you doing here, lad?'

'I've got a few things I need to tell you!' I shouted next to his ear.

'Oh, have you now? Let me just get these orders and then we'll talk.'

'Let me help you!'

I helped Peter for a while, until we reached a lull in the flow of customers.

'So, tell me then. Good news or bad news?'

'Mainly good.'

'Go on then!'

'Rebecca and I ... we're finally together, Peter.'

'Well, thank Christ for that, Jacques! Thought the day might never come. Congratulations, lad.'

'Thank you, Peter.' It was a relief to have such a genuine, positive response, especially after that day with Oliver. 'The only thing is Rebecca's asked me to come and live with her in Edinburgh. We're going to get a flat, so ...'

'So, what's the problem? You've got to go, haven't you? I mean, you'll be missed, of course, but grab your chance, Jacques!'

'Thank you, Peter. I will! I'm not quite sure where I'll get work yet, although I'll get something. The main thing for me is to be with Rebecca. You know I'm not really ambitious when it comes to the world.'

'You're right, Jacques. You start in the right place, where your heart is. If you branch out from that, well and good. If you decide not to, you're still in the right place, aren't you? Though, stay open to the possibilities, lad. The confidence that comes from love can help us achieve things it does us good to achieve. It's not so much a matter of vaulting ambition as becoming the best man that you can become. Anyway, less philosophy! You're even more capable of working things out than The Boatman is. How did Anna react to the news?'

'Anna accepts it. I think she's pleased for us. She said that she's suspected it for some time.'

'Doesn't miss a trick, does she? And Oliver?'

'He took it badly. I don't know if we'll ever be on speaking terms again. But I don't care.'

'Doesn't surprise me, from what I've seen and heard. I have the impression that Oliver needs to feel constantly in control.'

'Yes, that's the way he is. He can also be contradictory. On the one hand, he argues that other people's views matter to him, while on the other, he doesn't quite accept that they really exist in the way that he does himself.'

'Try your best to forget about him, Jacques. You're your own man. Perhaps what your own father might have told you, if he was alive?'

'Something like that, probably. They'd have liked Rebecca, my parents. Although, it's almost an impossible thought that if they were still here, Rebecca and I might not have met at all.'

'Know what you mean. Sets the mind spinning that does. Now, how about a drink, Jacques? Champagne? I'll give you another bottle to take back to Rebecca, but let's have a glass now. A salute from one treasured offspring of *la belle* France to another?'

'Yes, Peter. A glass of champagne,' I agreed.

Epilogue

June 2005

My story has been a simple one. I have no reason to believe that my future will be radically different. Although some people might point to the difficulties and especially the grief I had to endure in my early years, I have been fortunate to discover in life what most mattered to me, to prize the connections to those who I have loved and who have loved me, above all else.

I have never been a particularly ambitious person, a fact that some have, some will, interpret as a fault. There is no doubt that I have been privileged, have had the freedom that can be afforded by the inheritance of a degree of material wealth. While I am attracted to philosophy, I have been driven to live for the experience rather than the abstract idea, to be affirmed in relationship rather than at the height of a publicly admired achievement or a grand dream. I have loved to play music, to paint – in such moments, the ego is most easily forgotten. I have found a woman to love, who loves me in return.

Two months after Rebecca asked me to live with her in Edinburgh, I joined her. We rented a small flat in Marchmont, I found a job in a piano bar. In time, Rebecca qualified as a doctor, got a medical post in Edinburgh. I continued to paint. More nudes, some entirely drawn from imagination, some based on drawings of Rebecca. Scenes buzzing with greens, blazing with yellows. Multiplying buds and bulbs. Skies intense with thunder, radiant with unequivocal sunlight. Interplays of darkness and light. Reflections of inner landscapes, expanding freedom, life's tones and rhythms. With Rebecca's encouragement, I began to exhibit and sell my work.

We married in June 1998, when I was twenty-four and Rebecca was twenty-five, in a simple registry office ceremony. As well as Anna and Peter, we were joined by Wheelie and Mitch and some of Rebecca's friends from Edinburgh.

'Never thought you'd get there before me, Jacques!' Wheelie declared, amiably, as we celebrated in a little bar afterwards. He was dressed more elegantly than I was, of course, in a well-cut suit and a silk cravat, and made me a present of a box of fine Cuban cigars. He had just started a tentative relationship with a fellow journalist, 'a perfect English rose, Jacques'. Surprisingly, she was his own age. 'I mean, Mitchie here was always a bit of a late developer, but, let me just say, in this case, the best man has definitely won!'

'Yes, congratulations, you dark old French horse!' Mitch added, good-humouredly. He had started teaching history at a school in Manchester, liked to travel as much as he could, said he was making the most of his 'bachelor lifestyle'. 'Have to say my bet was on you from the beginning, Jacques!'

Anna and Peter continued their own relationship when Rebecca and I left Chester. They carried on appreciating food and wine, began to travel together occasionally to the Mediterranean, each urging the other to gradually loosen their hold on their careers, to experience simple pleasures, to discover the new. They still lived separately. 'It doesn't mean that we think any less of each other because we don't live under the same roof, Jacques,' Anna told me repeatedly. 'Peter and I simply have to have our own space.'

Sadly, last year Anna died. Insidiously, the breast cancer that we hoped had left her forever returned. Peter, Rebecca and I have struggled in our own ways to come to terms with her absence. I still find it strange to think that the austere figure who reluctantly, albeit dutifully, included me in her life, became a person I increasingly looked to and grew fond of. While never a replacement for my own mother, Anna's constancy and integrity, and paradoxically her capacity for detachment, allowed me to find my own identity, to learn to trust my passion for the things I was naturally drawn to.

I was with her just before she died. Her final words to me were, 'I've been lucky. I've had a ball these last years, haven't I? I'm ready … as far as a person can be ready. Look after Rebecca and Peter for me. And yourself, Jacques, dear. Have a good life.'

Oliver didn't communicate with Rebecca and me for many years. It didn't surprise me to learn from Anna that he parted company with Emily and predictably rapidly attached himself to yet another 'someone else'. He sent us a Christmas card with no personal message, which included, below his own, the signature of someone called Miranda, the year after we married – a fact that he obviously couldn't bring himself to acknowledge, let alone celebrate. We now have what Rebecca refers to as 'a strictly cardboard, non-contact relationship' with him. Although, undoubtedly much less ill-intentioned, Matthew has a similar approach.

Following Anna's death, Rebecca and I have returned to live in our old home. Mrs Chadwick has long retired. Rebecca and I clean the place much less efficiently and cook for ourselves. We have planted roses, peonies, thick-stemmed daisies and tulip bulbs in the garden. Recently we have set up a small chicken run, with six hens. We grow lettuces, potatoes and many different varieties of beans. I was ignorant of the fact before Rebecca told me – apparently the Pythagoreans believed that souls could be reincarnated in beans.

When you look out of the kitchen window now, you can see the statue of a stone nude, carrying a basket of fruit on her head, that I bought Rebecca for her thirtieth birthday. 'This is a big house.

Perhaps one day we might have someone else to join us – and I don't mean a housekeeper!' Rebecca has hinted, increasingly.

It is impossible to know what our future holds. I am excited by the thought that one day we might have a child, although I tell Rebecca what I truly believe, that it will always be enough that she and I can simply live together, that I would be equally content with that. It is what I most hoped for, what I once believed would never be possible. Our relationship has become the main touchstone of my life.

Rebecca has a job in a hospital in Manchester. She has decided to train to be a paediatrician. 'It'll be difficult, Jacques. But I think I can do it. I want to look after sick babies. Give them the best chance of a quality of life, if possible.' I have returned to work at Keys with Peter. He wants me to consider taking over from him soon. I suspect that I probably will.

I continue to paint and have sold more of my work. I still play Beethoven every day and have become particularly attached to his beautiful Sonata No. 24, in F Sharp Minor. My mind and my hands return to the piece, obsessively. There is always something to perfect, another nuance to discover. I have also expanded my repertoire to include more Schubert, Satie, Debussy. Rebecca never tires of 'Liebesträume No. 3'.

I will never forget Stephen Reid. Even now, when I listen to music, I still hear his quiet, thoughtful voice, imagine the conversations we would have had. The photograph of him and Mack that his father gave me stands in a silver frame on the top shelf of the bookcase where I keep my music. Occasionally I have tried to picture how he might have looked as an older man, but have never been able to do so. In my mind he is, will probably always be, dependably seventeen.

While I find other ideas of immortality questionable, I believe that in this way, those we have loved survive. Through patterns of relationship and invested feeling they have become permanent parts of us. Our dialogues must carry on indefinitely, irrespective of physical absence. When I sit behind the Bechstein I think unfailingly of Maman. When I go into a bookshop and see a collection of fairy tales, I remember Papa. I am still able to picture in detail the rooms of our apartment. Flashes of my childhood in Neuilly continue to come back to me. I suspect that they always will.

I have never come to believe in God, but in experiences of music and particularly of love, I have found myself closest to hope, touching the realities connecting with those primal metaphors of human aspiration, 'miracle' and 'resurrection'. Love changes us, gives us the opportunity and the reason to begin again.

Acknowledgements

Richard, Hannah, Rory and MJ, for their constant encouragement, interest and ideas.

All my family and friends who understand the value of the story and the dream. Thanks especially to Peter and Bronagh, Karen Williams, Jon Clayton, Sam Hughes, Randolph Ellis, and Gillian Little, for positive reflections and for sharing their own creativity.

Literary agents, Susan and Paul Feldstein, of The Feldstein Agency, Bangor, for their guidance, energy and ongoing commitment.

Twenty7 Books/Bonnier publishers. Particular thanks to my dedicated editor, Claire Johnson-Creek, and also to Joel Richardson.